DARKNESS FALLING

Bria Ferguson

Paperback Edition ISBN-13: 979-8-9887181-1-6

eBook Edition ISBN-13: 979-8-9887181-0-9

Cover design by Kimberly Killion

Dedicated to my parents, for always believing in me.

CONTENTS

CHAPTER 1

February 2010

Lex

The ghost tour of the French Quarter ends outside the Witch Queen's house. I'd have expected her to set up in one of the more sprawling mansions in the Garden District, but, apparently, she prefers the Quarter. We hardly need the tour guide's explanation of where we are, though, even if we hadn't already scoped it out this afternoon, after we dropped our bags at our hotel. But preparations and tours aside, the crowd of protesters gathered on the street outside would have given it away.

They aren't quite a mob with torches and pitchforks, but their hand-crafted signs are a modern-day facsimile. I even spot a couple with "Exodus 22:18" scrawled in bright red letters. They don't put the text of the verse explicitly on the sign, "Thou shalt not suffer a witch to live," for anyone who can't quote it chapter and verse because

1

that would constitute a threat. Or hate speech. I'm not sure how referencing it isn't an equal threat, or equally hateful, but the law shaves very fine lines when it comes to supernatural rights. That they recognize any threat at all is mostly at the insistence of local populations who depend on the supernatural community. There's at least one case in federal court challenging the restriction against the verse and others like it as an impermissible restriction on both speech and religion. I can't wait to see what the Supreme Court does with that.

"Oh, look. It's your father's favorite verse," I murmur to Mike, nodding at one of the signs.

"Fun," he mutters back, his hand going to the small of my back, almost protectively. It's sweet, if unnecessary. I've gotten by for eighteen years pretending to be a mundane human. If no one back home has cottoned on to my being a witch, no one in a city teeming with tourists is going to figure it out as we wind up a ghost tour of all things. Even if they do, I'm one among many here. Still, I lean into the touch, not willing to take any of his for granted. He knows how much his touches ground me, keep me from getting too stuck in my head and emotions, so he's not stingy with them, by any means, but each one is still precious. I'm always convinced that, eventually, he's going to be tired of people assuming we're a couple and pull away. He tells me not to be an idiot, and I guess he wouldn't be here in New Orleans with me now, preparing to go through a sacred ritual with me in under twenty-four hours, if he had any doubts about his commitment to our bond.

My gaze flicks beyond the protesters to the line of men and women in uniform separating them from the Witch Queen's gates. The Magic Corps, known more colloquially as "MagCorps," is the elite branch of the US Military reserved for witches, shifters, and human mages who are able to qualify, mages like Mike. Apparently, a lot of mages have only minor talents—able to sense or even see magic, but less able to use it productively, so Mike's acceptance is a coup for both him and my parents, who trained him. A lot of mages, maybe even most, never get recognized and go on to live mundane human lives with just glimmers of what they think of as heightened intuition. We don't really know. For all our understanding of the science of supernatural species has advanced precipitously in the modern age, precious little is known about unidentified mages. Most mundane, i.e. non-magical, humans don't even know they exist.

I want to study our future comrades to see if I can get any estimate on the ratio of species represented, curious, mostly, about the mages and if I can identify them, but Mike is pulling me gently away from the protesters, like he's afraid I'm going to do something impulsive and stupid. I admit that I have been known to have an impulsivity problem, but MagCorps presence or not, I'm not going to launch in and incite something. It won't help to bring about more peaceful relations. If anything, it'll just give the protesters more evidence for why we're dangerous. It's not worth it, as my dad always says. He's a history teacher, interested primarily in various civil rights-type eras, so he should know. More a fan of MLK than Malcolm X, my dad.

Mike says something else I don't catch, his brown eyes steady on Queen Esther's house.

"Hmmm?" I pull my gaze away from the guide and the co-eds flocking around him now that the tour is done, refocusing on my companion who, if I can be allowed to be biased since he is my soulmate and all, puts the admittedly handsome tour guide to shame. We are both going to have to cut our hair in the next two weeks, shaping it into the high and tight cut our drill instructor overlords will expect at Parris Island. But, for now, for tonight, Mike's brown hair is still in his usual shaggy cut, ruffled from the wind in a way that makes my fingers itch to smooth it down. As if in a final "hurrah" before our strictly regimented future hits us, he's gone without shaving for a couple of days, and he's giving off a kind of pirate vibe I dig. I quell my itching fingers by sliding them through my own blond curls, catching them on a tangle or two that pull sharply. The minor pain is a good reminder to focus. And behave.

"Vampires, Lex," he says patiently, reaching out to tap my nose to get my attention, but clearly looking to change the subject away from his father's bigotry and the protesters who echo it. "I'm disappointed no one's tried to suck my blood tonight, yet. What's the point of this town without vampires?" A zing skitters along my nerves at the teasing touch to my nose, light as it is, and the silver cord I can always see linking his heart to mine glows a little brighter.

"I bet she'd be happy to try," I say, nodding to the red-headed co-ed who's given up on getting the tour guide's attention and is edging toward Mike, looking like she's eyeing him as an alternative for her evening's fun. It takes a lot of willpower, but I don't step in to block her view, or snarl something like, "Mine" at her. He isn't mine, after all. Not that way. "Besides, you've got witches and shifters all over town. Don't get greedy." I'm willing to allow the change of subject to something almost silly if it takes the worried frown off his face and restores the smile that had been there all night until we wound up here.

Mike huffs a half laugh, then reaches for my arm and tugs me further away from the house and its hostile ring and down the crowded street toward the live music dancing its way to my ears. The co-ed looks disappointed, and I can't resist the triumphant look I send her since he barely gave her a glance before leaving with me. Like a sore loser, she flips me off. Mike misses it all. "I'm being serious, Lex."

"Seriously, man. I told you. There's no such thing as vampires anymore." I have told him this more than once, but think I manage not to sound exasperated as we walk under another iron balcony and dodge the red Solo cup tossed down by a drunken reveler. The town is gearing up for Mardi Gras, and it's obvious by how rowdy the crowd is.

"Why couldn't some of the stories tonight have been about vampires?" he asks, almost insistent in pursuing his theory.

Christ, he is stubborn.

"Because vampires died out during the Burning Times, when the Church was hunting down all supernaturals. Witches and shifters barely survived, as species; the vampires didn't. I've been telling you that since we were ten."

"You don't know everything. Some could've survived."

"I never said I knew everything. But if there were still a third supernatural species out there, I'm pretty sure we'd know. The three courts were closely entwined back then. It's not like vampires were the Fae, with a whole other realm to retreat to when the Church drove them out."

"Maybe they just prefer to stay in the closet, coffin, or whatever the appropriate metaphor is," Mike insists, looking over at me before linking our arms and making the spectral silver cord tying us together hum in pleasure, brightening. He stares at the space where I can see it and know he can, too. Him being able to see it is why we're here and why I, at least, am following him to Parris Island instead of heading to the University of Virginia to major in history like my parents wish I would. It's so much safer than going to war, and, even with MagCorps training being almost two years beyond the three months we'll spend at Marine Basic Training, they are very likely to deploy us fairly quickly after we're trained. Afghanistan and Iraq both need a continuous supply of manpower to maintain the gains the United States has made, after all. "What was that?"

"What was what?" I ask, genuinely unsure what he's talking about, but glad we're off the subject of the sexy undead, for now.

"It glowed brighter. The cord."

"It does that when we're touching. You've never noticed?" I mean, it's done that since we were five. That's thirteen years; it's nothing new.

He shakes his head slowly. "Not in particular."

"Huh. Well, it makes it happy." It makes me happy, too, but I bite those words back, still afraid of spooking my straight best friend, even if he is my soulmate. Plato and Aristotle were all about the platonic soulmate, after all. Maybe they knew more than we do. Or maybe platonic soulmates are as rare as Mike's elusive vampires. To be fair, they aren't unheard of, but I've never met another platonic pair. Oh, wait. There are no vampires anymore, so that analogy doesn't work, unless Mike ever decides to try pinch hitting for my team and joins me in the delightfully freeing fields of bisexuality.

"Huh," he echoes, though he sounds intrigued. "I didn't realize it felt things."

It doesn't. I do. I'm still not stepping into that emotional quagmire, but I also don't want to lie to him. "It's a reflection of us. When we're close, it hums more, vibrates higher. Like, when you went off to camp without me when we were twelve…"

"I didn't have a choice in that!"

This conversation has happened more times than any about vampires, so I hold up one placating hand. "I wasn't casting blame, just trying to remind you how dull and thin it got while we were apart. You noticed that."

"I did."

"This is just the opposite effect."

"We've touched plenty of times, and I never saw it get brighter."

"I'm not responsible for explaining your past lack of attention." I shrug, but also snuggle closer to him as we move through a crowd of drunken tourists. The parade floats won't be out for days, but apparently two girls are practicing for it by flashing their breasts at people on the balconies. I briefly appreciate the view until Mike tugs me onward, giving me an exasperated look for my distractibility—like he wasn't also looking. The cord lights up again once I'm snuggled against Mike's side until it's bright enough even my twelve-year-old sister could see it if she were here, and she can only visibly see limited psychic and magical phenomena; her gifts are more intuitive than visual. That is true for a lot of supernats, as members of supernatural species are known both in and out of our community. Americans, always trying to shorten words, right? Anyway, not everyone manifests magical sight. Some witches gather their information about the supernatural world by feeling; shifters do it largely by scent. I don't know what other mages do. We've never met one that we know of. Beyond that, the strength of Mike's talent borders on unique. I can do some of what he can, like identifying different species on sight, but I just notice things, I guess. I can't tell you for certain what even gives it away, most of the time. He sees actual colors of auras, can read them to indicate both species and mood. That's getting into Seer territory, but his gift is firmly in the present. Neither of us has a lick of talent for seeing the future. Seriously, we're laughably inept with tarot cards or any other kind of divination. Meanwhile, what my sister, Lizzie, even untrained, can do with a tarot deck is eerie. The cord linking me and Mike, though? That I've been able to see for as long as I can remember, even if I don't really remember noticing it before we met. I was five, so, I don't really remember a lot from before we met. But since I do see others' cords, I guess I have some level of visual talent.

"So, the more we touch, the brighter it gets?" His question pulls my wandering mind back to the moment.

"Yep."

"So, if we ever fucked...?"

The question might be hesitant, but it comes from so far out of left field that I draw in the humid air too quickly and start coughing as I choke on my own spit. I mean, okay, maybe it is a natural question to ask as a conversation progression, but it mirrors my own inner lamentation about the lack of fucking too closely for comfort. Mike stops walking to pat my back, and my shock dims the cord a little. Thankfully. If it had brightened at the idea, I might've had some explaining to do that I don't want to do. Honesty might be the best policy, but I don't want to scare him off. It also feels like I'd be putting unfair expectations on him.

"You okay?" he asks.

"Yeah. Just," I hesitate, trying to get to the question through my shock. "Where the fuck did that come from?"

Mike's turn to shrug, though I'll give him points for still holding my gaze, even when a linebacker in cargo shorts plows into us. Mike just tightens his hold on me, keeping me from stumbling while he explains. "I just was noticing it got brighter the more we touched and that was the most thorough touching I could think of."

"Right. Okay. Well, I don't know what it would do. I assume it would probably light up the room, but since I've never played voyeur to two soulmates having sex, I can't say for sure."

"Your parents?" He trails off again, like he doesn't know what he wants to ask, exactly.

"Ugh, no! Don't put that image in my mind!"

This time, he blushes. "No! I was just gonna say that your parents' cord gets brighter when they're snuggled up watching TV."

Oh, so he's noticed the varying brightness levels of other cords, but not the one rooted in his own heart. Okay, then.

"Yeah, they say that's normal."

"Maybe I've never noticed ours doing it because the others are so dull."

"Maybe." I study the second silver cords emerging from each of our hearts. "Have you noticed they're brighter? Have been ever since we got to the Quarter this afternoon."

He glances down at them, too. "Yeah, but I didn't want to ask. It's not like they're connected to anyone we've met. The ends still fade into nothing."

"Not yet, but we haven't actually met anyone. That'll be tomorrow when we go to the Queen's court. But it could still just be a proximity boost." I don't know if cords work that way, really, since I can't remember what my first one looked like before I met Mike, but I'm trying to logic my way through the question of "wtf is going on?"

"You mean like they're in New Orleans?"

"Would make sense. Town's full of witches and shifters, and it's Vows and Bindings Week for both courts, which means there's a slew of witches our age in town to pledge their allegiance to the Queen. Shifters, too, for...whatever they do to mark their sixteenth year." Probably also just pledging allegiance to their Queen, but we don't generally hang out in each other's courts without a specific reason, so they might have a whole other secret ritual I know nothing about.

"It's weird how they do whatever two years earlier than the witches."

"It's not weird," I correct. "Shifters mature faster because of their animal side, so they get recognized as adults two years earlier. Used to be a lot earlier than that, but they gave in to cultural pressures to extend the concept of childhood as the mundane humans did." It was no longer appropriate to marry your kids off at puberty or send them to work after elementary school, and humans would've noticed if shifters kept doing it. "Witches are closer to mundane humans except for our magical cores, so we get to follow your customs for being considered mature. Uncle Sam says we can enlist in his military at eighteen, so Queen Esther says we'd better pledge our fealty to her, first. Shifter recruits have just already taken care of that before the U.S. military will take them."

Mike looks a little troubled, and I wish we'd already formally bonded so I could feel more of whatever is going on with him. He'll probably tell me, eventually, but I'll never win any awards for my patience.

"So, our third could be a sixteen-year-old shifter?"

Ah. He's hung up on the age thing.

"Our third could be a baby born yesterday," I return, mostly to tease him. "But soulbonds aren't usually locked in until puberty," Despite ours having been. We're different in multiple ways. "So, given the state of our silver cords, your scenario is probably more likely, especially since it's likely he or she is a shifter." Triads with a mage in them, like Mike, are rare, but they usually include a witch and a shifter for maximum stability. Legend has it the earliest triads—the ones we actually have myths about—were always witches, shifters and vampires, the three acknowledged supernatural species. Mages weren't really around back then—or, if they were, folks just thought they were weak witches, not another species. So, triads with one member from each distinct supernatural species made for the most stable bonds, the strongest ability to combine powers, and, thus, they had the most exploits that became legends. The heroes supernats revere were almost all members of triads who could share powers across species. Or maybe, science tells us now, our legendary heroes were just hybrids or tribrids – the first shifter witches or even vampires who were also witches and could take animal forms, which sounds like something from a bad YA vampire series if you ask me. But then, supernatural biology is weird. It doesn't follow mundane human genetic principles firmly. The magic interferes and does as it will. Trying to do supernat Punnett squares is the fastest way I know to give yourself a migraine.

There are a few hard-and-fast rules: shifters always follow the species of their mothers, and witches almost always beget witches. I say "almost," because some evidence suggests that if witches interbreed with mundane humans for too many generations, their children eventually lose the magical cores that make them witches, making them mundane humans, except that every now and then, someone will be born with the ability to manipulate magic again, even sans a magical core—a mage. Many times, they don't even know they once had a witch in the family. No one knows how many generations it might take, because we've only been able to conduct wide scientific studies in the last fifty years or so. Before that, we were all too deep in the broom closet, as it were, hiding our true natures from the mundane humans. Since we came out and revealed ourselves to the mundane world, more testing has been done. DNA testing surprised everyone by revealing that supernats aren't just people, we are, in fact, also human, just different subspecies than mundane humans. Mundanes are Homo sapiens sapiens; witches are Homo sapiens arcanus; shifters are Homo sapiens whatever their animal type, like Homo sapiens lupus for wolf shifters. Mundane human scientists don't know about mages. Supernat scientists have cautiously designated them Homo sapiens magus but can't definitively say that they are a separate subspecies or if being a mage is just a recessive trait. There is actually heated debate on the subject in scientific circles, because there's no way to determine where mages might pop up. Like I said, supernatural Punnett squares are a bitch. Even the shifter mother thing doesn't make sense using them.

While I'm mentally meandering through history, literature, and science, it turns out Mike is still fretting over age of majority and/or consent issues. "What will we do if he or she is one of the newly 'adult' shifters?"

I don't have to see the air quotes to hear them. "First off, we don't have to do anything but be kind to him or her. Like, just because we find them doesn't mean we have to automatically and immediately fuck them." I mean, we aren't sleeping together, so that should kind of go without saying, shouldn't it?

"I-I know that." He blushes more, which is fucking adorable, and I take a moment to enjoy it before taking pity on him.

"We might end up with someone else who'll be a platonic soulmate for us." In fact, we probably will. Because that is my luck. Finding our third is my only shot at having the kind of relationship I grew up watching my parents have, where two soulmates fulfill what we're told by the romance and entertainment industry they're supposed to – being each other's fated mates, or whatever. I can't have that with Mike, no matter how much I dream of it, so, soulmate number two has to be it. I won't mind sharing them with Mike. Though, for his sake, I hope they are a girl. It would suck for him to have a bi-guy and a gay guy as his soulmates when he isn't interested in anyone's dick but his own. With my luck, we'll end up with another straight guy. If so, the question I've been asking since I was twelve, when I realized I wanted to kiss Mike, but he wasn't into me like that, will be answered: am I cursed? Because why else would the love of my life not swing in my direction?

So, I am hoping for a straight or bisexual girl, so Mike can have the romantic ideal and I'll have a second chance at the non-platonic ideal love, too. Maybe she'll even keep me from breaking my heart on Mike's stalwart straightness. Granted, compatible sexualities don't guarantee romantic love, even for soulmates, and even if it is the norm.

"You think that'd happen twice?" Mike sounds glum, which I take to mean he wants that ideal love, too.

Probably, but I don't say that. "I doubt it. Triune souls are meant to be sacred matches."

"I thought soulmates in general were sacred."

"Well, yeah, but everyone says triads are the most balanced unions, so, we need someone to unionize with." Mike blinks at my wildly inaccurate use of 'unionize,' so I correct myself. "Unite with. Biblically."

Mike snorts. "If it's such a big deal, then why...?"

He trails off, and I mentally curse, because what if he'd been intending to end that question with an inquiry about why we weren't Biblically united, his straightness be damned? I doubt it, but still. It's not like him, trailing off mid-sentence. That's more my thing because, eventually, my brain does catch up with my mouth.

"Are you having second thoughts about the binding ceremony?" I ask, worrying. Please, Goddess, let his answer be "no." I want everything with this man, and if a ritually cemented soulbond is the most I can have, I'll take it. Losing even that would break me.

"Of course not." His free hand rubs through his hair, mussing it more, as his other squeezes my arm like he's trying to reassure me. "I know I should have this stuff down by now—you've been explaining it since we were five."

"I never mentioned 'uniting' at five!"

"Maybe not." Mike sighs and looks up at me again from where he'd been studying the ground in front of us. "But you did tell me we were going to get married when we grew up."

My skin burns from my chest to my cheeks. "And you said that boys couldn't marry boys."

"Well, except in a few places, they still can't, so the ceremony tomorrow is the closest we can get."

"Which turned out to be lucky." Because tying us together with ritual magic is far more binding than marriage for supernats. Divorce is a thing for supernats as much as mundane humans, while a soulbond severing is so rare as to be unheard of. But soul bindings don't come with the same baggage of expected romantic and sexual union that comes with marriage. Or, at least without the explicit expectation. It's not required. Soul bindings can go unconsummated, sexually speaking, without negatively affecting the ritual magic involved. I'm still willing to bet everyone else bonding tomorrow night will go celebrate all naked and sweaty. We'll probably watch a pay-per-view movie in the hotel room, or maybe Skype with our—Mike's—girlfriend Hannah. She is also kind of dating me, with Mike's knowledge. But no one else's, so she doesn't wind up caught in the gossip fodder that follows me and Mike around Staunton, Virginia.

"I guess so." Mike pulls away a little, and I frown and follow, snuggling against his side again, unwilling to agree to the physical separation when unnecessary. Granted, this physical touching is the shit that makes us ripe for the gossip mill back home, but here we're two anonymous guys in a bustling district of a big city. Even if some homophobic asshole tries to make an issue of it, we can defend ourselves handily. I'm a boxer and Mike has his black belt in Tae Kwon Do, never mind our facility with magic. Luckily for me, he's always been okay indulging my snuggly side and doesn't pull away again, and the silver cord between us hums happily as we walk, at least until a soft cry of distress nearby snags my and its attention.

Mike

I feel the cord perk up when Lex snuggles back into my side. I wonder what it'd do if I released his arm and put mine around his waist, instead. I wonder what he'd do. He seems particularly snuggly tonight. Hell, if I'm being honest, I wonder what I'd do, after I made the move, small as it would be. He's warm, pressed so close, a heat I can feel from my shoulder down. Our hips bang a little, but that's okay. It's just another reminder he's there.

The discussion about our second soulmate has just confirmed what I know. Lex wants love—beyond what Hannah gives him, beyond what I give him. Of course, he does. I do, too. For myself and for him. He deserves someone who can give him all the things I can't. He deserves someone who wants him, body and soul; someone who isn't confused about the body part of it and someone who isn't concerned about what anyone—parents, friends, the voices in their head—thinks about them being with him.

He freezes a second before I hear the cry he must have heard. It's not quite a scream, but it's clearly a sound of pain, though whether of a woman or cat, I'm not sure. Hell, in this town, it could easily be both. Lex's blue eyes meet mine, something more than worry in them, and I feel him shiver before he turns, scanning, trying to get a bead on the sound.

"This way!" He slides away from me, only to grab my hand, pulling me down the street until he cuts up one with less neon, and then into an alley.

I'm instantly on alert, remembering the tour guide's caution to stay where there's light and music, and we'll be fine. Wander out of the reach of the revelry, and we could find ourselves in danger. While he might have been talking about ghosts or supernats, he definitely gave the warning as the way to avoid the human criminals, too. I tense, ready for a fight, but let Lex pull me down the long alleyway as the faint sounds we heard grow louder, bracketed by taunting male voices.

"What's the matter, kitty, lost your claws?"

"Go ahead and scream, bitch. No one will hear you or care."

"Fuck off," a female voice snaps, though it's thick like she might be fighting tears. "You have no idea what you're getting yourself into..."

"Oh, look who's all tough." Another cry rings out and the sound of flesh on flesh—a hit, I think, trying to see in the dark. The cry cuts off with a strangled sound. "Not so much now, though, are you?"

Lex skids to a halt, taking in the scene under a broken streetlight. Four—no, five—young men, mundane humans, as far as I can tell, are ringed around a small female figure. I can't see much, just a white dress mired with filth, and a spill of inky hair that looks black in the gloom. She's on her knees, hands clasped behind her back, while one of the men holds her head back. Another is strangling her, while a third focuses on putting something around her neck. We take a few more steps, and I see the light glint off of something silver at her neck as the one putting it on her steps back. I feel sick when I recognize it—a collar. Her hands, I realize almost at the same time, are in cuffs that look heavy and black against her delicate wrists and fair skin.

I flash back to another alley, another girl, this one with braided black hair and ocher skin. The cuffs on her had been black, as well as thick and clunky, and they'd burned her skin—iron on a witch to cut her off from her magical core. She'd been beaten badly and doused with lighter fluid. One of her tormentors had lit a match before we got there. Lex had gone at them like a wild thing, kicking, punching, and biting. But he'd never pulled out his magic. He'd driven them off with physical skill alone, while I'd pulled the girl to safety. He'd only just been training a few months, but he'd had righteous fury on his side and a complete lack of fear. One of the boys had pulled a knife and things might've gone badly, only Lex made enough noise in his attack that someone called the cops. The boys tormenting the little witch had gotten off with a warning. Lex did a two-month stint in juvie for assault. Luckily, a friendly judge was willing to expunge his record, or he'd never have gotten into the Marine Corps.

He's not being as careful tonight, as the alley suddenly flares into sharp relief in the glow of four witchlights—like miniature suns lighting up the night, bright enough to blind as they each zing at one of the girls' assailants.

"More witches," the tallest man spits, coming to meet us. He's got an iron chain in his hand, and he spins it before trying to lash Lex with it.

"Let her go," Lex says, voice like a snarl.

"I don't think so." They've ringed him but haven't seen me, yet, which lets me jump in, bringing all my hand-to-hand training to bear. I take them by surprise, but they must have reinforcements because, before I can get to Lex, something hits me from behind, and the world goes black.

CHAPTER 2

Lex

I scream something as Mike goes down, and I feel the chain lash across my back, the iron burning where it hits the bare skin of my arms. I call up a fireball, ready to roast someone, my parents' cautions forgotten, but something harder hits me in the back again before I can launch it, and I fall with someone atop me. The breath gets knocked out of me, my lungs seizing up painfully, and my back aches and burns from where the heavy chain split my shirt and hit skin. The guy holding me down wrenches my arms behind me, and I feel cuffs slam around my wrists. My sense of my own magic disappears almost immediately, the witchlights disappearing without that connection, plunging the alley back into darkness, and I'm regretting not attacking them as soon as we entered the alleyway. The man hauls me up, then shoves me at the girl. My already aching back hits the brick wall, and I crash into her, unable to break my fall without hands or magic. I feel something in me snap into place, rushing out to meet some force in her, awareness zinging through me, leaving me breathless again even as my lungs remember how to breathe. I only note it distantly, though, more immediately concerned about the soulmate I already love than investigating this thrum of connection with someone new. I strain to see Mike in the dark, but he's just a lump on the ground, and I try not to choke on my own panic at my inability to go to him, to check on him. I can still see the cord, can still get a sense of his presence, so he's not dead, but that doesn't guarantee he's not hurt badly enough to change that. To distract myself, since panic is counterproductive, I turn as best I can to check on the girl, who I can still feel more than see.

A shifter, I realize, seeing the silver collar they've placed on her, to keep her from changing. The iron cuffs on her wrists suggest she's probably a shifter witch, at that, or the thugs are being over-cautious. Her dress is torn from shoulder to waist, and she's bleeding from a nasty cut on her mouth. It's not the right time to notice that she's gorgeous—all long black hair and blue eyes in a heartbreakingly lovely face. Those blue eyes reflect the streetlight, the way shifters' eyes do, seeming to glow in the darkness as she stares back at me, surprise sitting on her features, but, however dark it is, I can still see the fear there. A fair share of defiance, too, to be sure, but she's scared. Scared and young. Fourteen, maybe fifteen, at most.

"You shouldn't have come down here," she hisses at me.

"And let them do whatever they had planned to you?" Fury flares in me, sharper than expected. Sure, I hate bullies, and I'm tired of people thinking they have a right to do anything they want to us because we're "not human" (even though we are. Bigots don't really care about biology.). But looking at this girl, who seems so fragile in a collar and cuffs, makes me genuinely want to badly hurt the men hovering around us, leering. I might even want to kill them, and I'm angry and scared enough for both her and Mike that the thought of killing barely shocks me. My own peril doesn't matter in the rapid calculation my emotions are doing. Only she and Mike do.

The state of her dress, and the way her bra strap is barely hanging on to cover her, suggests at least some of what they had planned. Ballsy in New Orleans. Most states only recently made raping a supernat a crime—and it's still barely policed or enforced. The general public often thinks of shifters as lower than the animals they turn into, after all. And witches? Well, we've made pacts with Satan, or so they say, though I must've missed that negotiation while carrying out my altar boy duties at St. Francis of Assisi Church. Clearly, the general thinking goes, if a supernat claims to have been raped, it couldn't actually be rape, because the animals want it, and the witches deserve it. Only steady lobbying from the Queens has gotten the laws changed.

But in New Orleans, the seat of supernat power in the world? Well, the cops here are on the Queens' payrolls, the Queens' Courts have their own enforcers, as well, and hurting a young shifter like this girl can lead to a swift death sentence, without legal repercussions from mundane authorities for those carrying that sentence out. It's not perfect, even so, as these thugs prove, but it's better than back home.

"Well, now they're just going to kill, or sell, all three of us," she points out, voice dry. But I notice she's shifted closer, leaning a little into me, which makes the wisp of a cord between us brighten and hum.

"We were trying to rescue you!"

"Which is sweet, but who's going to rescue you?"

One of the goons throws Mike, also cuffed, down beside us. He groans, and I could sob with relief. He's not just alive but aware on some level, thank the Goddess.

"He is," I tell the girl, nodding at my unconscious soulmate. She snorts in disbelief.

"Shut up." One of the men backhands her, then punches me. My head bounces off the brick wall hard enough that I'm sure it's given me a concussion.

"Three for one's not bad," another says. "And the boys are pretty enough we might be able to sell them, too." He reaches out to grab me by my hair, tugging my head up hard enough to jerk my neck. Added to the incipient concussion, it makes me a little nauseated. "Especially this one."

Am I supposed to be flattered? I probably should be afraid, too; maybe the girl has more sense than I do. But Mike is moving, and soon, he'll be awake, and I'm still convinced there's nothing we can't do together, even injured.

"We'll need a bigger car to move all three of them. I'll call Davis."

One of them moves down the alley, leaving just the four others with us.

"Since we rounded up three of them, maybe Davis will let us have a little fun with her first," one of them says, reaching out to caress the girl's face. "We can't ship them out until tomorrow anyway." He keeps stroking her skin even as she flinches back, making my rage flare even brighter, but I have to bite back a cheer when he brushes his hand over her lips, and she bites him hard enough to draw blood. And maybe break a finger if the crunch I hear is anything to go by.

She gets backhanded again for her trouble, but the man she bit looks terrified, retreating across the alley.

"Fuck! What if she's infected me?"

"It doesn't work that way," one of his partners snaps. "You're born a shifter or not."

"Unless she's a werewolf!"

The girl spits at him. "Maybe I am a werewolf, and I'll gladly curse all of you with it." They back up a little, and she gives me a wry look, muttering, "Never thought I'd say that in a million years."

Now isn't the time to laugh, but I almost do anyway. Werewolves and shifters have a very uneasy relationship, mostly because lycanthropy is, indeed, a curse, forcing werewolves to shift on the night of the full moon, while shifters consider their ability to shift, or not, at will a gift.

"Lex?" Mike's voice is hoarse and scared, but he struggles to sit up, then leans against the wall. "You okay?"

"Never better," I assure him, even if it's a lie. "Can you feel the magic?"

"Not yours," he says. "Or hers."

"The iron's in the way, locking down our cores. What about the deeper magic?"

Mike has a rare gift, especially for a mage, of being able to directly tap into the ley lines--the lines of magical energy crisscrossing the globe. Unlike witches and shifters who are magic at their very cores, mages have the ability to manipulate and use magic from relics and artifacts or from other supernats. Or, in Mike's case, from the ley lines. Iron dampens a witch's magical core, cutting us off from our innate magic at our cores, which is usually what we use for anything magical that we do. We generally only use the ley lines to recharge if we deplete our cores. Theoretically, if a mage can do it, witches should be able to actively draw on and manipulate ley line magic, too. Maybe we could, once, but the skill has been lost somewhere in time. The goons have put Mike in iron cuffs, sure, but they won't affect his ability to do magic with the ley lines, which gives us an edge.

"Reverse transfer?" Mike asks.

"Worth trying," I agree. Normally, a witch would transfer his or her magic to their mage, but through playing around, we discovered that, in the event of an emergency, Mike can transfer ley line magic to me. I can't store it or hold it in reserve any more than he can, because ley line magic isn't meant to be held, but I can shape what he funnels to me. The act of transferring it somehow renders it usable the way raw magic isn't. Whether it will be enough tonight is another matter.

I feel it when he pushes it at me, and sigh, immediately working to craft it into a rough spell to get rid of my cuffs. Fast and hard would be to just burn through them, but that would wind up burning me even more than they already have, and it might not even work. I have no idea how much energy it would take to do that. What I start working on is more elegant—they put these cuffs on us, which mean they open and close somehow. So, I start working the magic into a kind of lockpick, fumbling around the edges of the cuffs to the thinner, weaker spot where they fasten. Mike feeds me more magic—more than I can hold without storing it; so much so that it starts to spill over.

The girl leaning against me gasps. "What...?"

I realize she is also siphoning the magic. It is transferring into her, same as it is to me, like Mike is sending it to her, too, either directly or through me.

"Work at the locks," I whisper to her and feel her nod.

It takes me a while to shape the magic into a key, and I start to worry that this Davis will show up before I can. Our captors are keeping their distance after the biting, and just laugh when they see me struggling, convinced there's nothing we can do.

I hear Mike sigh and feel the flex of his arms. "Got mine. You?"

"Almost. Don't do anything until I'm free, too, then we need to work together."

I feel the lock give, finally, and catch my cuffs before they can clang to the ground. The metal burns my palm as surely as it was doing my wrists, but I'm free and can feel my magic welling up, responding to my need to fight. I direct a little of it to my injuries, easing the pain, even though I can't work a proper healing spell on the fly, yet. After MagCorps training, maybe I'll be better prepared.

I hear the soft sound of cuffs dropping to my right, and the girl sighs. "So much better."

As soon as I set my cuffs on the ground, I flash her a smile. "Agreed."

Mike and I share a glance.

"Mobile?" he asks in our own shorthand where cities stand in for strategy.

I remember the fight in Mobile, Alabama quite well—witches don't duel outside of daytime soap operas and other melodramas—but no one got the memo to a couple of idiots in Mobile who'd come after me and Mike for supposedly hitting on their girlfriends by asking them for directions. Our strategy in the fight hadn't really been a great one, per se, especially since we were used to fighting mundane humans, not witches, but it built on how we'd fought our schoolyard bullies until they learned to leave us alone and make their homophobic jokes elsewhere. We found a rhythm in our magic to heighten our other skills. Unused to physical altercations, the assholes had no idea what hit them.

"Yep," I concur. "I'll take the ones on the right,"

"Works for me."

"What are you two going to do?" the girl whispers.

"Get us out of here," I tell her. "Close your eyes—I don't want chips of brick flying into them." And she probably shouldn't see what we do to the assholes, never mind the violence on TV and in movies these days.

"I can just shield," she says with a bit of a smirk curving her lips.

"That also works." I'm a little surprised, because outside of MagCorps, shielding isn't usually taught to young witches back home. I don't know why—it's always seemed to me that it should be.

"On three," Mike murmurs, before starting a quiet countdown.

Mike

When I give the signal, Lex moves, fast and low, cutting to the far right of the group of men, while I go the other way, trapping them between us. To my surprise, the girl moves, too, right in front of them so we've formed a sort of triangle with the wall as the base and the men in the center. I blink in surprise when I see the silver cord that usually shimmers between me and Lex sketching out all three legs of the triangle and encircling our former captors. The meaning of that hits me right before the girl—far too young—flashes me a smile and a coy wink, telling me she sees it or feels it, too. At least now I know how she was able to take in my transferred magic. Even now, I can feel her magic humming inside of her. I shake it off to deal with it later, focusing on our quarry. Lex's incandescent rage makes more sense, too, now that the pieces have slotted into place in my head. He's always defensive of those less able to protect themselves—a byproduct of years of bullying—and he gets angry at injustice, but the emotions rolling off him aren't like anything I've ever felt from him. They're almost strong enough to keep me from realizing he's injured. My own head is pounding from whatever they hit me with, but I can work around it.

The men already think we're all witches, so a magical barrage is the simplest way to bring the fight to them. Lex is a study in grace and precision, wielding his magic like a biting whip of white light lashing into them from first one angle, then the next. The thug up against him has a lead pipe as a weapon, and manages to get a few worrisome blows in, but Lex soon drives him back. The thug can't see the whip like I can, so he can't judge where the next strike might come from. He feels it when it hits, though, if his yelps are any indication. The girl is as graceful as Lex, and I almost get distracted when her arm and hand shimmer and shift smoothly into an agile leg and paw, covered in fluffy white fur with black markings on it and tipped by wicked-looking claws. I remember her soft cries of pain before we got here—the men are not nearly as quiet as she was, though I note that she's precise enough that none of the blood she draws comes from mortal wounds. She's a cat playing with mice she might or might not kill, literally. I snap the wrist of one guy and use Lex's magic to hurl the other into the wall, hard. Between the three of us, it's over fast—two of the guys are on the ground, bleeding and unconscious, but still breathing, while the others push past her and make a run for it. She bares her now-quite sharp teeth and looks like she's going to start after them, before she pauses, looking down at the two on the ground. Lex starts down the alley, until I call his name, and he comes back with a disgruntled frown, cranky I made him stop.

"Are you guys okay?" I ask, looking them both over, noting her hand and arm are back to human with the threat gone. She's got a busted lip and burns on the wrist of the arm that didn't shift, but otherwise seems okay. Lex, on the other hand, is favoring his right side, like his ribs hurt, with blood at his temple and burns on his wrists, too.

"Nothing a little salve from my Tante Marguerite won't fix up," the girl assures me, rubbing her burned wrist light-ly.

"Yeah, same," Lex adds. "I mean, not about Tante Marguerite, since I haven't got one of those, but a little salve, some ice and aspirin, and I should be fine. Maybe a healing spell or two."

Yeah, he's more hurt than he's letting on if he's planning on healing magic.

My own skin is unmarked, but their injuries cause such a flare of anger that I kick the guy on the ground, still clutching his pipe. The girl distracts me when she starts tugging at the silver collar. I can see welts on the skin of her neck, as Lex reaches to still her hands.

"Let me..." He's as gentle as can be as he finds the clasp on the collar and sets her fully free. The fact that she could even partially shift while wearing it is telling of impressive magical strength. "I'm Lex, and this is Mike. Can we walk you home?"

"Tante Marguerite's shop is just down the street," she says, giving him a sweet smile of thanks, touching her neck lightly. "She's a healer and runs a Voodoo shop, and you can get everything you need from her. So, you can walk me there. She'll see I get home safe. I need to talk to her anyway."

She takes the collar from him and breaks it in two, tossing it into the bag she retrieves from the ground. Then she winds her fingers through his and reaches for my hand. I let her have it, feeling the ping of awareness slide through me, much like the first time Lex and I touched. Her fingers are trembling, telling me she's not as fine as she's insisting.

"How old are you?" I can't help asking.

"Rude," she says, laughing. "A gentleman never asks a lady her age."

"He's going to have a fit imagining the worst," Lex tells her with a solemn nod, though I can feel his amusement flare.

"I'll be fifteen soon," she finally says with a sigh.

It could be worse, I think to myself, then drag up what Lex said less than an hour ago. All we have to do is be kind to her. Time will take care of the rest if it's meant to. A three-year age gap isn't the end of the world once she's finished growing up.

"Fifteen was a good year for us," Lex says, smiling at me over her head. I smile back, as he adds, "You didn't tell us your name."

"Didn't I? Sorry! It's Andrea, but you can call me Andie. Everyone does."

Something about that niggles at the back of my mind, like I should know it, but I leave it alone as she leads us out of the alley. As we reach the alley's exit, I hear low snarls and find myself hitting the ground all over again, hand torn from hers as a large weight hits my chest and pins me down. Given the bruising my back already took, getting the breath knocked out of me again hurts more than I'd care to admit. The ache is deep, and my lungs burn as they struggle to work right again. I hear Lex yelp in surprise, too, and a thud. When I look, he seems to have a shadow perched atop him. A shadow with a long swishing tail and a set of glowing green eyes. I look at what's got me pinned and find golden leonine eyes staring down at me from a face framed by an actual mane, baring impressive teeth.

"Stop it!" Andie's shout is sharp and commanding, and I swear I hear her growl. "Get off of them, now!"

The lion on top of me shimmers, and I find myself pinned instead by a guy who looks like a bodybuilder crossed with a surfer with shaggy blond hair. The eyes remain the same, though, if possibly more hostile. On the other side of Andie, the panther—I think it was a panther—on Lex becomes a guy with hair as black as Andie's falling to his waist. Both erstwhile big cats are naked.

"You're bleeding, my lady," the panther shifter tells her, snarling again. "And burned."

"And half-naked," adds Mr. Lion.

"Yeah, well, you're fully naked," she snaps. "If you want to be useful, three of the guys who did this took off that way." She points down the road after our attackers who'd run. "You can probably still pick up their scents, since they were bleeding. The other two are at the other end of the alley, also bleeding, and need to be secured. They're some of Davis's procurers. These two saved me. So—and do not make me repeat myself again—get off of them, now."

The two shifters grumble at the reprimand but do as ordered.

"Now, help them up, and get after the actual bad guys. They could be the link we've been searching for. I don't want to have ruined this dress for nothing."

They both give her startled and appalled looks, even as they haul us to our feet.

"We need to get you home, my lady," the lion protests.

"Lex and Mike are going to take me to Tante Marguerite's, and you know she'll call Mama. I'll get someone to come get the other two, and then I'll be home in no time. But if those three disappear, we'll lose the best leads we've had in months. Davis is possibly even on his way here now—they called him. But I don't think we can set a decent trap in time. They probably already tipped him off. Go!"

They grumble a moment, but quickly shift back into their feline forms before sniffing the ground and taking off in the direction the guys went. Andie huffs out a sigh, then takes our hands again.

"I'm sorry. It's their job to keep me safe, and they're probably going to get in trouble for losing me and letting me get hurt," she says, voice almost contrite. "Which isn't their fault. I gave them the slip."

"Why?" Lex asks. "You obviously know of this Davis guy, so he's a known danger?"

She nods. "He's a supernat trafficker. Sex and slave labor primarily. Mostly pubescent shifter girls, but some younger boys and witches. They've been disappearing at a higher-than-usual rate from this area of the Quarter, and we've heard rumors of overseas auctions advertised on the Internet backchannels."

"So, you, what?" I ask, a suspicion sinking in my stomach. "Thought it would be a good idea to slip away from guys protecting you and go wandering in the area they're known to go missing? What were you thinking?"

She spins to face me, all defiance and fury to match Lex's earlier display. Kitty has claws, indeed, as our attackers noted. "I was thinking that someone had to do something, and most girls aren't lucky enough to have security who'd start tracking them down immediately if they go missing."

"You set yourself out as bait," Lex says, voice a little choked, expression horrified. "You wanted to get taken."

"Well, not taken, exactly," she says, and she looks a touch contrite again, like she can hear the pain in his voice, too. "I thought Grégoire and Gervais would find me quicker than they did. And if they didn't, then I should be okay long enough for my mom or aunts to do a tracking spell and find me..."

"Which isn't guaranteed to work if they have the right wards," Lex reminds her, voice sharp.

"Okay. It wasn't my best plan," she concedes, "but some-one had to do something, and the cops weren't doing anything. Goddess only knows what the missing kids are going through. I had to at least try."

She turns in the opposite direction from where her bodyguards went and tugs us after her, presumably to her Tante Marguerite's shop.

CHAPTER 3

Lex

I still feel sick thinking about what could have happened to our newly discovered soulmate before we even found her when we reach a shadowed doorway. The window next to it is draped in red satin and lit with electric candles to show off a display of esoteric and occult merchandise. Nothing a real witch would use outside of very specific rituals, but the stuff most mundane humans think we use every day—lots of pentacles, black candles, a crystal ball, a cauldron, some herbs and incense. A rubber snake is coiled around a chalice, looking real enough to make me shudder. Tourist and poseur stuff. Tante Marguerite's shop, I presume.

Andie's stint of looking chastened has worn off on the short walk. Part of me understands her need for justice; part of me thinks she acted foolishly. Part of me wonders how a fourteen-year-old girl gets her own bodyguards. They called her "my lady," so her family must be rich and important, cheesy Voodoo shop aside. Shifter nobility is a little different from witches, and I'm fuzzy on how it works. Maybe she feels guilty for her privilege. Maybe she's even more impulsive than I am. Poor Mike, if so.

Another young woman about Andie's age is perched on a stool behind the counter, flipping through a fashion magazine. She drops it swiftly when the bell over the door jingles, one hand smoothing down her narrow black braids before a fey smile curves her lips.

"What boon are you seeking from the spirits tonight?" she asks in a heavily accented voice, sounding like every caricature of a voodoo priestess ever to grace a Hollywood production.

"I'd appreciate it if they'd keep Mama from grounding me until I'm sixteen," Andie says. "But I think that's beyond even them."

"What did you do now?" Most of the girl's Cajun accent drops away, leaving a softly accented drawl. She hops down and comes around the counter. Her gaze sweeps over me and Mike, assessing, and I see it linger on the spectral cord binding all three of us. One eyebrow arches. "Besides finding them. They didn't do that, did they?" Her hand waves a general encompassing of Andie's bloody and disheveled state.

"No! They saved me from some of Davis's guys."

The other girl sighs. "I thought you were just fooling about going after him."

"Well, I wasn't." Andie frowns, then gestures at the girl, looking up at me. "This is my cousin Tia. Tia, this is Lex and Mike." She points at each of us in turn.

"Well, you certainly don't do things by half, do you, cher?" An older woman steps through a curtain in the back of the room. "Grégoire already checked in. Your Mama's sending Anton here to fetch you."

Andie gives a dramatic sigh. "Ugh." She glances over at Mike. "Anton is one of my stepfathers. The strictest." Another sigh. "He's a wolf."

Wolf adults are known for their strictness with their pups, though I'm more intrigued by the idea of him being one of her stepfathers, and can't help but ask, "How many stepfathers do you have?"

"Two." Andie winds her fingers through mine more tightly. "Tia, can I borrow a dress before he gets here? Oh, and Tante, these are Lex and Mike. They need some healing. Guys, this is my Tante Marguerite."

"Borrow what you like," Tia says, waving a hand at some steps in the corner of the shop.

Andie looks reluctant to let go of us, but she finally does. "Stay until I'm changed?"

"Of course," Mike promises, watching her like she's some kind of revelation made human. Well, Homo sapiens Felidae, at least. Or whatever specific feline shifter she is.

They're all three shifters, I note, and all with the same blue eyes which are even more startlingly lovely against Tia and Marguerite's dark brown skin. All three witches, too. Voodoo is more religion than magic, so not all practitioners are witches, but it drew a lot of the free witches of color back in Colonial and antebellum days, from my understanding. The White witches wouldn't let them in their covens, and many had already embraced Catholicism, so they formed their own congregations in a space that allowed them to practice magic without condemnation.

I step forward when Andie releases my hand and offer it to Marguerite. "It's a pleasure to meet you, ma'am."

"Yes, it is." Mike pulls his gaze off Andie long enough to step forward, as well.

Marguerite shakes Mike's hand as he's closest, then takes mine. "Same. Andrea's been looking for you two for a long time. Thank you for helping her when her scheme got too real, as they say." She keeps a hold of my hand, gaze sharp on my face. "Your path diverged from its course tonight, cher. Shadows will settle around you, as you go along this new one, as darkness falls on us all. But stay true to your heart, to your people, and it will all come out right in the end."

I'm no stranger to Seers—my little sister has a form of the gift, after all, but I'm still taken aback a bit. Usually, you have to ask and pay a boon for a reading. "What? You can see all that in my future? Did meeting Andie change it for the worse?" That's even worse luck than if she'd not been someone I could see myself loving.

Marguerite hums something that sounds like agreement. Or dissent. Really, it's a fairly noncommittal sound. "Not worse, cher. And Andrea isn't the point of divergence—she was always there." Her fingers trace lightly over the burned skin of my right wrist. "These, though...they've darkened your destiny, but it's still a fateful one. Rocky and painful, yes, but you're never going to be forgotten with the mark you'll leave on this world, my prince."

"Prince?" Mike asks, when all I can do is gape at her. It's not necessarily the first thing I'd have reacted to—I'd like to hear scenarios where I can opt out of the "rocky and painful" part, if possible, but I suppose it's a good question.

"I see a crown," Marguerite says with a shrug. "And we have no kings. Unless you boys make yourselves a throne."

Mike

Marguerite's tone isn't joking, but Lex laughs at the idea of a throne, though there's something I don't like in his eyes as he gently untangles his hand from hers. "Maybe it's a clue about my Halloween costume this year?" The laughter can't hide the fact that there's already something shadowed in his eyes. I can't help but remember his visceral rage at the thugs, and a shiver races down my spine. Truthfully, I don't like the idea of shadows and darkness, let alone pain, ever touching him, even though I know pain is something everyone goes through in life.

"Maybe," Marguerite murmurs, good naturedly, letting him go. "Samhain is certain to be involved."

"Samhain's going to be involved in what?" Andie glides back into the room, cleaned up and in a casually elegant blue dress, with a high neckline and long sleeves that end in a point at her delicate wrists, covering the burn marks.

"My destiny," Lex tells her as he crosses to meet her. I can tell he's feeling the same pull to her as I do, and I'm glad of that.

"Destiny's a crock," Andie says, a little more vehemently than seems strictly necessary, sending a glare toward her aunt.

"Let me get you something for those burns," the Voodoo priestess says, slipping behind the counter where her—daughter? Granddaughter? whatever Tia is to her—has gone back to sitting. After about age 30, and until they hit their 70s or 80s, it's impossible to tell how old shifters are. Marguerite could be 35 or 65. "And look at those ribs and heads of you boys."

My ribs are fine, so I shoot Lex a look. He mouths an "I'm fine" at me before she bustles him to a seat.

She's just finished patching Lex and Andie up when the door opens and a tall, broad-shouldered man strides in. He's regal and imposing, even in jeans and a Saints t-shirt, and most definitely a wolf—Homo sapiens Lupus—if I've ever seen one. Not a witch, surprisingly, but still powerful. He's surely an alpha.

"Andrea? Your mother would like to speak with you." His voice is stern, but I see affection in his eyes as he gazes at his stepdaughter.

"Yes, sir," Andie says, before taking Lex's hand again and reaching for mine. "I didn't even ask—are you here for the vows and bindings or just touring?"

I don't ask how she knows we're not local, though I can tell Lex wants to.

"Vows and bindings," he tells her. "I'm making my vow to Queen Esther, and we're doing our binding ceremony."

Her smile is bright. "Good. Then I'll see you there." Up onto her tiptoes she goes before brushing a kiss over first Lex's cheek and then mine. "Save me a dance?"

"Of course," Lex promises.

My hand feels empty when hers slips away and she follows her stepfather out to the car waiting by the curb. Lex's must, too, as he reaches to wind our fingers together, like we can make up for her lack.

"I guess we should go," he says, and thanks Marguerite for treating his wounds, accepting the tonic she gives us for our heads before we take our leave and head back out into the night, aiming for our hotel. Outside, we can hear the music again, and I angle us toward it. It's in the right direction, at least.

After about ten minutes, we reach a crossroad near Jackson Square and St. Louis Cathedral and find the source of the music we've been hearing. A band plays on the corner opposite us, while performers dance in the middle of the crossroad. They're doing some kind of magic—the glow of it hangs in the air, throwing the neon signs of the nearby bars and the dancers' faces into sharp relief.

"They aren't summoning a crossroad demon, are they?" I'm only part way joking with the question. That's all tonight needs.

Lex huffs a laugh at me. "I don't think so, but I call dibs if Crowley shows up."

Having watched *Supernatural* with him, I understand the reference. The comment deserves an answer, but what to say that won't give my confused feelings away?

"You can have him," I settle on as thoroughly neutral.

Lex smiles at me, his dimples showing and his blue eyes warm with amusement and pleasure. The magic in the air is brushing up against his, turning his aura a soft orange color. Some kind of sex magic, then. Or desire-inducing, at least. Dangerous. But I don't pull him away. Maybe it also imparts courage to follow that dangerous desire. After our evening's adventures, desire feels a little less scary.

"Good. Because he's on my list if I'm ever in a relationship that demands monogamy."

"Your list?" If we ever took that step, I'd probably want monogamy, or only poly between the three of us. With multiple stepfathers, and two soulmates, Andie probably isn't going to demand monogamy from Lex, but I am already disinclined to share his attention with the lovers he sporadically takes. Still, I'm not surprised that Lex sounds mostly disgruntled at the idea. Hannah certainly doesn't ask it of him, and Lex has never shied away from playing the field.

"Of people I'm allowed to fuck without it being cheating."

"The fictional demon or Mark Sheppard?" I name the actor who plays the demon to get some clarity. It matters.

"The demon," Lex answers without hesitation.

"I'm sure that this future monogamy-demanding lover will be okay with that, given, I stress, the fictional part," I tell him, mock-solemn.

That wins me a laugh from him, and I feel the gloom from Lex's disinterest in changing our relationship start to lift.

It isn't like I'm even sure I want to change the relationship but thinking about the ceremony tomorrow forces me to consider it. Soulmate bonding rituals are sacred to supernats. More sacred than marriage, even, given the high incidence of polyamory and divorce, for that matter, in the community. Even the US government recognizes the importance of soulbonds, allowing soulmates to stay together, even if they are same-sex and pursue military careers. No "don't ask; don't tell" in the Magic Corps. Soulmates might find themselves separated for a temporary mission but are rarely assigned to a duty station or deployed separately.

I don't know why tomorrow's ceremony has me so nervous beyond its location—the Witch Queen's house—and officiant, also the Witch Queen. Lex and I are soulmates and bound together just by that, whether we formalize it or not. So, I won't be promising anything that isn't already a locked-in thing. I'm not afraid of the blood rite part of it, either; the pain won't be too bad, and hell, Lex and I swore ourselves blood brothers with blood when we were eleven, so this is also just more of the same. Maybe it's just the expectations that go along with it. I know we're the oddballs in a sea of romantic soulmates. Sure, platonic soulbonds do exist, but they're rare. All the other pairs participating in the ritual will probably be lovers. We've never even kissed, a fact I'm a little bitter about.

When your best friend/soulmate comes out to you as bisexual and then proceeds to date every other queer boy in town, but never so much as bats his eyelashes in your direction, it's a little hard on the ego. If he likes guys, then, shouldn't I – his damn soulmate and best friend – be at the top of the list? It isn't like he's secretly crushing on me, either. Lex sucks at secret crushes. When he developed a crush on Allan Thomas in tenth grade, but wasn't going to tell, because Allan was, at least as far as we knew, straight, I had to rescue him from a beating for sighing over Allan too much in gym class. I started training him to fight the next day, which broke my heart, because he's just...not meant to be a fighter, his performance tonight notwithstanding. Not that he hasn't turned out to be damn good at it, but I didn't want to see him touched by that violence. It's why I wish he was back in Virginia rather than going with me to South Carolina next week. It's highly likely that they'll ship us out soon after we're trained, and Lex shouldn't go to war. He's too good, too...pure isn't the right word, because that implies an innocence he's largely missing, but it's the best I can do. Fragile is even worse with its implication of weakness, but both are true. Lex has what my mom calls an artist's soul and is too often a slave to the vagaries of rapidly shifting emotions. No one's ever diagnosed him with anything, possibly because mundane human shrinks suck at supernat psychology, and there aren't any supernat shrinks near us back home. But they tested him for everything from ADHD to Bipolar Disorder, and he felt it to the point that he practiced for the psychological evaluation of our military intake.

I do not have an artist's soul, even though, like Lex, I also write music. I knew from the time I held my first toy gun that I was going to be a warrior. The eldest son in our family always joins the Marines, but my older brother, Brandon, has severe asthma, so the military expectation fell to me. There was no way my dad was letting me out of that family tradition. I've had enough of a fight defending my friendship with Lex from my dad who's convinced Lex is going to corrupt me and ultimately get me dishonorably discharged from the Marines for sodomy, or, at least, Article 133, Conduct Unbecoming an Officer and a Gentleman, which despite its name, applies to all service members, regardless of gender or rank. Unfortunately, Lex being a witch and us joining the Magic Corps after boot camp graduation isn't something I can use to reassure my father. He hates witches almost as much as he hates non-straight men. He says witches are Satan's minions or something and a threat to the country, maybe even the world. Gays are, too, according to him. Yeah, my dad, the bigot. Fun times.

Never mind that MagCorps is basically Special Forces, even if unacknowledged or revered as such. The USA might not be willing to grant supernats full citizenship, rights and protections, but the military will happily use them when it suits their own ends. Most people who don't like supernats explain their derision of MagCorps by claiming its servicemembers aren't genuinely impressive, like real special forces, but cheaters using their magic and enhanced abilities to show up regular human guys who work hard at what they do. No one ever understands how hard supernats must work at their power and abilities. It isn't like witches snap their fingers and have a fireball to throw. Well, Lex snaps his fingers and has a fireball to throw, but not when he first learned how to do it. That took years of practice and work and a few singed-off eyebrows—his and mine. And he isn't as precise in his targeting as he'll need to be in battle, either. Friendly fire is a problem with the witches, too. But that's part of what we'll learn at MagCorps training, which is basically like a Hogwarts-Naval Academy hybrid. Maybe Dumbledore's Army? I don't know. I didn't read the books, just heard about them a lot from Lex's little sister who thinks they are the best thing ever written. Lizzie wanted to tell us all about Dumbledore's Army, so we'd know how to fight Voldemort. Or Al-Qaeda and the Taliban. Maybe all three. That part of her lecture—complete with a PowerPoint—was unclear. Probably because she was eleven when she gave it and mixed fiction with CNN.

Lex bumps his hip against mine in an affectionate move that pulls me out of my head and back to the here and now. The music is still going, the magic of it still flowing through the crowd, tinging them all in orange. Listeners sway, not quite dancing, and some are kissing off to the side. Lex looks almost wistful. Unable to bear any hint of sadness on his part, I let go of his arm and shift behind him, feeling very daring as I drape my arms around his waist and encourage him to sway. He gives me a startled look over his shoulder, and I worry I've gone too far, but then he smiles and just leans back against me, letting me hold him. It isn't too much of a move—Lex has always been a cuddler and generous with physical affection—two reasons everyone back home assumes we're more than friends, even my girlfriend, whose only complaint is that we never let her watch. I've told her repeatedly there's nothing to watch, and she's the one who told me a few weeks ago that maybe there should be.

I realize the problem with my move about thirty seconds later when Lex does decide to half-sway in my arms. Given how he'd pressed back against me when I put my arms around him, his ass is now brushing against my groin. In anyone else, I'd consider it a deliberate tease, but the smile Lex gives me is genuinely innocent, not his "oh-look-how-innocent-I-am" smirk. He's just...happy about whatever is making him smile. Meeting Andie, us here, together. Who knows? I cant my hips back as subtly as I can to try and discourage any embarrassing reaction from me that might raise questions I don't have answers to.

I know that leaning in rather than back probably would lead to something that might answer those questions, but as much as part of me wants them answered, another part of me does not, too afraid of what the answer might be. I don't want it to be one that hurts Lex or that ruins what we have by making it messy, or by making me seem like anything other than someone who completely adores him. I don't want to lead him on if my upset over his lack of interest is ego rather than genuine desire for him to notice me so we can be together. I've always considered myself straight, though no one else I know thinks I am except Lex, including my own family. And, honestly, we've never explicitly talked about it except when he came out to me when we were twelve.

"I think I like boys," he'd whispered after chewing on his bottom lip for a long enough five minutes that I'd started to get worried. All I'd asked him was who he was thinking about asking to the dance—Mary Louise or Katie, who had been as far as I knew, the two girls we were both crushing on. I figured he'd take one, and I'd take the other, and all four of us would hang out and save each other from the awkwardness of seventh grade dances. I'd never been to one, but I'd seen enough in movies and on TV to know it would be awkward. Only now, it was probably going to be more so.

"Well, obviously," I'd returned, not as oblivious as I sounded, but unsure what to do with the twisting sensation his confession had set off in my gut. "You like me."

That was it, the point where he could—should—have confessed that, yes, indeed, he did like me, his damn fated soulmate, but he shook his head.

"I don't mean like how I like you," he tried explaining. "I mean like, I'd rather take Katie's brother to the dance than Katie. Or..." he'd paused, frowning, confusion flickering across his expression. "Or like maybe I'd like to take them both."

We barely have a grasp on bisexuality as an identity now; back then, he and I didn't even have a word for it. Same-sex relationships were familiar enough, being common among supernats and the bane of my father's existence, apparently, but no one had really shared the details of potential sexual orientations with us. Or at least not that they came in more than just two flavors. So, his confusion was probably understandable. To be fair to my twelve-year-old self, mine probably was, too.

"You mean, like, take him and dance with him, even to the slow songs?" I was thinking I needed to find Katie's brother and punch him a few times, so he kept his damn hands to himself.

"He kissed me after practice yesterday," Lex continued with his life-altering confession. "It was kinda nice."

"Nicer than kissing Katie at lunch last week?" Yep, Katie's brother was going down.

"Different. I'm not sure which one I liked more."

"My dad says boys kissing boys is wrong." I whispered, trying not to lean in and test how wrong it was for myself. I'd already gotten more than one lecture on it, starting with when Dad gave me the talk about sex in general and most recently when I'd asked if Lex could spend the night.

"Your dad also says 'Thou shalt not suffer a witch to live,'" he'd retorted.

"Yeah." I'd had no good response for that, because, if my dad knew I was dabbling in magic with Lex, he'd kick me out—probably pretty bruised up—sure as he would if I got Lex to stop biting his bottom lip so I could do it for him.

And I didn't know where that thought had come from, not then or any other time it has occurred to me since.

Tonight, at least, I can recognize the temptation to lean in for what it is. Possessiveness, pure and simple. My soul-mate, for me. Even if I'm not sure if I'm also bisexual, or Lex-sexual, or am just a jealous straight asshole who doesn't like it when Lex pays attention to anyone but me. I mean, when we're with Hannah, the few times she's been willing to have sex with us both at the same time, I think they're hot to watch, but that's like...live action porn, and I'm usually thinking about how it's my turn next with Hannah. I don't get jealous of her. On the other hand, I'm also not as weirded out by the proximity of Lex's dick to mine as I probably should be, either. And now there's Andie—this vibrant, beautiful, far-too-young girl who is apparently just as destined for us as we are for each other. After thirteen years of wondering about our third person, the question has been answered, at least partly. I don't know what that answer really means, though, for us or for Hannah.

"Sorry," Lex mutters, pulling a little bit away, though I'm not sure what he's apologizing for. I do note that his hips have stilled. "I didn't mean to make it weird."

I lean back in, resting my chin on his shoulder and just wanting to reassure him until the bond is glowing again with his happiness. "You didn't," I murmur, maybe a little too close to his ear, which makes him jerk away. I know how sensitive his ears are. I can't help but tease, just a little bit to see if he'll take the bait. If I tell him I'm...curious or whatever, but don't know if it's guys and my sexuality, or just him, then he'll feel like he's my sexual experiment, and I won't know if he wants me or is just helping me figure myself out. It'll go sideways if I can't handle the thought of sucking his dick or whatever. If he makes a move, then I know he wants me. But from the way he's jerked away, I guess that answer is "no," after all. Even if his aura is tinged more with orange now. I messed with his ear; of course, he's got orange in his aura. "Sorry."

He gives me a puzzled look, like he's not sure what I'm apologizing for, but I have already made it weird enough, so I just give him a shrug and point out one of the dancers twirling like some kind of dervish. He watches.

CHAPTER 4

Lex

There are more people in attendance for the ceremonies than I expected. I know there are four other pairs doing their binding ritual tonight, but I didn't expect the spectators. Do spectators even come to fealty vows, since I know there are a lot more of those than binding rituals tonight? It's like a royal wedding or something. Maybe one of the Queen's kids is doing their ritual tonight, and it is akin to that royal wedding, but, whatever the cause, it sends my anxiety sky high. Mike's been quiet since we got back to the hotel last night, settling down in the second bed instead of joining me the way he has every night we've spent in the same room since we were kids. He was just as quiet when we woke up this morning. When I asked him about it, worried, he just said he was nervous about meeting the Queen. I tried to reassure him, but he's still so quiet I don't think it worked.

Those of us making our vows to the Queen are called forward first, and Mike squeezes my hand before melting back into the crowd. A couple of dozen other young men and women my age step forward with me, and the herald, or whomever he is, lines us up by name so he can announce us as our formal introduction to the Queen. I wouldn't have thought the Queen's kids had to go through a formal fealty vow, but I guess I was wrong, because one of them—her eldest son, I think, Elias—comes down off the dais, leaving the other five, to join the line up ahead of me. As witch after witch moves forward at the sound of their name, footsteps silent on the cobblestone courtyard, I look around.

The house rises around us, ringing the circular courtyard, all gray stone that still looks warm in the glow of the torches spaced around to provide light. I can see the modern lights in the ceiling and lighting in some alcoves, so the torches on the wall and the bonfire in the firepit in the center of the courtyard must all be for atmosphere. If they were going for a spooky medieval castle in the heart of the French Quarter vibe, they succeeded. The whole Oath of Fealty hasn't changed since then, either. It's kind of like the Pledge of Allegiance, but with more consequence. It's binding, as a vow should be, and demands absolute loyalty. Punishment for breaking the vow can be anything from a fine to death depending on how serious the infraction. And that's just the legal punishment. The potential magical consequences are even more unnerving; the Goddess does not appreciate disloyalty to her anointed High Priestess, especially for vows sworn in her name. Not that I've ever known anyone to break their vow, so I can't say for sure what that might look like. I imagine it would be bad.

"Elias Jonathan Carmichael."

The prince—and Lizzie would be proud I remembered his name— moves forward before sinking to one knee in front of his mother and holding out his hands in supplication before reciting the oath every witch learns by heart long before we have to recite it. The Queen smiles as she steps forward to touch his hand and bid him rise. It softens her severe face, warming her icy gray eyes. The ritual repeats with the next witches in line as Prince Elias resumes his place on the dais with his siblings and a pretty brunette who smiles at him softly, as she links her arm with his, causing the silver cord between them to brighten. Maybe we're getting a royal binding tonight, after all.

"Alexander James Monroe."

I start when I hear my name a few minutes later, having gotten lost in the drone of voices and looking around at all the faces watching us, and move forward. Out of the corner of my eye, I see where Mike has moved to get a better view and snap a photo for my mom. It's allowed, so long as you're respectful and discreet. I move to stand before the queen, whose brow is slightly furrowed as she watches me. That makes my stomach clench with renewed nerves, but I can't worry about what she's thinking now. I kneel, holding my hands up and recite what I was taught, "I vow that I will be faithful to my Queen, never cause her harm and will observe my homage to her completely against all persons in good faith and without deceit. I promise to stand against those who oppose her, to obey her decrees faithfully and pledge my life to her service and will. May the Goddess strike me and my house down if I fail to honor my vow."

A chill races down my spine and I feel something snap in the air, and maybe inside of me. I can't help but remember the other oath I swore just a week ago at our MEPS: "I do solemnly swear that I will support and defend the Constitution of the United States against all enemies, foreign and domestic; that I will bear true faith and allegiance to the same; and that I will obey the orders of the President of the United States and the orders of the officers appointed over me, according to regulations and the Uniform Code of Military Justice. So help me God."

Hundreds of witches have sworn both oaths before me and hundreds will probably swear both after me, but the similarity still chills me, and I can't help but remember Matthew 6:24: "No one can serve two masters, for either he will hate one and love the other; or else he will be devoted to one and despise the other." But the Queen and the United States work together for the protection and benefit of all Americans, supernat and mundane human alike, so it's not like trying to serve two masters, right? Witches and shifters have their own Corps in the military, for fuck's sake. We're all on the same side and have been since the Revolutionary War. MagCorps even fought for the Union, leaving the Confederacy with no organized supernatural force, just scattered battalions that some generals allowed to serve, even though the policy of most of the South has been in line with Mike's dad—keen on not approving of witches to put it mildly. Never mind what they think of shifters. Even so, "so help me God" feels a lot less consequential than calling the Goddess down on me and my family if I break the vow. Christ only knows what that could look like. Words have power.

The Queen watches me for a moment then touches my hand, accepting my oath and gesturing for me to rise. Her herald goes to call the next in line, but she stays him with a lifted hand.

"Where is your mage, Monsieur Monroe?" Her voice sends another chill down my spine, for all that there is no overt threat in it.

I pull my gaze to hers, tensing and trying to figure out if my oath is going to be tested so soon. Before I can answer, I hear Mike behind me.

"Here, Your Majesty."

"Step closer."

She moves to Mike, and I want to throw myself between them. It was a risk, bringing him, but we hoped that our binding ceremony would pave the way for his acceptance in the community. Most mages must swear some kind of oath to the Queen before they are trained—to keep all they learn secret and not work against the community, if nothing else.

Most witches must swear to certain rules regarding training mages, as well. But most mages aren't discovered until they are solidly teenagers. No one has heard of a mage manifesting Sight and the ability to handle and manipulate magic as a child. My parents thought it might endanger Mike if anyone knew they'd found such an anomaly. But they couldn't leave a mage who was already manifesting the ability to manipulate a witch's magic untrained, either. So, the day they found us tossing a ball of magic around like a Nerf ball after school, and we'd told them about the silver cord between us, they'd stepped in to start Mike's training, without consulting anyone else. My mother is the High Priestess of our coven, so she would have had to consult with the High Priestess of Virginia, at the least, to find out what she should do, and even that felt risky to Mike. She wasn't willing to put him in danger. My parents would have taken him in if he hadn't had a seemingly unobjectionable home. But they'd done the next best thing and folded his training in with mine, so every day after school, we played with magic and grew our skills. They'd kept him a secret until time came to submit our application for a formal binding ceremony, to let us go to the relatively safer MagCorps than stay solely in the Marines. Now we are about to see if there is fallout from that.

"I want to hear your story, when you have a moment." She looks at me. "Both of you."

"Yes, Your Majesty," I say quickly.

"Hmm. For now, mage—what is your name again?"

"Michael Mathis, Your Majesty."

"For now, Michael Mathis, will you pledge yourself to me and to our community? It's a little late for the mage oath, but better late than never."

"I don't actually know the oath, but I'm happy to pledge whatever you need from me."

"The herald will lead you through it. Kneel." She points at the ground at her feet, and Mike sinks to one knee without hesitating. "Don't worry. It's basically the same as Alexander vowed."

The herald steps forward and leads Mike through the oath, phrase by phrase. "I, Michael Mathis, vow that I will be faithful to my Queen, never cause her or her people harm and will keep secret the mysteries of the community I now join. I promise to stand against those who oppose them, to obey my Queen's decrees faithfully and pledge my use of magic to her service and will. May the Goddess strike me and my house down if I fail to honor my vow."

Another chill slides down my spine. If I was my sister with her intuitive gifts, I might call it a premonition, but my powers of prescience are as dull as dishwater. Queen

Esther touches Mike's cheek in acceptance, then bids him rise. She dismisses us both with a wave of her hand, then moves back to the foot of the dais to receive the next vow.

Mike reaches for my hand, while I go over the words he vowed in my head, trying to make sure he didn't promise anything dangerous to account for my chill, but I think it's just the solemnity of the vow coupled with the fact that I know he doesn't really believe in the Goddess. I wind our fingers together as he tugs me back to join the others who have made their vow. A few whispers follow us, but I can't make out what they are and don't care. Another hour or two and then the binding rituals will begin.

Mike

I don't have any of the cake or punch laid out for the newly sworn witches—and me. I know this is just a rite of passage for Lex, but I wasn't expecting it and am a little thrown. Like the upcoming ceremony, I'm not uncomfortable with it—I've kept the witches' secrets for thirteen years now; I'm not going to just start blabbing them around. Everyone knows they exist, at least, but there are things I learned, things I know that aren't common knowledge. Even that mages like me exist is mostly a secret, because if people knew that otherwise mundane humans could be born with the ability to see and use magic, even if they have none of their own, they'd all start demanding their letters from Hogwarts, hounding any witches they knew until no one had any peace. There'd probably be a run on magical arti-facts, too.

Mages are extremely rare from what I understand. Mag-Corps has a healthy number of them, but they're gathered from all across the country. Unlike witches and shifters, we have no magic within us, no magical core. Instead, we can manipulate and use magic from other sources—a witch or shifter who shares it with us or magical artifacts—something or someone with stored magic we can access, basically. I watch Lex drink the punch and chat with one of the kids who I assume is one of the Queen's children, since he'd been up on the dais with the others. He's younger than the one who'd made his vow by a year or two, with light brown hair almost as curly as Lex's and hazel eyes. He's handsome enough, though the tilt of his chin seems a little arrogant. He also appears to be grilling Lex, and I move to rescue him, just as the herald calls for the soulmate pairs to come forward.

Moment of truth or whatever.

Lex smiles at the younger man, then moves to me, winding our fingers back together. His hands are trembling a bit, but the smile he gives me seems steady enough. We're led to the third ritual circle in a row of five of them that are already laid out, if not closed. Once we step in, the priestess closes the circle behind us and calls each of the quarters, summoning the elements and spirits of the watchtowers to protect and bear witness to the ceremonies. I notice the prince who'd made his vow—Elias?—is in the first circle with the pretty brunette who'd been by his side. The Queen, in her role as High Priestess of the Goddess, her representative here on Earth, goes to her son and his soulmate first, guiding them through the ceremony.

Even though I have memorized these vows, I didn't realize just how very much they do seem like a wedding until I'm watching Elias' ceremony. Each rite takes about twenty minutes so it's a while before the Queen gets to us. She goes through the same opening spiel about the sacredness of soulmates and how they form the bedrock of the supernatural community and how blessed we are to have found our mate out of all the people in the wide world. I feel Lex flinch at the word "mate," and want to ask what's wrong, but his fingers tighten in mine, and I hold my peace.

The Queen finally addresses us with the ritual admonishment. "Alexander, Michael, let there be no mistake. This binding is not to be entered into lightheartedly. The vows you make today signify that your souls are bound eternally. You make these vows today with the understanding that you are committing to be a partner to one another, and to honor the connection your souls now share with one another. These vows are sacred, and they should not easily be broken, as you make them to one another in the sight of these witnesses."

Christ, this is more serious than some of the weddings I've been to. I'm starting to understand what Lex's parents meant when they told us the soulmate binding ritual was more respected than a marriage among supernats. Marriages still happen, even if only to get the governmental perks for being married, but they always give way to a soulmate binding, which takes precedence. A lot of supernats make both work—one of the main reasons for the polyamory in the community—but a marriage is generally considered more a legal contract than a spiritual binding of two into one, like the Christian church sees it.

"Knowing this, Alexander and Michael, is it your intent to enter into this commitment to one another?"

There's not a thought of hesitation as I answer with Lex. "It is."

She steps in close with her athame and cuts each of us on our left palms. We press them together, as directed, and she binds our hands with a silken cord that doesn't quite soak up the blood that's sluggishly flowing between us. A few drops fall to the flagstones.

"Then make your vows to one another."

Like for a wedding, Lex said we could write our own vows, but since I'd never seen one of these rituals, I'd voted to go with the ones his parents said were the standard.

As the witch, Lex goes first, and I can see the magic spool out from him, all pinks and reds and blues, love, and sincerity. Vulnerability. "Michael, I vow to honor and respect you and to never break that honor. I vow to share your pain as much as your joy and seek to ease it. I vow to share your burdens so our spirits may grow together in this union. I vow to share your laughter and look for the brightness and good in you, always. I may make you angry sometimes; I may cause you pain, but I vow that will never be my intent. I will protect you whatever may come and put you before all. You are the other half of my soul, of myself, and I recognize you as such, before the Goddess and all these witnesses. May the Goddess strike me and my house down if I fail to honor my vow. So mote it be."

I can see the magic flare all around us at his final words, something locking into place that I didn't even know was missing. The silver cord between us thickens and seems to swirl, with rainbows reflecting in its depth. Lex gives me a small smile, squeezing my hands and I squeeze back just as the Queen prompts me with a nod.

The vows are the same as he made to me, and I'm proud of myself that my voice doesn't shake the way Lex's hands are trembling again. His part is done, so his nerves surprise me, but I can't chase down that rabbit hole to figure out what's wrong until later.

"...So mote it be."

If I thought something locked into place after Lex's vows and that the cord reacted to him, that's nothing compared to what it does as I finish mine. The cord is nearly twice as thick as it was before we started. There's no going back from this now, and I wouldn't have it any other way. I vaguely hear the Queen giving her spiel about the consequence of our vows—but I listened in the first two rituals, so that's okay. I do hear the part that's straight out of Christian weddings, if tweaked, about what the Goddess joins, let no one put asunder, and I thrill a bit at the permanence that means: no one can separate us now, not the Marine Corps, not the Mag Corps, not my dad, not even her.

We do the ring exchange next, after the queen removes the bindings at our hands—on right hands, not left, though soulmates who marry usually wear both rings together, like their binding rings are engagement rings. Those who don't still have their left hand free for their future spouse. Then the Queen is making her pronouncement. The other two pairs before us had kissed without any prompting, but when she finishes the pronouncement, she says quietly, "Please seal your bond with a kiss."

Lex looks startled and then apologetic when he meets my eyes. I'm a little thrilled, because it lets me see what it's like with it being ritual rather than suddenly out of desire or whatever. We've exchanged kisses on the cheeks before, and it's not unusual for one of us to drop a kiss on the other's head while we're snuggling, so this isn't that different, right?

The moment Lex's lips touch mine, I know how wrong I am. Lightning zings along my nerves, and I feel like I've been punched in the gut. It's no more of a kiss than that, just a brush of lips on lips. Innocent. Chaste. And I'm disappointed when it ends.

Lex looks shocked when I pull back, and I hope it's because the kiss gut-punched him, too. I smile, and he seems to relax. Then people are cheering, the circle is opened, and the Queen moves on to the next pair.

"Sorry about the kiss," Lex whispers as we're swept toward the reception hall where dinner will apparently be served once all the bindings are done. "I didn't expect that. I hope it wasn't too awkward for you?"

What is this man even talking about? But he seems genuinely worried, and I can't stand that.

"It's fine, Lex. No big deal."

I can't decipher his expression then, but I feel something that's almost disappointment, and I don't think it's mine. What the hell? I know Mr. and Mrs. Monroe said the bond would turn more empathic once we formalized it, but I'm not actually feeling what Lex feels, right?

"Okay. Good. Come on, I'm starving."

Me, too.

CHAPTER 5

Lex

The reception hall is off the courtyard and bigger than should be able to fit in a house in the Quarter. I'm tempted to check for the Doctor and wonder if the Queen is doing dimensional magic of some kind. I've heard it's theoretically possible, but the books all say no one's cracked it, yet. But if anyone could, she could.

Something's up with the bond, I notice, as we walk across the dance floor toward the buffet table. It's more solid, which is great, and it's like I can almost feel Mike and what he's feeling, which I know is a possibility on some level, but I didn't expect it this quickly or without us working on it. The cord is humming and still reflecting multiple colors back instead of just silver. I like it, I decide, as Mike scans the room before going still.

"Who is that?"

I follow his gaze to the most beautiful woman I've ever seen. I'd say she was the hottest babe I've ever seen, but there's something too dignified about her for that. She's a little younger looking than Queen Esther, though not by a lot—definitely a good decade older than us, but I like someone with more experience and a woman like that has things to teach. I can just tell. However, given she's surrounded by three very handsome men who all manage to appear to be touching her, even if they aren't, I'm guessing she's not on the market. She looks familiar, somehow, and then the man standing behind her leans forward, his gaze meeting mine. He nods, and I recognize him from last night. Anton. Andie's stepfather. Why the woman looks so familiar hits me then, too. Add a few decades onto Andie and you'd have this woman.

Mike seems to answer his own question a moment later. "Shifter, right?"

Mike's only ever seen a few shifters, Andie, Marguerite and Tia included, so I can understand him not being sure at a glance, even with his gifts. I nod. "Yeah. Shifter. Feline of some kind, by the way she moves." I should mention what I've figured out, but some part of me is curious if he can work it out on his own, too.

"And her eyes."

I hadn't noticed her eyes, yet, too entranced by the rest of her. Her hair falls in a curtain of black silk down to her waist, with just a hint of curl, like Andie's. Her skin is creamy and darker than her daughter's, but not so dark as Marguerite and Tia's. It's perfect. Her nose tilts just a touch and her lips are fuller than Andie's and look like they laugh a lot. I look at her eyes and catch a glow of blue when the light flashes in them.

"That's my mom," a familiar, amused voice says behind us.

I spin, a little embarrassed at being caught gaping and glad I didn't say anything I was thinking. I smile at finding Andie standing there. She looks younger than last night, in comparison with her mother, more knees and elbows and early teen coltishness that's still feline and alluring in the tilt of her head and teasing smile.

She's biting back a laugh as she adds, with an apologetic grimace, "Queen Eleanor. My mom."

"Your Highness," I say automatically, bowing, as I would have last night, if she'd told us who she was. I hear Mike's sharp indrawn breath and see him mimic my bow out of the corner of my eye. Trying to fit the pieces together, I try desperately to remember what I know about the Shifter Queen's family. She has three husbands, I know, which makes sense of the men surrounding her—and Andie's comment about her two stepfathers. One of her husbands is her soulmate and her consort. She married the other two for political reasons. First, the Alpha of alphas, the leader of the wolf shifters—Anton, I'm guessing. Her third husband is a witch and one of Queen Esther's cousins, I think. Before this moment, I'd only have known she had a daughter because my sister is somewhat obsessed with the royal families, and Andie is just two years older than her. "Princess Andrea. I apologize for not recognizing you last night. And any inappropriate over-familiarity."

She nods at her name, and there's a hint of regality in it, like the Crown Princess of the shifters should have, but then it disappears in a flash of her bright smile, causing irrepressible effervescence to bubble up. I feel a pang in my chest, somewhere near the root of the silver cord. "Andie's fine. Like I said." She turns that eager smile on Mike. "I didn't realize you were the unsanctioned mage. I was hoping we'd get to meet when I heard you'd be here. I've never met a renegade before."

Mike's good with kids—a weird thing to think about our soulmate—and laughs. "I'm not sure I'm the renegade here. I was just a kid who could see magic."

"Still, that's cool. Was it because you're soulmates?"

"My parents think so," I interject, not liking losing her attention, even to Mike. "They think our finding each other somehow triggered his abilities to reveal themselves earlier than usual."

"That's so romantic," she says with a sigh, though she frowns a little after that moment's sigh. "But you barely even kissed at the end of your ceremony. That was disappointing. You'll have to do better when it's our turn."

Christ, she's as bad a Hannah, maybe worse, if you consider she's younger. Still, I suppose she has a right if anyone does. I can't explain that without raising questions I'm not ready to answer, yet. Still, there's a clear question in her eyes that I want to ease.

"Too many people staring at us," Mike says, pulling her attention back to him. "It wasn't the time to put on a show."

"Oh." She sighs a little again, then flashes him a teasing smile. "I'm just making it clear I expect to put on a show at my binding ceremony, so you'd better use the next couple of years to work up to it. It has to be compellingly romantic and sexy, okay?"

Mike turns red but tries to nod.

I laugh and bow again. "Understood. I'll try to help him get over his shyness."

"You could take the first step and kiss him more properly now. I'd like to see—something to believe in and remember for the cold years of waiting I still have."

Precocious little thing, isn't she?

Mike makes a slightly choking sound, drawing her attention and concern. "Are you okay?"

"He's a little worried at your being so much younger than us," I tell her. Not that three-and-a-half years is so much, really, in the grand scheme of things.

She makes a sound somewhere between a snort and a giggle. "Why? Is this one of those human morality things?"

"You're still a kid," Mike manages to protest.

"Hardly," she returns. "It's less than two years to reaching my majority—the point at which I could become Queen, rule over a whole species if, Goddess forbid, anything happened to my mom. Less than two years until I'm considered mature enough for that kind of power. That's not something you can say about a kid."

The full implication of her identity only hits me then. She's going to be one of the Queens. Our destinies just changed dramatically, indeed, though Marguerite pointed out it wasn't Andie herself who changed mine, as she was always part of it. So, maybe it's just that I've recognized what that destiny at least partly entails. Maybe that's what Marguerite meant, calling me "my prince." Though the title would only apply if Andie chooses me as her consort. There's nothing requiring her to do so—though, by tradition, it would be either me or Mike, and is more likely to be me—I don't think a mage has ever been made a consort. It might be a little too radical.

The DJ shifts the music to something slower and Andie holds out her hand, this time palm up, her look a little imperious. "We should dance. And talk. I've been looking for you since I knew what a soulmate was and all I know is your names, that you're careless with your own safety when it comes to saving damsels in distress, and that you don't like putting on sexy shows for people."

Well, fuck. That cinches it. I am, indeed, cursed.

Mike

Be kind to her. Lex's comments from last night come back to me. Yes, she's even younger than what I was already worried about, but that's okay because we don't have to do anything but be nice to her. Lex and I knew we were soulmates in kindergarten. Our kiss today was our first one ever. There's nothing inherently wrong with having a younger teen as our soulmate. We just have to be kind. Time will take care of the rest.

However, that she's a princess changes things in ways that will take some getting used to. Her bodyguards from last night make more sense, now, and I glance around until I catch sight of them in the shadows, watching us suspiciously.

"Seriously, guys. Breathe," she says softly, somehow not upset at our dismay. If anything, she looks more amused. "I'm not going to drag you off and try and seduce you, and I already know you don't like public displays. But you promised me a dance last night. It's my first ball, and I don't want to sit with my mom all night." Her smile quirks. "We can even leave room for Jesus or whatever they say, if it'll make you more comfortable. I promise, no one's going to execute you for touching me." The call-back to what the chaperones always told us at dances to keep us from pressing too close together makes me laugh. It's so incongruous, especially coming from a shifter witch and a princess, though I guess they say it to teens down here, too.

"Lex is the better dancer. He actually knows some steps. I just...sway."

Something snaps into place for Lex, and he smiles, taking her hand. "Don't run away," he tells me...almost flirtatiously, before leading her out on the dance floor.

Her mom is watching closely, intent on them. That's a little terrifying because, as I recall, the royal shifters all turn into leopards of some sort, and she's watching Lex like he's a threat, or prey. However, Lex does indeed leave room for Jesus and starts waltzing Andie around the space gracefully. Her mom still watches, but a small smile finally curls her lips. Until Queen Esther sweeps into the room, that is, looking around it and frowning when she spots Lex and Andie. People get out of her way as she makes her way to Queen Eleanor. Their conversation is in furious whispers and Andie's dad and stepdads close ranks around them. Esther's younger son, who Lex was chatting with before, trails behind his mother, also frowning as he watches Andie and Lex intently.

Well, shit. Is our new little soulmate already spoken for? That'd be as awkward as her being fourteen. I don't know all the rules, except that soulmates are supposed to trump all relationships, because they're ordained by the Goddess. They're destiny, which is why supernats would find mine and Lex's lack of romance so odd. Of course, romance is out of the question with Andie, too, for three or four more years, at least, though I suspect we'll have a hard time convincing her there's any need to wait after her sixteenth birthday. So, given we've got a girlfriend, Andie should be able to have a boyfriend. But said boyfriend shouldn't be glaring when she dances with Lex. She steps back from Lex when the music ends, cheeks pinkening, and he looks over at the young man. His bow is exaggerated as he hands her over to the boy, but he gives her one of what I think of as his special smiles, kisses her cheek, and whispers something that makes her giggle before he lets her go. If looks could kill, the princeling would be up on murder charges, but Lex doesn't seem to notice as he makes his way back to me.

I intercept him, putting one hand to his hip and drawing him close. His eyes widen as he looks at me, but I'm still watching everyone watching us.

"My turn," I tell him as his brows knit together in a frown, and he looks at me with questions in his eyes.

"You want to dance...? To a slow song?"

"Yep. It's our reception, after all. I'm sure somewhere there's a rule about first dances."

For a moment, I think he is going to pull away, but then he shrugs and presses in closer than I pulled him in to begin with. Jesus is not getting between us, apparently. I try not to find the press and sway of his hips distracting, but it's hard not to think about how perfectly he fits in my arms, and it should be weird, but it's not, even when he lays his head on my shoulder. Queen Esther nods approvingly, looking happier, and I can't help glancing toward Andie and the princeling. She's also watching us with an approving smile.

"What was that about with Andie and the boy?" I ask, hoping Lex got the story.

"Hmm...? Oh, apparently, they're betrothed."

"Like to be married?"

"That's usually what that means, yeah."

"She's just a kid!"

"She's a princess. He's a prince. Royalty have different customs. Plus, apparently, they're supposed to heal the rift between the shifters and witches, which is ridiculous since he's also a shifter and she's also a witch, but she said something about the Seers at their births saying they'd fulfill the prophecy about the supernat Messiah."

"The what now?" As far as I know, there's only one messiah, and he doesn't have a tail, which a kid of two shifters would.

"It's an old prophecy," Lex explains, "That someday there'll be a messiah born as a scion of both royal houses who'll be an avatar for the Goddess and unite the supernatural Courts and help them prevail against the human world."

"The human world needs prevailing against? I thought we were all getting along save for a few fire and brimstone types." Like Dad.

Lex shrugs, though his voice stays quiet, barely audible over the music. "I don't know. Maybe it will get worse. I just know that every supernat kid grows up hearing about the prophecy, and Andie's supposed to be the messiah's mom or whatever."

"You've never mentioned it before."

"I didn't think it was important or relevant to us. It had nothing to do with us, and I didn't want you to think my family was anti-human or anything."

"It's something to do with us now."

"And now I'm telling you about it." Lex lifts his head from my shoulder, and I hear the exaggerated patience in his voice.

I tangle my fingers in his curls more tightly than necessary and tug his head back down. "How does her being our soulmate affect things?"

"I don't think it does." He settles back against me with only a moment's resistance. "I mean, we could maybe make a fuss about it, but since we only have the claim over her that she allows, and none until she's legally an adult, no one would likely listen. She doesn't seem upset about it. More resigned, but she says Nick's a good guy and they're friends. Plus, he's met his soulmate already, too, and is in love with her. So, things should work out, if we find we want them to, when the time comes."

"The princeling's name is 'Nick'?"

"That's what Andie called him."

I decide to let it go, because getting jealous over Lex's flings is bad enough. I'm not going to glare at some kid for dancing with another kid who might grow up to love me, one day many years from now.

"We should figure out some way to get to know her better after we're gone, like, letters or at least emails or something. You said we just need to be kind to her and ignoring her doesn't seem kind."

Lex turns his head and nuzzles my neck a little, which is damn distracting, humming something I take as agreement. "She doesn't seem likely to let us ignore her." I manage not to flinch as his lips shape the words against my throat, but it's a near thing. I don't think I'm imagining that I can feel him there, emotionally, alongside my own feelings, and that's going to take some time to get used to, to be able to sort out what's him from what's me. Right now, though, an overwhelming feeling of peace is sliding through me from both of us. There's maybe a hint of dismay that our situation has just gotten more complicated—her other destiny and age aside. Andie's still the next Shifter Queen, and that's always going to come with complications. But we've found her, and we've solidified the bond between the two of us into a formal binding. Dismay and my own confusion over things aside, the general emotion humming between us as we dance is contentment.

CHAPTER 6

July 2010

Lex

The trail is shaded, which is pleasant after the stretch of time we spent in barren fields two weeks ago. I step over a tree root and down a natural step, taking care as I put weight on my left ankle. I sprained it badly during the Crucible—our final challenge at Basic Training and aggravated it severely by marching ten more miles on it before getting it checked out at medical. But I made it through, and Mike and I are now both officially members of the U.S. Marine Corps. We've got twelve days of leave before we have to report for MagCorps training, so we're back home, despite my suggestion that we go to Disney World.

Instead of Disney, though, we agree we need to see Hannah before she heads to college, and we head into a year-long program. It's suddenly odd to think of, having found Andie. Neither of us is sure how to handle the relationships. Andie isn't our girlfriend, and we always knew we had another soulmate out there, but somehow it feels different since she has a face and a name. Like, it's not really fair to Hannah that we're bound to one another and have Andie working on growing up. And it's not fair to Andie if our hearts are taken up with someone else, someone who might be expecting something more from at least one of us than we can give.

So far—which has only been the 30-minute drive to the trailhead and the time gathering our gear in the parking lot—we have been able to fill the air by telling Hannah about Basic Training and the crushing nature of the Crucible. She'd kissed us both when we picked her up, not caring that her folks were watching disapprovingly from their battered white porch.

We're hiking to our favorite campground, planning on spending the weekend and doing some stargazing. When we run out of stories from Basic, Hannah tells us about her early orientation in Charlottesville, and about meeting her roommate for the first time. The day is warm, but the shade of the trees helps and, after Louisiana and South Carolina, even Virginia doesn't feel quite as humid.

"How was New Orleans?" Hannah asks when we stop at an overlook for lunch. "You were there when all the protests were going on, weren't you? What was it they said—something about young witches and shifters pledging loyalty to the Queens?"

Mike freezes in the middle of taking a drink of water, so I jump in.

"Yeah. They do it every year right before Mardi Gras. We came across a couple of demonstrations, but it wasn't too bad."

"It's a shame you couldn't have gone for Mardi Gras instead."

"It conflicted with our report date for Basic," Mike tells her, having regained his ability to speak. "But we want to go back again in a couple of years, so maybe we'll plan to stay for Mardi Gras then."

"Why not just plan it for Mardi Gras? All three of us could go."

She's never asked anything so close to the supernatural before, and part of me wants to tell her.

"We could do that," Mike says instead, maybe guessing she'll have forgotten by then. Given that'll be about the time Andie might expect a binding ceremony, hopefully Hannah forgets by then. "But it was really cool to see all the supernats in town. Still had a party vibe, you know, with less throwing up in the streets."

"I didn't think you liked supernats." Hannah sounds surprised. "Your dad's always complaining about them."

"I'm not my dad!"

"Of course not..."

It's not the distraction I'd have chosen, but my urge to confess eases back while they make up, and Hannah lets it drop, or seems to.

When we're setting up our tent for the night, the next moment comes. "What's with the matching rings? You guys finally declaring you're friends forever in the face of the toxic masculinity of Basic Training?"

I play with my ring, spinning it around my finger. "Something like that."

"You two have always been close, of course, but it does seem like something's changed."

Mike focuses on the tent studiously, so I tackle that. "Basic training was hell, yeah. But the common challenges did make us closer. Brothers-in-arms, even if those arms weren't firing live rounds, y'know? The rings were just something we found in New Orleans and thought would be good to commemorate our time there."

She smiles but doesn't look quite convinced. "Just so long as you didn't run off to Vermont without telling me."

"They're not on our left hands," Mike points out.

"No, they aren't," she acknowledges. "But I think they look good on both of you."

He finishes getting the tent up while she grabs us beers out of the cooler, and we settle in to watch the sunset, then the stars for a bit.

After the Crucible, I could've used a break from tents, but here we are, after dark falls, in a tent again, though this one is in a much better location, with better company, especially since Hannah stopped asking questions after sunset. As we turn in, we've got an air mattress to sleep on and a naked girl on it with us, so I'm not complaining. The two six-packs of a local microbrew don't hurt, either. Well, one six-pack now.

I'm especially not complaining when Hannah slides down to wrap her mouth around my dick, tonguing at me while her hand fondles my balls. I can see Mike stroking between her legs, but his eyes are on where her mouth meets my dick and I can pretend the hungry look in his eyes is for me, not just the free show. I wind my hands through Hannah's red hair and fall back on the mattress with a moan. Her pale skin is a creamy bridge between me and Mike, and if she catches me looking at him as much as her, it's our secret. She knows how I feel, has even tried to play wingman for me a time or two, though Mike seems oblivious, which is for the best.

She moans around me at something his fingers are doing, and my balls tighten. I stave off an orgasm, barely, and she pulls off.

"I want to try something I saw online…"

"Well, that's not ominous," Mike murmurs, then chuckles. She pulls away from him just enough to swing a leg over me and shifts to press my dick against her slick folds.

"I want you both to fuck me, together."

Oh, Goddess, I'm going to come just from the idea.

"You were in a better position for that a second ago."

This man is adorable or willfully obtuse to not know what she's suggesting. Offering.

"I think she's talking about double penetration, Mike."

His eyes widen, and he swallows before I feel his hand slide between her legs again. His fingertips brush over the head of my dick, seemingly accidentally, and I bite back a whimper. I can feel his fingers dip into her, getting some of her slickness on his fingers before he drags them back to tease at her puckered opening.

"Yeah?"

Hannah rocks a little, enough that the head of my dick slides into her, and I clutch tight at her hips, not wanting to go farther until I know what Mike will do.

"Yeah," she says on a breathy little moan, pushing back against his fingers. "Please? I missed you and you're going to be gone for months again. I just want to make tonight one we all remember."

It doesn't take long for Mike to get on board, though he still takes careful time to prepare her and himself—slipping on a condom and lubing it up. I can feel his fingers stroking me through the layers of her skin that separate us, and it takes literal magic for me to stay still. Finally, after what feels like years, he presses into her and, finally, so do I.

It's as close as I'm going to get to this between us, and I'm in heaven as each of his thrusts all but run his dick against mine. Hannah's going to have bruises tomorrow from where my fingers are gripping her. She drops her forehead to my shoulder and rocks back to meet us both. I loosen my grip on her, sliding my fingers between us to play with her clit, wanting this to be good for her, too.

Mike's plastered against her back, his hands at her waist, and I can't help but tangle our fingers together against her skin. He gives me a startled look—we've never touched during one of these 3-ways, but I notice he doesn't pull away. It's messy and uncoordinated, at first, but we eventually find a rhythm that works for us all. Hannah murmurs encouragement between moans, seemingly intent on showing us she's enjoying this as much as we are.

Mike's pupils are blown from more than the dark, and he and I finally find a rhythm, moving against each other through her. He holds her and me both, and I keep working my fingers against her until she's the one to fly apart first, coming hard. The way her walls spasm around me, coupled with the hard thrust of Mike's cock is enough to have me cresting over the edge, spilling into her as my vision whites out a bit at the edges. Mike keeps fucking her as she and I twitch in the aftermath of our orgasms, but it isn't long before he, too, comes with a shout. I manage to pry my eyes open long enough to watch him, then catch the triumphant smile she gives me.

I kiss her sweet lips, murmuring my deep and abiding affection through the words we rarely say aloud. Mike's not so shy, telling her how amazing she is and how much he loves her. He's still looking at me, though, so I let myself bask and pretend.

Eventually, we pull apart and I snag some of the camp washcloths we brought to clean us all up. I don't go so far as trying to clean Mike up, but our fingers brush as I hand him the cloth and he smiles at me without any of the embarrassment I'm always afraid I'll see there.

"Thank you," Hannah murmurs. "Now I have a memory to keep me warm all the time we'll be apart."

"And so do we," I tell her, brushing a kiss over her lips. I nibble down her neck and run into Mike coming around from the back. Before I can pull back, he nibbles a kiss against my lips, nipping at my lower lip.

"So do we," he agrees, even as I try not to chase after his lips but pull back before the post-coital haze wears off and he realizes what he's done.

Mike

Hannah looks smugger than I've ever seen her, and I'm not sure if that's from the sex or me kissing Lex. Lex looks like he's ready to bolt, and my stomach twists. He'd seemed into it in the moment, but maybe he's worried now we crossed a line he didn't want to cross. I disentangle from Hannah a bit to brush my fingers through his hair.

"Okay?"

He laughs, a little disbelieving sound, even as he pulls back away from me. "Um, yeah. Obviously." He runs his hand down Hannah's side, untangling the grip he's had on my other hand. "Wow. Watching things like that's how you kept yourself entertained while we were gone, babe?"

Hannah stretches and rolls to her back, leaving my abandoned hand to just rest on the mattress, bereft of the warmth of both Lex's grip and her skin. "Yep."

"What will you do while we're gone this time?"

She smirks as she stretches. "I got a toy that'll recreate this, so I expect I'll spend a lot of money on batteries, if I can find enough alone time in the dorms."

"When do you move?"

"Six more weeks." Hannah tilts her head to brush a kiss over Lex's lips. "I still wish you were coming with me."

"Me too," I say, because I'm still not thrilled at the idea of dragging Lex off to war when he's smart enough to do what he loves and deserves a normal college experience. He keeps saying we can go when our enlistment is up, that we can use our GI bills, but I was never meant for college, not like the two of them and Brandon, my brilliant brother.

Lex frowns at me over Hannah's shoulder. "Well, I made my choice, and I don't regret it."

"You're both too thin," Hannah chides us.

"We'll gain the weight back in advanced training," Lex assures her. "The last few weeks of basic were rough, but it won't be so bad where we're going next."

"I wish you'd tell me where that was."

"We can't, sweetheart," I tell her, brushing a kiss over her shoulder.

In truth, we could, but Lex's family is still firmly in the broom closet, given anti-supernat sentiment around here. It's not so bad if you're over the mountain in Charlottesville, but in Staunton, they'd be subject to all sorts of abuse.

Hannah wouldn't care, but Lex's parents don't want anyone to know, for Lizzie's sake, and Lex and I honor that. But it's hard, keeping stuff from Hannah. Maybe she's not our soulmate, but I still love her, and I think Lex does, too, and it sucks to feel like there's this major part of ourselves we have to keep from her. I didn't know how to respond to her questions earlier, letting Lex respond instead. Maybe it was a coward's move, but his secret is bigger than mine, as is his potential danger.

"Just promise you'll be careful. Both of you."

So, we promise, even if I'm not sure we'll be able to keep that promise. I knew what to expect from boot camp, but neither of us knows what to expect at MagCorps.

CHAPTER 7

July 2010

Lex

"And this'll be your room." The smiling young mage—Ronan something or other—opens a door for us that's about halfway down the hall of the sixth floor of the barracks. He's already shown us the chow hall, the gym, and the rec room.

"Our room?" I ask, feeling a flash of shock at the idea after twelve weeks in the squad bay with twenty-eight other guys.

"Sure," he says with a smile. "Go on in. Head's shared with the guys on the other side of you, who are me and my partner. Lock it if you're doing anything but hygiene. We'll do the same."

"Anything like...?" Mike asks. I don't clue him in, too happy we won't be sharing a bathroom with twenty-eight other guys anymore, either.

I move into the room and take it in. I expect to see two twin beds or even a bunk. I'm not prepared for the single queen-sized bed in the middle of the room. It looks comfortable, but there's only one. I come back out to ask Ronan about it.

"Anything like...blowing off steam." He arches one eyebrow, looking amused. "You're not at bootcamp anymore, boys."

"Oh, you mean like..." Mike swallows. "With each other."

"When we don't feel like using our bed." I stress the singular, which has Mike turning into the room and staring.

"Well, yeah, sometimes it's fun to get frisky in the showers," Ronan says, like I should know this.

"I wouldn't know." My lips feel numb. Mike's barely met my eyes in the two weeks since our camping trip with Hannah, and I'm convinced he's regretting every second of it. Definitely the kiss at the end. What is he going to do about this development?

"Ah, right. Straight from your folks' houses to boot camp and never had the chance, right?"

"Right." Mike answers for me, before I feel his hand on my lower back, which is reassuring. At least he's not heading for a bus home. "My dad is against anything we might do at my house and Lex has a little sister who can open any lock with her brain, so."

"I get it, man. I've got one of those myself, and my family doesn't know about me being a mage or that Isaac—my soulmate—is even a shifter, let alone a shifter-witch. They'd be okay with it—my parents are mundane humans, but our extended family are witches and the gene turned up in my little sister, too. No mages but me and one uncle, though. I just...never wanted to feel different from them, so I kept it to myself. It's a relief to be here and just be able to be ourselves, fully. You'll see."

"There's just the one bed?" I go back into the room, like I might have somehow missed a whole piece of furniture.

Ronan laughs. "Like I said, you're not in boot camp anymore. Welcome to MagCorps, boys. Chow's at six, sharp, so I'll see you then, and you can meet Isaac. I'm right next door if you need anything."

I wander back into our room and put down my rucksack on one of the footlockers. "Well, I knew it would be different here..."

"You weren't kidding when you said they supported soulmates."

I look up at Mike, feeling a flare of panic. He'll think I tricked him into something. "I didn't know. Swear."

"Didn't think you did by the face you were making." He drops his own pack and moves to my side, reaching out to ruffle his fingers through my curls. Something unclenches inside of me that I didn't know I was holding tight until this moment. I lean a little into his touch until he looks down and meets my eyes. His fingers still for a moment before he slowly extricates them. "It's not like we haven't shared a bed before. It'll be like sleeping over, just more permanent."

"Yeah, and it's plenty big enough for us to both have room." I bite my lower lip to keep it from trembling and giving my worry away. His gaze seems to fix on it, or maybe I'm just imagining things. Wishful thinking or whatever.

"Sure, it is." I almost don't hear the comment and when I do and look up, he's staring at the bed.

"Mike..." I wait for him to look at me again. "I didn't know. I figured we'd still be in a squad bay, but that no one would give us grief about being too close. That's..."

"Don't worry about it, Lex. Seriously. I know you didn't know, and I wouldn't care if you did. It's not a big deal to me. I promise." He squats down in front of me and puts a finger under my chin to make sure I'm looking at him. As if I'd want to look away. "We're soulmates, right? Bled and bound for the rest of our lives. Apparently, it comes with perks now that we're back in your world."

"It's your world now, too." He seems to forget that easily.

"Fine. Now that we're back in our world, and outta my dad's." He smiles and his thumb brushes my lower lip, sending a trembling wave of pleasure through me. Unfair, when I can't reciprocate.

"Thank Christ and the Goddess for that."

"Amen." He pushes to his feet, still smiling at me. "Why don't you start unpacking? I'm gonna go grab a soda from the vending machine. You want one?"

I shake my head. "No. They're still too sweet tasting after so long without."

"We gotta get your sweet tooth back."

"And lose these chiseled abs I literally bled for? Bite your tongue."

He smiles and turns to go, and I think I must be hearing things because I swear, I hear him mutter something about how he'd rather bite mine.

Mike

There are so many flashing danger signs in my head I might as well be Will Robinson. I haven't been able to stop thinking about that night in the tent since it happened, and now I have to find a way to sleep while still not being able to touch him the way I want to touch him. Even just now, it was all I could do to not try and kiss away his worried look. Maybe I should have, and we'd just figure it out. If he wasn't the most important person in the world to me, I'd be more willing to consider it.

I've been trying to explore more on my own—watching gay porn instead of straight, checking other objectively good-looking guys out—but none of it does anything for me. The only porn that was even a little appealing was one where one of the guys looked like Lex. I wasn't disgusted by the rest or anything, but it didn't turn me on. Surely, if I were bisexual, something would've triggered in my head? It's been the same with hot guys. I can acknowledge they're hot without feeling my masculinity threatened or whatever, but I'm not attracted to them. Lex? Lex, I can't look at for too long or I have an obvious and awkward boner. Lex, I sometimes have to physically stop myself from touching, have to make myself walk away before I push him up against the nearest wall and kiss him until he can't stay standing.

If I'm strictly honest, it's kind of always been this way for me, even with girls. Don't get me wrong – I like sex. I like sex a lot, and I've had plenty of crushes in my life, but it's like...the crush comes first and then I start feeling the attraction. I knew Hannah for five years before I started thinking about her that way. It's almost like I've got to like someone before I want to fuck them, which seems backwards from how most of the guys I know are. Lex doesn't even usually care if he gets someone's name before he's trying to find somewhere to get naked if he finds them attractive. I mean, he ultimately does fall in love even harder than I do, but for sex? He can happily do just sex and move on. I don't usually want to have it until I don't want to move on.

Maybe I'm just weird that way. Maybe the reason I don't want to kiss any other guys is that I don't have any others I'm particularly close to. Most of the guys I might've gotten close to in my life were…wary of me because of Lex, because they assumed he was my boyfriend, and they didn't want to get too close to the queer guys. I figured if that mattered so much to them, then I didn't care to get to know them, because they'd probably be jerks to Lex like the bullies in middle school. I don't have time for those kinds of guys. Like the guys in our company in basic training, for another example. Band of brothers, my ass. Even our drill instructor turned into a dick about it, giving us extra work for "probably being fags."

Maybe we'll do better here? Where they can tease about fully expecting us to make use of the shower for recreational activities and where they talk openly about their same sex partners and using magic and it's all just seen as normal.

They only gave us one bed. One nice bed at that. Maybe that'll be enough of a push to at least talk about what happened with Hannah. Maybe Lex will stop being skittish and tell me what's wrong. Maybe it won't be that he's pissed I kissed him, or that he feels sorry for me for wanting him when he doesn't want me. Maybe, maybe, maybe. At some point, I may just have to man up and ask. Talk about my, ugh, feelings. Listen as he talks about his. Maybe it'll be better than I anticipate. Maybe he's just as scared of scaring me off as I am of scaring him. Wouldn't that be a cruel irony?

Actually, that would be amazing. Because then we could be on the same page, and I wouldn't have to keep trying to come up with ways to test the waters.

Too bad testing the waters seems far safer to my heart.

He knocks on the door, and I jump.

"We should head down to chow soon. We could sit with Ronan and his partner—Isaac—if they have space?"

I hate that his voice lifts, making it a question. He's so excited at the hope of not being an outcast. They'd better not turn out to be dicks like at boot camp and home. I may not love the idea of sharing him with a wide group of friends, of losing some of his attention; I've never had to, but it'd be worth it for him to be happy. He deserves everyone to see him shine like I do.

"Yeah. That'd be cool. He seems nice."

Lex's smile is bright in agreement. "Yeah. I think we made the right move, applying for MagCorps, even if we can't tell your dad, yet. After we're through training, they'll have to let us—he'll see the Corps patch on our uniforms, if nothing else."

"You think we can tell?"

"It's MagCorps, not the CIA or MI-6. I don't think there's a NOC list we're on, or a bunch of undercover missions we'd be sent on."

"But your folks..."

His face falls. "Maybe your folks would be so embarrassed by the assumptions people would make about them that they wouldn't tell."

"Or my dad would just tell me to quit."

"He can't do that. Not anymore. You're safest with me, now that we're bound, and Queen Esther won't let us go back to being regular infantry grunts."

"You sure about that?" I ask, hopeful, but my dad has always ruled my life so strongly, it's hard to imagine him not doing so anymore.

"She has partial control of MagCorps, and it's the only place where the U.S. military recognizes her authority over us, so. Yeah. Pretty sure," Lex tells me with a wry smile.

"Always comes down to power."

"Makes the world go 'round," Lex quips.

"Thought that was love," I comment.

"Wouldn't that be nice?"

We make it to chow on time and get an overall nice welcome. Ronan waves us over to where he's sitting with a young man who has sandy blond curls a bit like Lex's but paired with pretty golden-brown eyes. He looks more like an artist than a soldier, down to the scarf loosely tossed around his neck, but his grip is strong, and he meets my eyes with almost a challenge in his. I check out his aura and nod to myself. It reminds me of Andie's stepfather, and Ronan did say he was a shifter. Wolf, by my guess. I drop my gaze to the side, not showing submission, but not challenging him, either. When he smiles, the artist is back, and I guess I pass muster. Lex clasps his hand with a friendly smile before settling in the chair between us. No challenge for him, just a flash of dimples on both sides. We all chat for a while, exchanging stories. Turns out the other pair met in boot camp in San Diego and discovered they were soulmates. A mage and a shifter, they were always bound for MagCorps, but had to request reassignment when they got here to be put together.

"We're technically all Charlie Company, but they call our squad the Soulmate Squad. Most of the others are made up of singles or unbonded pairs. Only bonded pairs get assigned together once we graduate." Ronan gestures around at the other guys sitting at the tables around us. Well, mostly guys. There are two pairs of girls and about three guy-and-girl pairings. "The other soulmates hang with us because they know they could be separated at any moment. I think they think we somehow give them cover."

"Why wouldn't they just choose to do the binding ceremony?" Even if Lex and I aren't romantically linked, not binding my life to his didn't even feel like an option. I can't imagine skipping it if we were a couple.

"Bad timing for some of them," Isaac says with a wry smile. "Or just not being sure of each other, yet. A lot of them just found each other in the last year or two. Some less than that."

Having met Andie helps me contextualize their reasoning a little. Even if she wasn't just fourteen, I don't know that I'd have wanted to hop right to pledging to be her partner for life. Sure, she and Lex seem to assume we will do the ritual with her at some point, but I'd like to get to know her better before making a sacred vow to her. She's our soulmate, true, but even after a few other conversations before leaving for boot camp, we don't really know her. Then again, we're also Triune souls—I'm not sure if we could choose not to do the ceremony without causing a political crisis. I file it away to ask Lex more about later.

"But you two haven't known each other long..." Lex looks at Isaac and seems as confused as I feel. Then again, we're different just because of the length of time we've known.

"We like to live on the edge," Isaac tells him with a friendly, but sharp, grin,

Ronan leans in. "Rumor has it you two found each other when you were in kindergarten. I said there's no way."

"Well, then, I hope you didn't put much money on it, because rumors are true." Lex looks damn proud of himself, like it was all his doing, rather than fate. Or even just luck. "We were in the same class, and we sat next to each other at lunch and just...he asked if I could see a silver cord going from my chest to his and what it was. The rest is history."

"Pay up, babe." Isaac holds out his hand to Ronan.

"I'll pay up later, upstairs."

Lex chokes on a laugh, though the smile he sends me is delighted. "Can we keep them?"

I'm not sure we need them, or maybe I don't, but... Lex might. "If you want them, you can have them."

He flutters his lashes at me, reaching out to rest a hand on my arm. "You spoil me."

"Only the best for my baby." I smile at him, even as he blinks, like he didn't expect me to play along.

"Well, well, well." A voice comes from behind me. "I guess those rumors at boot camp were true, after all. When did the lovebirds of Bravo Company get here?"

The words are malicious, kind of, but the tone is more delighted than anything, as I spin, ready to take on anyone who's daring to start upsetting Lex again. Standing there are a man and a woman I vaguely recognize, maybe from chow times, but I couldn't tell you their names. They weren't in our company. They seem to know us, though, as the girl looks around at where we're sitting.

"Shit, you're soulmates?"

"Yes." Lex's voice suggests he's not fucking around. We might be new here, but he's with his people now. Our people.

"And witches?"

"I am. Mike's a mage."

There's a murmur that rises around us at that, like the one from New Orleans when I made my oath to the Queen. I can hear the whispers start about my being human from several directions. No matter. They'd all have found out soon enough. Even with my level of magic manipulation, I can't fake being a witch and our instructors would know that. It's not like I'm the only one here—Ronan said he was a mage, too, and these two don't seem to have magical cores, either. I'm not sure what the surprise is for, then. Maybe they just think I'm a renegade, like Andie did.

"That's cool, man," the guy says, stepping forward to offer his hand. "So are we. I'm Daniel and this is my sister Vera. Our soulmates are witches. Over there." He tilts his chin over at two girls sitting at the next table. "They went through basic last year and served for a year without us, waiting to come here."

"I told you they'd split us up if I fell behind." Lex's whisper in my ear makes me jump, and I put a hand on his leg to quell his outrage. It didn't happen, so there's no point in worrying about it. A bit of healing magic from his mom, and his ankle had been good as new as soon as we got home.

"We heard the rumors about a witch in Bravo Company, but didn't believe it," Vera says. "I wish we'd met you there. Would've been nice to have someone who understood."

"Well, we're all here now." Lex doesn't sound like he particularly wants to be friends. Maybe they didn't know us then, but their introductory words here are ones he'll hold against them, even if they weren't meant maliciously. Or maybe he's just as thrown as I am about finally meeting more mages. We know they exist, obviously, but Ronan, Daniel and Vera are the first we've met.

"We are." Daniel gives Lex a small smile, a touch conciliatory, then turns back to me. "We should chat sometime. Vera and I haven't ever met another mage before."

Lex puts his hand over mine, wrapping our fingers together. I squeeze his hand, trying to reassure him I'm not going to run off with new best friends.

"Well, you'll meet plenty here," Isaac interjects, leaning forward. "MagCorps prides itself on being fully integrated and strives to keep a balance between all three remaining species."

"Like a huge triad?" Lex glances over at our new friend.

"Exactly." Ronan is nodding, and Vera and Daniel retreat to their soulmates two tables over.

"They hassle you at boot camp?" Isaac asks.

"No." Lex takes a breath. "I mean, guys in our company did, but I barely remember seeing them."

"I can't believe I didn't see they were mages," I say, feeling myself frown. Magic users have a particular glow to their aura that I can see clearly in Ronan and the siblings. It's the same as witches have, but duller and only at the outer edges of their auras. The witches in the room shine brighter, as well as at their cores, like a glowing ball of energy, or a witchlight, in their solar plexus chakra, right between their hearts and groins. Granted, having never seen a mage before, I might not have recognized what I was seeing, but the magical tinge should've been enough to make me try and figure it out. "I know I saw them at chow or around during PT, but I never noticed..."

"You didn't have much reason to be using your Sight, either, while we were there," Lex says, squeezing my hand again and reminding me I'm still holding his. I don't let go.

"I don't usually turn it off." Lex's parents taught me how to turn off my sight when our kindergarten teacher told my parents I was easily distracted. Magic had been so new to me and Lex so bright, that I'd had a hard time looking away.

"You should probably start here," Ronan says. "I've heard the high concentration of supernats using magic can give mages a migraine if they don't tone it down."

"Thanks." It's good to know.

We finish out dinner with our suitemates, then play Call of Duty in the rec room until it's time for lights out; apparently, they do still regiment our days somewhat here. PT, physical training, is at 0600, and we do it as a group, just like the regular services. We still haven't met the superiors who'll be training us, but I'm a little less nervous after our warm welcome.

Then I'm nervous all over again after lights out when I can feel the warmth of Lex's body so close and hear him breathing in the dark. I manage to fall asleep after a long while contemplating the ceiling, only to wake up at 0530 wrapped around Lex, holding him tight in my arms like a giant teddy bear. This would be awkward at any point, but it's made doubly so by the fact that my morning wood presses right up against his ass, and he's not staying still or pulling away, but pushes back against me with his hips rocking just a bit in his sleep.

So much for this not being awkward. It's not the first time we've woken up like this, to be honest, but it is the first time since that night and the first time since I developed this obsession with wanting to nibble on his skin—the skin that's right up against my lips, courtesy of how I've curled around him in my sleep.

Fuck.

CHAPTER 8

Lex

I wake up slowly, a little disoriented by the warm, hard body at my back. Usually, this only happens when I let someone take me home, but I also remember what I've done unless I've been partying a little too hard. I don't honestly think there is such a thing as partying too hard, but Mike does and has a lot to say about my doing so some days. Mike...

Fuck. I'm awake now, and I know where I am, but I'm not used to Mike being the snuggly one. Sure, we've shared a bed before and even woken up snuggled together, but I'm usually the one who's moved to snuggle into him. The only times I've woken up with him holding me are after particularly bad nightmares when he's stayed with me, knowing that his presence can keep the bad dreams at bay. But I didn't have a nightmare last night. We just showered and brushed our teeth and went to bed and now this. Now this warmth and closeness and the temptation to just snuggle back into him and the hard length of his cock pressing against my ass in a far too tempting manner.

Whatever the temptation, I don't mean to wiggle back into him, but my body does it before I can second guess it and make a better choice. I feel his catch of breath against my skin and can't catch my own when, instead of politely pulling back, his arms tighten around me and tug me impossibly closer. Any closer and our boxer briefs might not be an impediment to getting to know one another on a whole new level. Goddess knows I want that, but I don't want to take advantage of his morning wood and friction. He's probably not even awake, yet.

"Lex?" The whiskey rasp of his voice against my skin as he hesitantly says my name makes me shiver, and I swear I hear him bite back a groan.

"Hmmm?" I'm not sure I can manage words.

"You're awake." He starts to loosen his grip on me, and I find myself clutching his arm to keep it in place.

"Sort of." My words probably get at least partially lost in my pillow, but he seems to take them as the affirmative answer they are.

"PT's in half an hour, so we should get up."

I groan at that. We shouldn't be late, especially on our first day, but all I want to do is rock my hips back into him again, to feel him there where I've been sure he belongs since I discovered what two guys could do together. "Don't wanna."

"That much is obvious, but I'd rather not be scrubbing toilets our first day."

"Mmph. But warm and comfortable. Cold outside." Also, no press of Mike's dick outside.

"It's July. In D.C. 'Cold' is not a word I'd use," he says dryly. "Also, you can't possibly be comfortable the way I'm poking you."

"Can."

"Seriously?"

"Can."

"Wanna talk about that?"

"Nope. Shhh."

Teeth scrape over my skin in a teasing bite that makes me shiver again. "Up."

"Oh, I'm up. Slide your hand a little lower, and you'll see."

"Christ, Lex. Now is not the time."

I reluctantly squirm away from him and roll over on my back to look at him. I notice he keeps his hand on me, dragging it over my skin as I roll until it's resting on my stomach, burning my skin. The silver cord between us seems to be pulsing. "Fine. Get up, then. Rude as that is."

"How is it rude?"

I arch an eyebrow and nod down at my own erection, now tenting my underwear.

"You're blaming that on me?"

"You rub your dick against a guy's ass like that and reactions will occur." Obviously. This isn't personal, I try to say with my eyes. He doesn't seem to be buying it.

"So, now, it's what? Rude if I don't take care of it?"

"I'd take care of you..." Really, really good care. Better care than anyone's ever taken. Well, shit, my eyes are not sending safe and sane messages.

"That's sweet, but you'll be fine if you'll just get up and get your mind off my dick."

But I like torturing myself thinking about his dick. Thankfully, my lips don't say that. I'm not sure what my eyes say, so I make myself look away before they give me away. "Fine. Consider my mind elsewhere."

"Thank you." He rolls away from me and moves to the head. "Get up and get dressed. We roll out for downstairs in ten minutes."

I sigh and try to do what he's said, but my mind is whirling. What was that? Maybe he didn't realize I was serious, so his straight-guy defenses didn't kick in? Maybe the bond is affecting him more than it used to? Maybe he liked the same things I liked that night in the tent with Hannah, and that kiss was supposed to be a clue that I somehow missed for fear of reading too much into it? Maybe I should press this a bit sometime when we're not in a rush for work? Maybe something more subtle than just waving at my erection in invitation next time? Except, if something that blatant didn't get a reaction, what chance does a subtle invitation have? At least it didn't get a negative reaction, either. That's got to be a plus. He didn't panic and push me away. And there was that teasing bite, though it was kinda like the kiss in the tent—he could just be being playful. Do straight guys kiss each other playfully when they have a threesome with a girl? Is it just some transgressive thrill to play with or a more serious overture? And how the fuck can I figure that out? It's not like I can just ask, Hey Mike, wanna try making out for real? And I shouldn't make a potentially unwelcome move on him if I'm misreading the signals. If he were bi, I'd know how to read what he's putting off, but he's not, so I don't.

I manage to get myself into my PT clothes by the time Mike's done in the bathroom and go to take care of my needs while he dresses. We make it downstairs just in time to fall in with our new squad and face our new drill instructor. Somewhere on the five-mile run, I start to feel my head clear from the morning, especially as I push myself to keep up with the shifters, which is a ridiculous endeavor. They're out-pacing all of us without even breathing hard. By the time we're on the deck, knocking out pushups, my cheeks are burning from more than exertion, and I can't believe how not-cool I acted in bed. I can't quite meet Mike's eyes as he holds my feet while I do sit-ups, but he's not quite meeting mine, either. Other pairs around us are rewarding each other for meeting fitness goals with quick kisses that get them an eyeroll from the drill instructor, but no reprimand unless they linger. At least no one's asking why we aren't being more affectionate, but it seems to earn us some approval from our taskmaster as he appoints Mike as our squad leader for the week. Mike looks both thrilled and terrified, and I realize again how much he's stepping into my world, now. At least the military trappings are familiar, even if the easy attitudes of those around us aren't.

We get chow before hitting the showers and getting dressed in our uniforms for the day's training. We start in the classroom with a class in magical theory and its battle applications. I assume this class is going to be basic because even witches get no formal magical schooling, non-witch shifters get no magic training at all, and most of the mages are probably only in their second or third years of learning magic, Still, I settle in my desk with my notebook open, hoping to learn something new. Mike's tapping his foot a little, an outward sign that he's nervous, when he shouldn't be. He's got more training than any of the other mages here, so this should be a breeze for both of us, at least this first day.

It is not a breeze.

Mike

When it comes to understanding their natures and magic, most witches and shifters are homeschooled. Mages are too, as we're usually taught magic by witches, unless we happen to be found by another mage first. Thus, most of my magical knowledge comes from Lex's parents. They're both well-versed in both magical theory and history, so Lex and I both expect to be well-prepared for these first weeks of training, in the classroom, at least.

I slide into the desk next to Lex's, taking up my usual classroom position between him and the door. There's no real rhyme or reason to the placement. It's where I sat in first grade, when our teacher assigned us seats and through the years it just became a habit. Here, the other soulmate pairs sit with one another, too, so the habit doesn't need changing. I set down the notebook I bought just for these classes, and before I can start my fruitless search through my pockets for a pen, Lex hands me his ever-present second one with a smile. His fingers brush against mine when he pulls back and linger. It is definitely deliberate.

I'd managed to get my libido back under control during PT, but that touch, that drag of skin against skin, as innocent as it is, relights the fire that I'd woken up to this morning. I am never going to be able to play this cool enough, especially if he's going to start flirting. It's so new it makes me wonder if it's that night with Hannah or being here surrounded by all these other pairs of soulmates for the first time. Most of our lives, people have assumed we were a couple when we weren't, and they'd reviled us for it much of the time. Now, here we are where the assumption, again, is that we are a couple, and, this time, everyone thinks that is a good, or even normal, thing. Maybe Lex is just tired of always being the different one. It makes sense that he'd want to fit in, finally, when we are somewhere we can, somewhere he can totally be himself, like Ronan had said yesterday.

I have to remember that doesn't automatically mean he suddenly wants to be with me. I glance over at him, speculating, and catch his bright smile. It pulls my own out of me, because how can I not smile back when his dimples are flashing like that?

Someone in uniform—a captain—steps to the front of the room. "What is it that separates witches and shifters from mundane humans?"

"Our magical core, sir," Isaac answers after raising his hand. "And y'know, whatever genome markers differentiate subspecies."

"And what is a magical core?" The teacher scans the room.

I know this, but a long habit from high school keeps me from raising my hand.

"Private Johnson?"

I turn to see Vera putting her hand down. "It's the inner reservoir of magic witches and shifters have that they use to fuel their magic."

"And what else?"

Vera looks to her brother who just shrugs. I have some idea, but I'm not sure if it's what the teacher is going for, so I don't raise my hand.

"I don't know, sir," Vera admits. "That's all I was taught."

"That's the problem for a lot of you," he tells her, not unkindly. "But it's important that you know, particularly so you can support your soulmate." He scans the room again. "Private Monroe?"

"It's what fuels not just our magic, but our lives. Without magic in our core, a witch or shifter will die. Our bodies stop functioning. That's why depletion is so serious."

"Yes, exactly. Whereas with mundane humans, their neurological functions seem to keep all systems running, with witches and shifters, it's magic itself that keeps even neurological functions running."

"What about mages? They're human, technically, but can perform magic... Private Mathis?"

I'm not expecting to be called on, but I sit up straighter. "Mages don't have a detectable magical core, sir." Though, apparently, we still have some genetic markers that separate us from purely mundane humans. "Rather, they can access stored magical energy and manipulate it."

"Stored in what?"

"Magical artifacts or the magical cores of their partners or familiars, should they have them. Even ley lines with enough practice."

"Ley lines?"

"Yes, sir. Magical streams crisscrossing the Earth..." I trail off as the captain arches an eyebrow at me.

"I know what ley lines are, Private."

"Yes, sir. Sorry, sir. It sounded like there was a question there."

"General understanding of magical theory says only witches can access the ley lines to replenish their magical cores more quickly. Shifters can only access them passively, like through osmosis, for the same purpose. There's nothing in the science or lore about mages and ley lines."

"Oh, yes, sir. I don't think most are trained to be able to access them."

"But you are?"

"Uh, yes, sir?" Because the Monroes had started training me so young, they'd run past the standard mage curriculum before I hit puberty. So, they'd started letting me sit in on Lex's lessons, including the one on ley lines and charging from them. They were stunned when I proved able to pull magic from them and use it. I couldn't store magic up like a witch and couldn't keep pulling an endless supply from the ley lines, but I could siphon off enough to do a bit more magic if my artifacts—mostly amulets—were drained and it wasn't safe to pull more from Lex. I could technically start with ley line magic, of course, but the Monroes discouraged that because there wasn't anything to explain how I was doing it or if it could have any unintended consequences for me or Lex. One consequence was that it quickly exhausted me, physically. I often wonder if that is just an endurance thing that I can improve on, but I haven't had a lot of time to try doing that, yet.

"You'll have to demonstrate that when we get to practical applications, Private."

"Yes, sir. Happy to, sir."

The murmurs are just background noise around me. I'd been prepared for this, knowing I'm far beyond most mages in training. We'll all catch up and even out eventually. I just have a head start, but I've maxed out what I can do, as far as we can tell. Yeah, I can draw on the ley lines, but only for three or four things before I'm physically exhausted, like the human body isn't meant to channel that much magic. Unlike amulets—or Lex's core—which have limited magic, ley lines are a virtually unlimited source of magic, and no one has been able to teach me how to pull just the discrete amounts instead of tugging at the whole thing. I vow to try and practice that more before I demonstrate.

"So, witches draw on their own core, some say even their souls, and mages on magic stored in something other than themselves. What happens if a witch depletes their magical core?"

"Death," Ronan says succinctly. "At least eventually. Magical coma usually, first, while their bodies try to recharge. If they can't, it can be fatal."

The captain nods. "So, what are the implications of that for the partnerships in this room?"

I do raise my hand for this because it has been drilled into me. When I'm called on, I lay out the rules as they were taught to me. "If a mage and a witch are partnered, the mage should monitor his witch's core, never siphoning too much and, should his or her witch go down, take what power he or she has to protect their witch until the witch can pull in enough ambient or ley line magic to restore their magical equilibrium."

"That's correct. Most of you have come to us from the Marines this round."

"Oorah." The battle cry is an automatic reflex around the room, and the captain smiles.

"Yes. So, I know you're all skilled in combat evacuations." Probably, so are the other branches, but after the Crucible, which only we have, it is a point of pride not to admit that others might be able to do what we can. "In MagCorps, you have to take magical depletion into consideration in combat. It's very easy to lose track of your magical supply in a combat situation. When the witches go down, the wider shields often go down, so the others in your squad will have to fill in the gaps—be security—while the fallen witch is evacuated. This is one reason MagCorps prefers bonded soulmates—bonded witches can pull on their soulmates much the same way a mage can, even if their partner is a mage without a magical core of his or her own. Whatever it is that serves as the biological equivalent to a core in humans can feed a witch's core until they can reach the healers for some restorative work. Bonded witches, thus, are safer in the field since the bond allows for the immediate transfer. If their partner is another witch or a shifter, then they have a second magical core to keep them upright, too."

The captain pauses, looking around the room. "Those of you without a bonded partner might want to seriously consider making that commitment if you want to be successful in MagCorps—for both of your sakes and safety. Yes, soulmates can share energy, even without the binding, but it must be more intentional, and it's a moving piece you have to keep track of in the middle of the most stressful situation you'll ever be in. Bonded pairs share more organically, without conscious thought. The magic is just there to use, so to speak."

Vera and her brother look a bit dispirited, and I wonder why they aren't bound to their witches already. Yeah, it's a big commitment, but I wouldn't dream of attempting to not just survive but fight in the supernat world without that bond in place. Mages who aren't bound to their soulmates, or, worse, mages without soulmates are second-class citizens, if that, in this world. We're humans operating in a society made up of people who are not, strictly speaking, human, as that species is generally understood, and who have historically been heavily mistreated and misunderstood by humans. While fueled by one organization, namely the Catholic church, humans carried out the witch and "werewolf" trials and executions, particularly in Europe. A lot of shifters were lumped in under the "werewolf" category and killed, and the vampires were driven to extinction. Some of the accusers might well have been mages, but most were undoubtedly mundane humans. In a lot of supernat's minds, because we lack a magical core, mages are more like mundane humans, who continue to persecute supernats than we are like supernats. Since we aren't usually identified until well into puberty, we grow up largely in the human world, and a lot of supernats fear that leaves us prone to anti-supernatural biases. Blood will tell, as they say, and if push came to shove, and the level of persecution rose again, a lot of supernats worry which community we would choose. Is it any wonder, then, that they want us formally bonded to members of their community before granting us protection and rights in their world?

"Sir?" Isaac's hand is up, and he waits for acknowledgement to go on. "What about shifters?"

"What about shifters, McCall?"

"Where do they fit in on the whole MagCorps battlefield scenario?"

The captain nods a little. "Shifter-witches operate largely like non-shifter witches, unless their shifter abilities are necessary. Shifters who aren't witches, but who wish to serve in MagCorps do so based on their animal-type. In combat, that means predators function either as, basically, infantry or foot soldiers, or—and both predators and prey can do this—by bonding with a witch as a familiar, offering up their own magical core to supplement their witch's. In that case, they operate much like mages, responsible for monitoring their witch and getting him or her out of there, but they obviously can't cast their own shields for security, so they must learn to rely on the larger squad. You all learned to rely on your squads in Basic Training, but human squads operate a little differently from us, and that's what we'll be teaching you first in maneuvers and magic training. In here, with me, we'll be looking at the theory behind what you'll be doing in field training. The better you understand the science of magic, if you will, the more effectively you can use it."

I glance at Lex, who is beaming, eating this up. He's always loved learning and has a head for theoretical concepts I've never quite replicated. But if I want to keep him safe in combat, I need to be able to do more than carry him out if he gets shot. This is especially true since Lex's likelihood of being shot is less in MagCorps, given our use of shields. He's far more at risk of magic depletion due to his tendency to get wrapped up in what he's doing and fail to pay attention to things like his magic levels. I long ago accepted that reminding Lex to focus was going to be one of my life's most consistent tasks.

The captain shifts a little bit away from magical cores to things other than overuse that can lead to depletion for witches and shifters, things that we need to be prepared for, even if it's unlikely we'll face them any time soon. This is stuff I didn't know, and I take a lot of notes, thinking of how it could affect not just Lex, but Andie, too.

Before we go, the captain gives us all a vial of something with instructions to drink it after dinner to reduce one impediment between us and our partner.

I'm still thinking about it all after dinner and video games, when Lex and I are back in our room, ready for bed, propped up in it. Lex is reading the course packet from our MagCorps history class like it's the latest best-selling thriller.

"Did you know that General Washington was the first military leader to recognize the usefulness of an entity like MagCorps?"

"Pretty sure you've told me that before, yeah."

"No, I mean, okay, yeah. I knew the basic fact, but this has a copy of his letter to Benedict Arnold letting him in on the existence of witches and shifters and offering a strategy to use them to turn the tide on the British. I mean, I knew a lot of presidents and military leaders knew about supernats before the general public, but this letter, seeing him explain it—tell the secret to someone else is fascinating."

"The traitor?"

"Hmm?"

"Benedict Arnold."

"Oh, yeah. But before he was a traitor, he was a major general in the Continental Army and in charge of West Point. Washington trusted him completely, which is why his name is still a synonym for traitor today."

"Okay..." I suppose this is interesting, but I'm still fretting over possible things that could hurt Lex.

"Speaking of things we're learning, did you know about all the pieces of the iron and silver thing?" Obviously, we knew iron could cut a witch off from their core and burn their skin, but I didn't know it could drain their cores, leading to rapid depletion, or that silver could also do that to shifters, not just keep them from changing. They aren't just inhibitors, but poison.

"Huh? Oh, yeah, sure. Every witch learns to stay away from cold iron as a kid, to avoid getting sick. I bet shifters do the same with silver."

"How come I never knew?"

He looks up, blinking at me. "Didn't you? You knew the iron cuffs meant we couldn't do magic..."

"I didn't know the full extent of it."

That makes him frown and close the packet he's reading. "I don't know. Maybe Mom and Dad didn't think it was something that would affect you or that you needed to know. It's sort of our biggest weakness."

"Did they think I'd use it against you?"

"No!" He looks shocked at the idea. "They know you'd never hurt me, not as my soulmate. That would be just about the biggest betrayal possible. Far bigger than Benedict Arnold's."

"I would never hurt you, no, but maybe they didn't think I could be trusted not to hurt another witch..."

"Maybe," his tone is doubtful, though. "Or maybe they didn't want to upset you or make you worry about me on the playground equipment."

"Is that why you got dizzy on the see-saw sometimes?"

"Yeah," he admits, giving me a sheepish smile. "Mostly if my hands were already scraped or the burns got blisters that broke, so the iron leeched into my system."

"I wouldn't have wanted to play on it if I knew it would hurt you!"

"I knew what it could do and made my own choice." He's trying to shift away, now, like my upset is something to get away from.

I reach out to snag his right hand and tug him back to me. He rolls into me, with a lack of grace, off-balance, and I content myself with studying the palm of his hand, tracing a fingertip over where the skin must have been burned and painful—even though we never played for long on the infernal equipment, and now I know why. My fingertip catches on the silver ring I placed there, and I trace it lightly.

"So, if we get one of these for Andie one day, we'll have to pick a different metal."

"Y-yes." For some reason, he's a little breathless, and when I look up, he's watching me with eyes that are nearly black, his pupils are blown so wide. "Probably platinum or white gold if we want hers to match ours, visually. The silver would burn her, sure as iron will me, like that fucking collar did."

"And her. She's susceptible to both, as a shifter-witch, right?" I drag my fingertip over his palm to see what he does, and he catches his breath.

"Right." He swallows and shivers, tugging at his hand a little, like he wants to get free, but when I let go, he doesn't move away, so I reach out to brush a still-wet-from-the-shower curl off his forehead. "Mike..."

The feeling in the air is a familiar one, though the players in the scene are new. Lex's breathing has sped up, and he wets his lips in a nervous gesture as I recapture his hand and go back to inspecting it by touch, like I can still find and soothe those long-ago blisters. The scent of his soap—something spicy and rich I always associate with him—is all I can smell, and it seems to be working its way deep into my lungs and from there to my core, warming me like the scent of nutmeg in a baking pie. Lex curls his fingers in to protect his palm, but that just tangles them up with mine and now we're holding on to each other's hands while he's half-rolled into me in the dip of the bed.

"Mike." He says again, barely more than breathing out my name, and this time I hear him.

"Yeah?"

"What are you doing? My hand is fine. It hasn't been hurt since Marguerite treated it in New Orleans."

"Maybe I just want to hold it."

"Since when?" For some reason, his voice cracks a little, and when I look up to meet his gaze, there's something fragile there I just want to protect.

"I don't know. Since..." How honest to be?

"Since?" He's not letting me get away with trailing off, and I wonder why. Usually, he doesn't press me.

"Since always, I guess."

"You've never, before."

"I was scared, before." I guess we're giving full honesty, then, and I haven't even had a drink.

"And you're not scared anymore?"

"Oh, fuck, yeah. I'm terrified. But maybe I'm tired of letting it hold me back from what I want."

He swallows again and pulls a little away before letting himself roll down into the dip of the bed fully, to land pressed up against me. "What do you want?"

That's the question, isn't it? And I don't have a clear answer. "To hold your hand. To have the right to hold it whenever I want to."

"You're my soulmate," he says, tone drier than the desert. "My bonded soulmate, at that. If anyone has the right to hold my hand, it's you."

"To the world, your world, that is, yeah."

"Our world." His voice is soft with the correction, but it's a clear correction, nonetheless.

"It doesn't feel like mine, yet," I confess. "It's still too new and I've got too much in the human world. Brandon, my folks, Hannah." Not that I know what to do about Hannah anymore. There was a time I thought I'd marry her, but now that we've found Andie, now that Lex and I are bound together, that doesn't seem fair to her. "It's the world I know. I barely know the rules of this one. I know how to use magic and the ways to take care of you, but it's not like I really socialized with the wider supernat community in Staunton."

He stills at the mention of Hannah's name, and when I finish trying to explain my thought and look up, he's blushing. It's adorable.

"We ever gonna talk about that night in Shenandoah?" I ask.

"No," he says, before backpedaling, "I mean, what is there to say?"

"I liked it. More than I would have thought."

"Well, sure. It was hot." He seems to have recovered his equilibrium faster than I have. "I never would have expected her to be into it."

"Me either, but I definitely was."

"So was I." His voice is quiet again, though he's stopped trying to pull his hand away and doesn't start again when I go back to stroking it.

"I felt a little guilty, actually, about how much I was," I tell him, just as quiet.

"Oh? Why?"

"Because I should've been taking care of her, but all I could look at was you."

He flushes again and won't look at me, and I wonder if I'm misreading his silence. "I took care of her."

"I know, but that wasn't my point. She felt good. You..." He lifts his head to look at me, waiting when I hesitate. "Felt better."

His teeth sink back into his lower lip. "Oh. I did?"

"Yeah."

"Well, friction. I mean, like this morning. That's just natural, Mike." He seems like he's trying to reassure me, but I'm not sure of what. "It doesn't mean anything. It's okay."

What is he even talking about? "What if I want it to mean something?" He blinks and doesn't answer for a long minute, so I press on. "What if I'm tired of everyone assuming I've got something, and I don't even know what I'm missing?"

"Wh-what?" Now he is trying to pull away, and there's a mix of hope and terror on his face.

"What if I want to know what I'm missing?"

"Is that all?"

"I don't know, okay? I just know I'm getting tired of wanting to touch you and holding myself back because I'm afraid of scaring you off. But you weren't scared this morning."

He sure looks scared now. "I wasn't awake this morning."

"What are you afraid of?"

"That you'll wake up in the morning and realize saying all of this was a mistake."

"That depends on you," I tell him,

"How so?"

"If you run, if you get mad and don't want to be bound to me anymore because it's too awkward or you feel too sorry for me, then, yeah. I'll think it was a mistake, because it cost me the most important thing in the world."

His gaze is perfectly serious when it meets my own. "I could never want to undo our binding. You're the most important thing in the world to me too, and I--I don't want to take advantage of anything you're feeling or thinking or make you regret binding your life to mine."

"Jesus." I have to stifle a laugh and slide my hand out of his to cradle his cheek. "I don't know why I feel what I feel. That's what I'm most afraid of. That it's some side effect from everyone's expectations or, I don't know, some confusion in my own wiring. I-I don't think I like guys, in general? But I get distracted a lot of the time by how much I want to touch you. And I don't want you to think you're just some experimental game for me. You're precious to me."

Christ, what the hell am I saying, and why am I saying it? It's like I can't stop myself, though.

Lex laughs. "If you want to experiment and went off to experiment with anyone else but me, I'd want to kill that person."

"I really had to stop myself from beating up Tommy Bowman."

"Who?"

"Katie's brother." I can't believe I have to remind him. "The first boy who kissed you?"

"Oh, right." He's flushed, but this time it doesn't seem like embarrassment. "Why'd you want to beat him up?"

"Because he made you want to kiss boys, but you never wanted to kiss me."

"Are you kidding me? I've spent the last six years trying not to kiss you. A dozen times a day."

"Why hold back?"

"Because what asshole puts the moves on his straight best friend and puts you in the position of having to reject me or do something you don't want to?"

"I want to."

He stills again, watching me closely. "You do?"

"Yeah. I mean, I can't promise I'll love it or want to do everything or that I won't get freaked out at some point, but I want to kiss you. I've wanted to kiss you since we were thirteen. Why did you think I kissed you in the tent?"

"I thought it was an accident." He trails off and looks away, and I can't have that. Reaching out, I tuck my fingers under his chin and make him look at me again.

"It wasn't an accident."

"Oh." For a minute, he just seems to sit there, processing, then he tilts his head into my hand and wets his lips. "Why don't we give it another try, then, without the misunderstanding?"

My nerves start firing at that point, but no way in hell am I backing down, now. I think vaguely of the potion or whatever we all drank after supper, but try to dismiss it, because Lex is leaning in, his gaze on my lips, and that's far more important. "What do you think was in the vial?"

"Huh?" He looks a little put out that I've cut off his move.

"The vial the captain gave us. You don't think he roofied us, do you?"

"As far as I know, there aren't any magical aphrodisiacs. He did say it was something to reduce impediments between partners, but pretty sure everyone else is fucking already, so that wouldn't make sense. Maybe it's some kind of truth serum?" He doesn't seem all that concerned.

"So, you really want to do this?"

"Goddess, yes. So, just shut up and kiss me, okay? We'll figure out the vial later."

That's good enough for me, and I wind my fingers in his hair and tug him across to me.

CHAPTER 9

Lex

Mike's got me wondering about the vial we drank, but I know that this feeling tightening in my core isn't new or the product of any magical drug. This is anticipation, and it's what I feel every time Mike touches me. I'm a little shocked I said the things I said but glad if this is the result total honesty gets me. Mike's fears of freaking out if we go too far too fast have me ready to slam the breaks on, but a kiss seems tame enough as an initial experiment.

His lips brush mine and it's like that night in the tent, only a hundred times more, because this time I'm not wondering if it's an accident. Michael Mathis is kissing me, and he's wanted to kiss me as long as I've been waiting for him to, and if we'd just both been a little braver, maybe we could have been doing this all along. Or maybe not, because his dad might have refused to let us see each other, or the teasing at school might have gotten to him when it was true, or any other number of things that could have gone wrong. Now? Now is the perfect time when we're bound, together, and away from all the bigotry and pressure.

His fingers are tight in my hair and the slight pull is perfect, leading me to press closer to him and slide my arms around his neck. He nibbles a little at my lips, keeping the kiss light and still mostly chaste, until the light swipe of his tongue over my lower lip has me parting my lips for him.

Then our tongues are tangling, and I can taste the mint of his toothpaste and something else that's just him. His teeth scrape my lower lip, and I can't hold back the moan that elicits as pleasure crackles along my nerves. I return the favor, nipping lightly, and his fingers slide to my hip and hold on tightly there.

Our bodies are pressed flush against one another, and the cotton of his boxer briefs leaves nothing to my imagination about if he's enjoying this. He's hard, thrusting against my hip and that makes me want everything. But...no. That's too much, too fast, and if he's worried about freaking out, then we need to go slowly.

It's hard to keep that in mind when his hands slide to cradle my ass and then pull me even tighter against him, so that our erections slide against one another, only thin fabric separating us. I try to ease back, and he lets me, but with a questioning murmur.

"It's too much," I say against his lips.

When he lifts his head, I chase after his mouth, keeping my words there. "I've been waiting for this kiss all my life, and I mean to savor it without rushing on to something else."

He lets me shift just enough that we're not rutting against each other and goes back to kissing me in a way that makes me hate the boundaries I just set, even if I know they're for a good cause. Where his kiss was turning demanding, he eases back from it without stopping. It's less and more at the same time: less demand, more tease; less take, more give; less me, more him. Another moan breaks free from my lips, and I'm murmuring "yes," over and over. I tangle my hands in his hair like I've always wanted to and swipe my tongue over his lower lip like I'm trying to memorize it. Maybe I am, just in case he wakes up and realizes this isn't all he expected it to be, even if it's more than I even imagined.

Mike

I've fantasized about this kiss since the moment Lex told me about kissing Tommy Bowman. Admittedly, my early fantasies didn't have quite this much tongue and teeth, but I've grown up since then. One part of my brain is noticing the differences in kissing a guy—the slight roughness of his lips, the stubble under my fingers, the more masculine scent of his skin—while another part still tries to figure out where I got the courage to tell Lex the truth. The third part wants the other two to shut up so it can just luxuriate in the kiss.

I don't fully understand why Lex slowed us back down when it's so clear we're both aching for more. His reasoning makes sense to the part of me that is waiting for me to freak out about this, but I'm so far from freaking out, I'm not even hesitating. Besides, this is quite possibly the most erotic kiss of my life, with the thrust of his tongue against mine and the burn of his hot fingers on my skin as he slides his hand under my shirt.

There are levels we can move on to, I guess. I return the touch, rucking up his shirt so I can stroke his chest feeling the hardness of muscle there under skin that's just a touch warmer than mine. He's always run warmer than I do, and I can't help but wonder if it's a witch thing or a Lex thing, but then his fingers are sliding along the waistband of my boxer briefs, and I think I whimper.

"Thought we were just savoring the kiss..."

"We are. Doesn't mean I can't tease us both just a bit." Lex's fingers drag across my lower abs, so damn close to the tip of my dick I swear I can almost feel them brush it before they're retreating up to my chest.

"Cruel, Lex. Just cruel."

He chuckles against my lips, but two can play the teasing game. I break the kiss to drag my lips along his jaw, savoring the roughness there, then up to his earlobe. I've watched Hannah send him higher like this, and I emulate what she does, catching his earlobe in my teeth and teasing it with my tongue.

The reaction is near instantaneous as his fingers dig into my skin and he presses into me with a moan.

"Two can play at this game," I say before nipping at his earlobe again.

His hands move to clutch at my shoulders, and he holds on, undulating up against me like he's searching for the friction he shut down earlier. He stills after just a minute, like he's trying to get control back, and I pull his earlobe into my mouth to suckle.

"Fuck. Christ. Fuck." His words are soft pants against my skin before he pulls away. "I'm not playing gay chicken with you, Mike."

It feels like being doused in cold water, and I immediately retreat a little, even though neither of us actually lets go. "That's not what this is."

"That's what it feels like, like we're escalating to the point where you finally freak out."

"I'm not freaking out."

"Yet."

"Maybe not ever. Maybe this is what I've been wanting for years, too."

"You don't even know if you're bi."

"I'm not going to figure it out running drill scenarios in my head."

"Look." He pulls away and runs his hands through his curls as he sits up. "I want this. I want you. And if the only way that happens is for me to be your experimental game, then I'm okay with that."

I try to interject, but I don't know what to say.

"I'd rather you figure it out with me than someone else." It's a soft admission, and he reaches out a tentative hand for mine, looking at me with troubled blue eyes. "But maybe you get caught up in the moment, and we end up going farther than you're comfortable with come daylight. I'd rather we take things slow, so if we hit a wall where you've gone as far as you're comfortable, we don't hurt ourselves on it."

"What does slow mean?"

"For right now?"

"Yeah."

"Maybe we should just stick to kissing and cuddling and not try to rile each other up to the point where we need to get off so badly, we can't think."

"I think I'm okay with some dry humping or even mutual hand jobs." What he's saying makes sense, but I can't help the protest when my dick is as hard as it is.

He groans, falling back on the pillow in a dramatic flop. His hands scrub at his face, like he's trying to push away that image. "Okay. But I need you to really think about that when you're not thinking with your dick."

"I've thought about it a lot, before now."

He gives me a skeptical look. "Well, think about it some more. And when you can say, 'Lex, I am ready to go to second base,' before we start getting turned on, we can do that. Because maybe you've thought about it before, but you've never acted on it before now, because you're still not sure if it's really you or our bond or whatever else you're worried about."

"Fine." I know I sound petulant, but I'm aching for more of his touches, and now it feels like even kissing is being cut off for the night.

He sighs and reaches out to run his fingers through my hair. After a moment, I lean into the touch and he flips off the lamp, then snuggles down beside me, curling into my side and resting his head where my chest and shoulder join. I can't help but curl my arm around him, holding him close.

"For the record?" His voice is just a whisper in the dark.

"Yeah?"

"That was the best kiss I've ever had."

I turn my head and brush a kiss over his forehead, and he wraps his arm around my waist. "Me too."

CHAPTER 10

Lex

Falling asleep in Mike's arms has always been one of my favorite things from the time we were just kids. Doing so while exchanging small kisses is amazing. His fingers keep playing in my hair and his other hand just keeps smoothing down my back like he does when I'm upset. Not being upset, I can appreciate the touches better. It's enough to lull me easily to sleep and into dreams where I'm not an idiot who stops the man of my dreams when he wants to sex me up.

No, I know it's the right call. I really would rather be the person helping him figure himself out than someone else, but I also don't want him freaking out in the middle of something he hasn't thought through. I know he might, still, when it comes down to it, but that's a risk you always take with sex—that someone might change their minds or not like how you do something. I feel better about that if he's at least sure he wants to try.

I'm still wrapped up in Mike's arms the next morning when there's a knock on our door. Mike calls for whomever to enter, and Ronan and Isaac spill through the door. I start to push away from Mike, but his arms tighten around me and keep me where I am, so I just burrow more under the covers and into him.

"Well, I guess that answers that question," Isaac says, taking the two of us in.

"I told you they were together," Ronan says in response. "They're soulmates who went through the same binding ritual we did. You don't do that if you're not committed to one another."

"Friends can be committed."

"Uh, what's up guys?" Mike asks, as I study our two not-quite-welcome guests. It's too damn early to be sociable. They... don't look well, to be honest. Both are a little pale and haggard with dark circles under their eyes. They're in uniform, but not really looking pressed and ship shape.

"What happened to you?" Maybe it's not the most tactful question, but I refuse to be held accountable for things I say pre-coffee.

"What do you mean?" Isaac asks, trying to act like nothing's wrong.

"You look like shit," Mike tells them, running fingers through my hair.

"You two drank the vial Captain Parsons gave us, right?" Ronan asks. "I remember we all downed them together."

"Yeah, what of it? What were they?"

"Nothing strange happened? You didn't find yourself having unexpected discussions and... confessions?" Ronan watches us both closely, and I manage to shrug.

"We had a very nice conversation, actually," I tell him. "Got a few misconceptions cleared up."

"And then fell asleep in each other's arms like everything was fine?" Isaac looks suspicious, but I just nod.

"Yeah. Why? What happened to you two?"

"Oh, we got a few misconceptions cleared up, too," Ronan says with a disgruntled look at Isaac. "Particularly surrounding what he thinks of my father."

"Yeah, we didn't touch that," Mike says, forcing a laugh. "But Lex isn't really shy about his opinions about my dad."

"He's kind of a dick," I say, just to prove Mike's point, and because it's true.

"I can't even argue with him about that," Mike says with a nod.

"Yeah, well, I can argue about Isaac's assessment of my dad."

"And did," Isaac adds. "Argue, I mean. And then threw out a few assessments of his own about my family and my fitness for duty."

"I never said you weren't fit for duty."

"No, you just said I maybe should have gone to college."

"Only because you were actually excited we're going to have to write papers for Captain Parsons and Major Greeley. No one that is sane gets excited about writing."

"Oh, so now I'm insane?" Isaac steps into Ronan's space and I look up at Mike in alarm. He disentangles from me and moves to step between the other soulmates.

"It seems like you two had a tough night, but maybe it's better to have it out rather than festering inside?"

"Was it festering, though?" Ronan asks. "They're hardly life-changing issues."

"I don't know, man." Mike lifts his hands in a pacifying gesture. "I know the shit Lex and I hashed out last night was."

"And, yet you seem fine this morning."

"We kept going until we understood each other better," I try to offer, unsure if I should be butting in, but knowing that mine and Mike's conversation could have gone a lot more poorly than it did. "We got to the root of some stuff that was hurting both of us, and now, hopefully, we'll be stronger than we were."

"Yeah, well. We're not there, yet," Isaac says on a grumble.

"I'm the last person to give relationship advice," Mike says. "But you two love each other, so. Maybe try to put the hurt aside and just keep talking. Or figure it's like one of those wounds you've got to get the gunk out of so you can heal. And, as you heal, you're stronger for it."

I'm so proud of him for even trying to help our new friends, for putting himself in the line of fire. He looks bemused as to why I'm beaming at him, but I can't not.

"Maybe," Ronan says with a grudging nod. "We just wanted to see if you two survived the night. Glad you fared better than us."

"You'll get there if you want to," I say with a small smile. Like Ronan had admitted a minute ago, their issues don't seem all that earth-shattering.

"Yeah." Isaac sounds doubtful, but he reaches for Ronan's hand to pull him back out of our room. "See you downstairs. PT in 20 minutes."

"What the fuck was in that vial?" Mike asks as I slip out of bed and reach for my PT clothes.

"Something that got people to spill their secrets it seems like. I guess other people's secrets weren't as... harmless as ours."

"Ours could've gone bad."

"Yeah, but it didn't, and I'm glad we got it all out there." Not least because we're finally on the same page about us and it's a page I never thought we'd be on, no matter how much I hoped.

"Me too. It just seems like an unnecessary thing to force on us without warning."

"Maybe so." It's hard for me to not see the whole thing through our experience, and Ronan and Isaac have seemed so close I have to believe they'll pull through this. "It doesn't bother you that I don't like your dad, right?"

"Lex, I don't like my dad. Why would you, after how he's treated you through the years?"

"And that's without knowing I'm a witch."

Mike sits next to me on the bed while I'm pulling on my running shoes, mirroring my movements. He bumps his shoulder lightly into mine. "Good morning, by the way."

"Good morning..."

Before I can get more than that out, he's leaning in to kiss me softly, and I really could get used to this. "Let's go show the captain we're better than ever. If his goal was to cause trouble, he failed with us."

He stands and offers me his hand, and I slide mine into his, winding our fingers together as we head out hand in hand and I won't say anything against the captain if he's to thank for this. Surely our friends will pull through this, too. What they learned couldn't have been that much of a surprise, right?

Mike

It's a little odd to be walking hand-in-hand with Lex again—we haven't done this since elementary school when the other kids started taunting us for it. Lex was the one to pull away then, but he's gripping my hand now like I might try to run away. I don't have any intention of going anywhere, but I don't mind the tight grip. He only lets go as we fall into formation, but he stays as close as allowed as we start a calisthenic warm up.

PT has a weird feel this morning. A few other pairs look as rough as Isaac and Ronan, and people who ran together yesterday seem inclined to split up. Lex and I pace each other, and I'm glad to see Isaac and Ronan staying close, too. They seem like good guys, and Lex could use friends he can totally be himself with.

By the time we get back from breakfast, the bathroom door is locked and Lex smirks.

"Good for them, working stuff out."

"Maybe we could lock it once they're done?" I ask, both nervous and hopeful.

It takes Lex a minute to answer me. "Maybe another day, but we're not there, yet."

"When will we be?"

"I told you last night. When you can tell me you're ready to move on to something more when you're not riled up."

"We just got back from breakfast."

His gaze drops down to the front of my shorts. "And what were you thinking about at breakfast?"

My cheeks feel hot, and I look away.

"If you can't say it, you can't do it."

"Fine. I was thinking about helping you wash your hair after we got back up here."

"No offense, Mike, but I've seen your hair. Don't think I'm letting you touch mine."

But I notice he's smiling, and I'll take the win.

The door's unlocked soon enough thereafter for me to wonder if we know them well enough to tease about how fast they were done. I let Lex hit the shower first, since he's vetoed sharing, but he opens the door to let me in when he's done. He's got a towel slung low around his waist, and I find myself looking at the bare expanse of skin in a new light. This? This is nothing new. This has been every gym class since we were twelve, only with even less of a view. But I'm able to look my fill, rather than glancing away anytime anyone looks at me, and I enjoy the privilege.

I can tell when he notices, because a flush creeps up his chest to stain his cheeks. He goes on about his business like I'm not there, shaving and brushing his teeth with the economical movements we perfected in basic.

He doesn't bother with modesty as he dresses, and the slide of fabric revealing and covering his dick and his ass like a fan in a burlesque show is intoxicating to watch. I shower fast so as not to miss any more than necessary. He makes no move to hide that he's watching me in return, and since it's the first time I've ever noticed him watching, I wonder how good he's gotten at covertly observing me, because from what he said last night, I have to think he's snuck a few peeks before.

The classroom is half full when we get down there. We're starting with Major Greeley's class, which is the MagCorps history class Lex and Isaac were both geeking out about. I notice Isaac seems a little more subdued about it today, but Lex is on the edge of his seat taking notes at a furious pace that has me wondering if he's trying to capture every one of the Major's words. After wrapping up the lecture, the Major pauses, looking out across the classroom.

"Rough night for some of you?"

He's met with some grumbles, but no one openly complains.

"As I'm sure you've figured out, the potion Captain Parsons gave you all was a form of a truth potion. It's meant to ferret out the secrets you're hiding most from the most important person to you. So, no matter what you revealed to your partner last night, you can each rest in the assurance that you are their most important person. Now, if some of you called your mother to confess your deepest and darkest, I don't have much consolation to offer your soulmate."

That gets a few weak chuckles, and Isaac raises his hand.

"Yes, Private McCall?"

"To what end, sir? As you observed, a lot of us had a rough night, so. Why put us through that?"

"Intimacy. Trust. In this squad, in MagCorps, your soulmate is the person you have to rely on 100% of the time, the person you have to depend on to always have your back. You can't do that if you're keeping secrets from one another. Even ones that seem petty in dawn's early light. You're going to go through training these next few months that will make the Crucible seem like child's play and then it's very likely you'll deploy to a war zone where your lives depend on each other and the rest of this squad. Secrets have a way of coming out under stress. Better to have them out now, in the safety of what is basically orientation week. Gives you time to process and deal with the fallout in a low-stakes situation." He looks around the room where half our squadmates are studying the floor. "I encourage you to make sure you deal with it. Remember you've bound your lives to this person. Trust them. Trust your bond. Work it out. Or enjoy it if your secrets coalesced around sexual positions you were too embarrassed to admit you want to try."

A sea of quick, indrawn breaths precedes a few nervous titters, like no one's sure a major in the Marines really just said that to a squad of privates, many of whom are paired up in same sex couples. When I glance at Lex, he grins at me and drops his eyelid in a wink. I know I'm blushing from the burn on my skin. Hell, I'd be glad to just get to touching dicks. I can't think about positions, or my pants will be far too tight. I feel like a teenager just hitting puberty. I mean, I am still technically a teenager, but, after basic training, it's hard to still think of myself as that young. But next thing you know, I'll be having wet dreams again, which won't be at all embarrassing when I share a bed with the inevitable subject of them.

We get through the day's classes, and the other pairs are slowly starting to talk to one another again. By the time we're done with evening chow and have retreated to the rec room, everyone seems over the worst of their upset, so a lot of talking must've been happening between classes. We didn't have Captain Parsons' class today, maybe to keep him from being the focus of our ire. But me, I kinda want to thank the guy, especially when Lex takes in the room and the dearth of seats and makes himself comfortable on my lap while we play games on the system set up in there. One by one, the other pairs filter out until it's just us and the siblings from Parris Island—just them, apart from their soulmates. Even after some seats free up, Lex stays on my lap. Once the siblings are gone, we start a game against each other, and the asshole starts trying to distract me by nibbling on my neck and teasing his fingers through my hair and down the back of my neck. I lose quickly, but that's okay, because he lets me switch the game off and lead him back to our room.

"I'd like to get to second base," I tell him, as seriously as I can, remembering his words from last night.

"You sure?"

"Yes." Eventually, he's going to have to trust me that I know where my comfort zone lies. It doesn't border touching Lex's dick with my hand. I'm nervous about trying to give a blow job, but hand jobs seem more exciting than nerve-wracking.

"Okay." His words might be casual, but I notice he isn't slow to sit down and start pulling off his combat boots.

"Uh uh," I say, stopping him when he starts to undo his uniform top. "Let me."

His hands fall and he tilts his head, watching me with expectant eyes. When I start undoing his buttons, though, he quickly returns the favor. He frowns when his fingers fumble, and his teeth catch his lower lip and bite down in concentration. Watching him distracts me, and I realize I've paused in my efforts to get him out of his uniform.

If I'm going to be fumbling and pausing anyway, I should be getting something out of it, so I duck my head and kiss him, scraping my teeth over his lip to get him to stop chewing on it so I can replace his teeth with my own. He quickly catches on to what I want, lips parting for mine, and I notice his fingers are moving with more assurance as I feel my uniform top part and cool air hit my undershirt. He pushes the top off my shoulders, then starts tugging at my undershirt as his tongue slips into my mouth with a sensual stroke against mine. I remember what I'm supposed to be doing and jerk a little too hard, popping one button off his uniform.

"You're sewing that back on," he says, then laughs. He pushes my hands away and gets his shirt undone far more efficiently. Then, he's back to pushing my undershirt up, running the palms of his hands up my sides, then over my chest as he goes.

I realize he's going to have to stop touching me to get his uniform top off, so I break the kiss to tug my undershirt off and toss it aside.

"Your turn."

He grins and drops his uniform shirt on the floor, then tugs off his own t-shirt and tosses it in the rough direction of his laundry bag.

With both our chests bare, he moves back in, pressing me against the bed, until I'm forced to sit down. He straddles me and then I have arms full of Lex, pressing skin to skin. It's been a whirlwind from the door to the bed, but as he settles on my lap, something changes. His kisses soften and slow down, like he's savoring again the way he mentioned wanting to last night. Yet, they're still just as hungry. It feels like he can't get enough of the way our mouths meet and meld. His fingers slide down my chest in a slow exploration, fingertips teasing through the hair of my happy trail before he drags them back upward. Demonstrating that he's paid attention to our times with Hannah, he flicks one of my nipples with a blunt fingernail, setting off sparklers racing to my belly. I need something to hold onto in the flare of arousal, and my options are him or the comforter-covered pillows I'm leaning against. I choose him, hands latching on to his waist, curving against the hard line of his abs, still more chiseled than ever after weeks of privation and training.

His skin is as warm as I remember, even in the cool room, soft and supple over firm muscle. I take this time to do some exploratory stroking of my own, finding I delight in his hard lines and sharp angles instead of soft slopes and gentle curves. When my thumb brushes over his nipple, there's no round, full breast in my hand, but I don't miss it. I can't wish for anything to be different when he's breathing soft moans into the minimal air between us.

He keeps up the teasing touches as his kisses firm again, teeth returning to nip and nibble in sharp contrast to the slide of his tongue against mine. When he captures my tongue in a playful move and sucks on it in a suggestive gesture, it's my turn to moan and rock my hips upward, trying to remind him where we were going with this. He sucks on my tongue again as his fingers slip down to my belt. His movements are precise and efficient without being hurried. Before I have time to check if I'm nervous, he's got my belt undone and is working on my fly. Any nerves that might have wanted to rear their heads can't overcome the anticipation as I feel his fingers working to get fabric out of the way. He gets my pants undone and starts on his own, which I probably should have been working on, but he's got them undone fast enough that I'm almost jealous at wondering how he got efficient at that.

His teeth scrape my lower lip and then he nibbles along my jaw. The nibbles turn to nuzzles at the sensitive spot where my jaw and earlobe meet. I'm almost too into it to hear his question.

"Are you still sure?"

"Touch me, Lex, please."

He hums something that must be an affirmative since his fingers slide their way into my pants. He's a little too efficient at getting past the fabric without any seeming effort, but when he palms my already hard dick, I forget to worry about how he's so much smoother at this than I am. I'm just going to enjoy his experience because he's mine, now. I try to copy his movements, but it takes me a little longer to get my hand in his pants. When my fingers brush the velvet hardness of his dick, I still, not because I'm unsure if I want to continue, but because I'm suddenly unsure of how to continue. The angle is all wrong, even before I've got him fully in hand. I scramble to do that first, pulling his dick free of his pants and wrapping my hand around it. Then I'm floundering again. Meanwhile, he's making it impossible to think my way to a solution, because those nimble, piano-trained fingers of his are playing me like a maestro. His grip is warm and firm, his strokes sure, slow, and steady, and I quickly go from half to full mast.

He seems to intuit my dilemma, as his free hand slides back and wraps around the one I've got around his dick.

"Like this." The words are almost whispered against my lips as he starts to stroke my hand up and down his dick, setting a slow and easy pace. When he lets go, he reaches behind himself and fishes something out of his back pocket. His hand moves away from me, but before I can protest, I hear the pop of a cap opening and then his hand is back on me, cooler, but slick, now.

"You just had that in your pocket?"

"I grabbed it when you hit the head, just in case." He backs up just enough to give me a cheeky grin before tightening his grip on me a little.

Again, I'm going to relish his experience and forward thinking. We both were Boy Scouts, but his level of preparation clearly exceeds mine tonight.

"Give me some..."

He squirts some lube into my hand before I wrap my fingers securely back around him. I restart the strokes he demonstrated and am rewarded by one of those breathy moans I could get addicted to. My hand glides more easily, and he strokes me in time with my own movements on him. Just when I think it can't get better, he shifts on my lap and scoots in closer, so our hands are bumping up against one another.

"Try this..."

He opens his hand, and I follow suit, curious. Then he winds our fingers together and our hands form a cage around both of our dicks, pressing them together as he leads us back into those slow, dragging strokes. The angle is still all wrong, but the heat of his dick against mine makes up for it, especially when he rocks his hips forward and slides them together in a counterpoint to the rhythm his hand has set. I'm a bit more pinned down with him straddling my legs and how I'm sinking into the bed, so I can't quite match his movement, but I try. I also turn my head to recapture his lips, wanting to feel as much as hear his moans.

For a time, there's just the glide of skin against skin and those soft sounds he makes. I echo him with moans of my own which build with the urgency building at my core. It's too much and not enough all at once, and I gasp his name in something like a plea.

"Lex..."

"I know. I've got you."

He shifts up more on his knees, changing the angle, and I fuck up into our joined hands the way I did into Hannah that night in the tent. The feeling of this is similar, only I can feel Lex so much more as he moves against me. If I were a better person, I might feel guilty at thinking this is better, but my guilt is tempered both by my pleasure and my surety that this is what Hannah has been trying to engineer for months. She knows how Lex feels and suspects how I do. I can see that now, but she slips from my mind now that everything is Lex: the nip of his lips, the hard heat of his dick and the way he's leaking pre-cum into the cage of our hands. He speeds up both his thrusts and the stroke of our hands, his moans coming shorter and sharper, and I have watched him come enough times to know he's close. I am, too, and my balls tighten in anticipation. Still, I'm not quite expecting the hot ropes of spend that splash up my chest or how it feels when it's my arms he's shuddering in. He murmurs my name as his shudders turn to small shivers, and both his hand and hips still for a moment before he resumes stroking my dick, fingers tightening their hold as he pushes me toward and then over the edge and I'm decorating his chest in turn.

Only then does he slow his fingers, loosen his grip, though he still doesn't fully break contact. His lips stay against mine, with pleased little hums slipping between us. I don't want to break the moment, so I hold him until I feel him start to shift away. He's always the one to pull away first, to go get washcloths or start pulling his clothes on. Not tonight.

I don't quite have the leverage to lift him, but when he stands, I stand with him, turn him, and push him back on the bed.

"Stay here, okay?"

He nods without words, and I tuck myself back in my pants and hurry to the bathroom, coming back with a warm washcloth to clean us both off so we can cuddle without sticking together. When I get back, he's got his socks off and is getting rid of his pants to switch them out for sleep shorts. I let him, then wipe down his chest first, then his dick to get the lube off. I tuck him back in the shorts, clean myself off and get into my sleep pants. By the time I'm ready for bed, he's under the covers, watching me with a pleased smile. I crawl under the covers, wrap my arms around him and pull him to rest against my chest. He offers no resistance, snuggling into me while I finally let myself bask in the afterglow.

"Everything okay?" he asks, looking up at me without any real worry, just the hint of concern. I know him well enough to know he's bracing for bad news, so I duck my head and kiss him.

"Everything's perfect. Not even a flicker of a freak out."

"I guess you were right, then, about what you were ready for."

"Maybe remember that next time."

Though I'm not completely sure what comes next—blow jobs? I don't feel any alarm at the idea of receiving one, and, as I examine it, my main anxiety about giving one is fear I'll suck at it – no pun intended.

"Yes, sir." His voice is just a sleepy murmur, and when I look down at where he's pillowed his head on my chest, I see his eyes are already closed.

"Hmm...I like that. You calling me 'sir.'"

"Aye, aye, sir," he says followed by a chuckle. "Though I don't think we're quite ready for role play or kink, yet."

"Probably not. But I'm filing it away."

"You do that."

"Yes, sir."

That gets me a full laugh. Then he snuggles in closer, and I wrap my arms around him and before I can think to thank him for an amazing time, he's asleep.

I guess I don't need to brush up on my pillow talk, then.

CHAPTER II

August 2010

Lex

One week later, I'm crawling through the muck in the woods, flat on my belly and hoping that I don't tumble into a copperhead den. It's the time of year when their babies are hatching, and I've been terrified of being swarmed by the deadly little things since I saw it happen to a mundane human kid I was playing with when I was six. Granted, being non-magical, he wasn't shielded, and I've got mine firmly in place. That's part of the drill we've been running most days this week—staying shielded in combat-like situations. It's a bit like the obstacle course at Parris Island, only they aren't firing blanks at us. We've all got protection spells on us from our instructors to ensure no one gets seriously hurt if someone can't keep up their shield. Speaking as someone who got distracted hurling offensive spells yesterday and let his shield drop, the pellets they're firing at us may not kill us or even break skin, but those fuckers leave some serious welts and bruises.

When they turn us loose in the field with mission objectives next week, we've heard rumors that we'll all be armed with paintball guns. One rumor says the paint pellets are coated in iron, so shields are useless, but none of us are sure we believe that. What would be the point, then? It becomes like the training we all already passed in basic, only using magic to ensure greater accuracy in our own shots.

Things have been good with Mike. To my delighted surprise, he hasn't freaked out, yet. We haven't really progressed to anything more than hand jobs, but we've taken to showering together, and he mostly seems delighted he gets to touch me. I'm working on trusting him to know his limits, but even though he's made noises about moving on, I'm not sure I'm ready. The more we fool around, the more I fall, and I was already so far gone that I was a hopeless case. They say falling in love with your best friend is sort of a rite of passage for those of us in the not-quite-straight middle of the sexuality spectrum. Maybe it's true; maybe it's not. It's not like I've done any random, controlled studies to test the theory. I'm also not sure that it's accurate to say I "fell" in love with Mike. There was no falling. There just... was. But I'm falling now, and it's fucking terrifying.

Touching him is addictive; I can't get enough. The more we do, the more I crave him, and the longer it goes on, the more I know it'll hurt when it ends. I wish I wasn't so sure it would. No one would understand if I tried to explain it. We're soulmates; we're ritually bound. We've sworn our lives to each other. If ever anyone should be secure in a relationship, it should be me. He's mine. I'm his. What could be simpler or surer? Maybe I'm just being pessimistic. Maybe I think I don't deserve good things, even though I've got no reason for thinking that. I try very hard to be a good person! Maybe I've wanted this for so long, I can't believe it's finally real. This goes beyond having good things. This feels like winning the lottery, and maybe it's just really hard to accept when all your dreams come true? Disney and Hollywood spend a lot of money to sell us on the idea of perfect love, and that there's someone for everyone. The whole existence of soulmates supports that even farther in the supernatural community. I should believe. Not to go all Fox Mulder, but I want to believe. But for all folks talk about girls' sexuality being fluid, you don't hear that much about guys, and Mike's never exhibited a speck of fluid inclination before. Maybe I really am worried the binding ceremony has fucked with his head, making him think he wants me, just because of how close we are. We're brainwashed to link that "you complete me" feeling to romantic love. What if that's what's going on here? It's not like I want him to prove his queer cred before declaring him my boyfriend. If he was out there kissing some other guy, I don't think I could be fully responsible for my actions. I know it wouldn't be pretty. But I mean, could he at least check out Isaac's very nice ass, and then tell me it's good, but mine's better? The qualifier about mine being better, besides being objectively true, is a necessary component to that occasional thought about Mike checking him out. It's a natural part of sexual attraction to at least glance, so long as you don't plan to touch. To be clear, I want him to want me and only me, except maybe for Andie, some day.

Even that, though, feels a bit like a threat, like I can't believe I won't end up with the two of them but still on the outside looking in, like I've often felt with Hannah, despite there being nothing she's ever done to make me feel that way. It's the easy freedom she has to be with him, to hold his hand, to kiss him in public, to call him her boyfriend to anyone she pleases. This is the first time I've been able to do that, notwithstanding it's the first time it's been true.

But when we go home for the holidays in a couple of months, all that will have to stop. Sure, Mike's an adult who can do as he pleases, so his dad can't really forbid him coming over to my place, and my parents will give us any privacy we want or need. But his dad can still make it very uncomfortable for Mike at home and could get even more hostile to me than he already is. Eventually, he'll probably find out about MagCorps, as connected as he still is to the Marine Corps and the various assignments we could get. Since there's significant anti-supernatural sentiment back home, that discovery doesn't bode well for either of us. It's funny how I never dreamed about being in the military, but it's this that's given me the clearest chance at a life I want. I just wish I could believe it's what Mike wants, too, as opposed to the wife and 2.5 kids I've always assumed he wants. To be fair to him, he's never talked about marriage or kids—not with Hannah, or in general. Maybe I'm just making way too many assumptions and making an ass of myself, if only in my own head.

A pellet breaks my thoughts when it hits the ground near my face, sending leaves and dirt flying up, but between my shield and safety glasses, nothing gets through.

"Switch over the shields and start the offensive." The order thunders over the loudspeaker, and I glance back at Mike. This is the new element for today—all week, the witches have been learning to hold our defensive shields while launching an attack, which isn't easy, as I learned so painfully, yesterday. Today, we're mixing it up, with partners shielding each other, so one provides security while the other attacks. Eventually, we'll move to teams, with half the team on offense and half on defense, but that gets a lot more complicated. Mike nods to indicate he's ready to take over defending us both, and I drop my shields. I feel his wash over me, the magic different—like mine, but not. I'm not sure if it's just the difference in people or a witch versus mage thing. My parents' shields also feel different than mine, but like with theirs, there's still something familiar about Mike's. I focus and consciously send him some of my magic, visualizing it flowing from me back to him, so he doesn't have to drain the amulet he's made that stores magic or pull from the ley lines which he's still working on being able to do smoothly while concentrating on other tasks, like supporting me.

Next to me, Ronan signals toward our target, while Isaac takes over shielding them. The initial goal is taking out enemy sentries—with "enemies" played by previous graduates and instructors and to switch back and forth between which of us is shielding and who is launching the offensive spells at our "enemies" at random signals the instructor running the drill gives. Ultimately, they explained, the drill will expand to a version of capture the flag, with magical offense and defense, but they aren't adding in strategy or much competition, yet. They really just want us to practice switching off who's shielding smoothly, maintaining a constant shield around partners, and to practice using magic in offensive maneuvers. I nod at Ronan and signal that I'll take the sentry on the left, leaving him the one on the right. Our opposition is also in four-man teams, trying to take us out to test our shields, but I don't see the other two. That in mind, I stay low as I start putting together a spell that should drop them—one that would be lethal if they weren't shielded against serious harm, like we are. They don't want us practicing with schoolyard magic. That won't do us any good in an actual battle.

I launch my spell and watch my target go down, while Ronan takes his out at the same time. Then we're looking for the other two. I feel the shields around me and Mike weaken, and I send him another stream of magic. I can see it turn the silver cord a sparkling purple as I steady it and keep it an open line of magic for him to draw on. He nods his thanks, then gestures to the right, where the other two members of our opponents' team are sneaking up on us.

I hiss Ronan's name to get his attention and point them out, but they attack before us, with pellets slamming into our shields in a steady onslaught, wearing them down.

"Switch," comes the order, and I swallow. We've never tried this while under attack, just in the classroom. The key is for Mike to keep his shield up until I have us shielded with one of my own. Then we'll switch places and he'll work on his offensive spells. I swallow and slam out a new shield around both of us, sending what looks to me like seeing a shimmery orb out from my center to wrap around us, just under the purple glow of Mike's existing shield. To anyone able to see magic, it would look like we're in the center of two amorphous witchlights, or colored hamster balls, or half of balls, I guess, since they end at the ground in a perfect circle around us. It clicks into place, with almost a physical snap echoing inside me, giving Mike relief and letting him drop his battered shield to regroup.

Mike and Isaac take over attacking, but after the pounding we took from our opponent's ammo draining their magical reserves, both of their spells are a little anemic. I try to feed Mike more magic, and that's when my grasp on the shield falters—I'm paying attention to the stream of magic, our opponents, and checking on Isaac and Ronan and, just for a heartbeat, the shield drops. Of course, that's when a shot comes from another direction entirely, cracking my safety goggles and flying into a nearby tree, blowing back bark on me. A piece slips between my goggles and my helmet, searing and slicing around my temple and left eye. I try to ignore it, but I hear Mike cry out as one of the pellets hits him and I panic, lifting to look back at him, which I know better than to do. Another pellet cracks against my helmet, right before I shield us both again.

"Monroe – you're dead! So is Mathis. McCall and Mason, you two finish up the mission, if you can."

Great. So now the whole squad knows I screwed up and got me and my partner killed. I grumble at myself, then turn around to check on Mike, finding it a little hard to do with my ears ringing from the shot to my helmet and blood dripping into my eye from the bark.

Mike

My neck is still hurting from the pellet shot when we make it to the showers a few hours later. But Lex has dried blood crusted on his face and a dazed look in his eyes that I don't like. Medical checked him out and said he was fine, but

I've seen him concussed before and am worried that shot to the helmet rang his bell more than metaphorically.

We'd gotten chewed out for putting our team at risk, and Lex has been quiet ever since. It's not like we didn't screw up at basic—it's inevitable when you're learning brand new skills. And today's exercise layered multiple new skills on top of one another. Shielding in general is still new to us—it's not something most witches or shifters learn outside of MagCorps, not at the level needed to stop a bullet, at least. Switching the shields between us while simultaneously attacking someone else—also a brand new skill—is something we just started doing this week and today was the first field exercise where we put it to the test. It wasn't just us struggling, either—over half the squad ended up dead. Ronan and Isaac took out the last two sentries, and then our position was overrun by multiple hostiles, and our friends died, too. Isaac's sister is a captain in MagCorps and told him the exercise is designed to make you fail at first, but that it gets easier. None of us are used to managing multiple magic streams at once. But Lex is still beating himself up, even after Isaac gives us all a pep talk.

"Hey..." I reach out and tug him under the water stream. "C'mere."

He doesn't resist me and slides in close, wrapping his arms around my waist and resting his head on my shoulder. We've been showering together for the last several days, but I'm still not used to the slick feel of his naked body pressed intimately against mine.

"How's your head?" I try to get him to look at me, wanting to check his pupils, but he won't lift his gaze off the floor.

"No worse than I deserve."

"How do you figure?"

"I got you killed."

"Only a little and not for real. I'd rather you did it here and now than in the desert when we don't have mega magic laid down to keep us safe." Though now I'm wondering why they don't use the same spells in war to keep the troops safer.

"It takes too much energy to run them for more than a couple of hours."

I blink and stare down at Lex. "Did you just read my mind?"

"No. I just know how you think."

"But seriously, if they can stop the bullets that get past our shields…"

"They can only do that in training, because of the number of them compared to us. In an actual battle, they've got to shield themselves, too, because they're also fighting."

"Right, that makes sense." But I'm still concerned about the question he hasn't answered. "How is your head feeling?"

"It hurts," he says with a sigh. "But mostly where I got cut, like pain radiating out from there more than the other, which is more general."

I run a finger down his cheek, and he finally looks at me. His eyes look normal, except for the one nearest the cut, which still looks bloodshot from the bark he got in it. That seems a normal reaction, so maybe Medical was right and he's fine. But screw it, it's my prerogative to worry. "We've got some Tylenol."

"Yeah, I took some. I think I mostly just need to wash this day off and sleep. You know now that they're done yelling, they'll still want to debrief what we did wrong tomorrow. What I did wrong, rather."

"You got distracted trying to steady the magic we were sharing. We're still having to learn how to do that under fire, just like we had to learn to navigate obstacles under fire and evacuate the wounded. Frankly, I think we're doing much better here."

"We died."

"I think you're forgetting how many times we 'died' in basic, and how many of those were all on me. As for today, I should be able to draw magic steadily without needing your help by now. We've been doing it for thirteen years."

"Not under fire or this much pressure."

"Hey—half the squad died, and that's not on you. A lot of people made mistakes. Next time, we'll make different ones. That's how you learn, right?"

"Right." He still sounds glum, and I hate that I can't seem to console him. "Here, turn around and let's get you cleaned up so we can go to bed."

He turns obediently and tips his head back into the water spray. I know he's hurting when he lets me wash his hair—with his preferred shampoo, not my bargain brand—without protest. By the time his hair is washed, and I've got the rag soaped up, he's a little less tense as I wash him off. He even steps back enough to get my shampoo and return the favor. He moves back in after rinsing my hair and drops a kiss on my collarbone.

"I'm sorry I got you killed."

"Hell, I'd prefer that to living without you, so don't you ever lift your head like that to check on me again, mister. You stay safe. That's the most important thing to me."

He makes a face but doesn't argue—a sure sign he's still in some pain. His fingers are a little bit frisky, though, when he starts washing me off, and he pays particular attention to my dick and my ass with the rag—enough that I have to ask, "Whatcha doin'?"

"Getting ready to apologize for getting you killed. Rinse."

I do as I'm told and then he's pressing close into my arms, nibbling at my collarbone. His lips move upward until he can kiss me, and I open my lips for him gladly. We've gotten past the semi-awkwardness of this, though I'm still relishing the newness of holding him in the shower. He urges me back until my back hits the cold tile wall while his fingers trace circles around my hipbones. They slowly slide inward until he draws just the tip of one finger up my rapidly hardening length.

Those teasing fingers stay on me even as his body pulls back. Then he sinks to his knees, looking up at me.

"That can't be comfortable..." Not on the hard tile floor with the almost mosaic-size tiles cutting into skin. But it sure is beautiful.

"I'm young. My knees can take it," he says with a cocky grin before giving me a more serious look. "I know we haven't discussed this, and I want to say I don't expect you to reciprocate, okay? If you want me to stop, just tell me."

Reciprocating has been my concern—not that I'm not willing to try, but this doesn't seem to be the time to debate that. I don't think I deserve this just for 'dying,' but he's hard, and I haven't even touched him. I also know, from one particular TMI night a couple of years ago, that he loves giving head. Call me selfish, but I'm going to let him do what he so obviously wants to do.

"I don't think that's going to be an issue," I somehow manage to say from a very dry mouth.

He smirks, a little cocky, then leans in. I'm not fully prepared for either the first swipe of his tongue or the view of him doing it. He takes things slow and easy at first, clearly learning what I like. I try to be as vocal as I can be without bothering our suitemates, both to guide and reward him. But he seems able to read my body language well enough not to need verbal guidance. When he takes me in to the hilt, to where I can feel my dick hitting the back of his throat, my knees almost give out. He peeks up at me from under wet lashes and I almost shoot my load at the sinful sight he makes there. Doesn't matter how long I live or what I go through, I'll never forget the sight of him like this.

His fingers aren't idle, either, cradling my balls and stroking back along my perineum. I maybe tense just a bit when his fingertip brushes my anus, but he hums an inquiry around my dick, and I relax again. This isn't totally uncharted territory. New with him and new with a guy, but I've gotten some adventurous blow jobs in my time. This is no different, except it's entirely different, because it's Lex. He just slides touches over me and goes back to deep throating me. Part of me wants to close my eyes and just feel what he's doing, but the other part wants to memorize how he looks for later when we might be apart. I definitely have some new material for my own fantasies. Or, rather, an update to already strong fantasies. What I'd imagined was so much less than the reality.

I want to hold on, make this last as long as possible, but he's too good, and it isn't long until I feel my balls tightening and the tension in my core that says I'm close. I say his name in warning, starting to pull back, but he just chases my movement and swallows me down again, sucking harder. I've avoided it until now to give him the freedom to move as he pleases, but now I wind my hands through his curls for something to hold on to. He slides up and down the length of my dick, and when I start to thrust, he hums, setting off vibrations that do me in. With a shout, I come into his hot mouth and watch as he endeavors to swallow everything I give him. He nuzzles at my groin, dropping soft kisses on my sensitive skin until my shivers stop. Only then do I notice he's washing cum off his hand from where he jerked himself off.

"Doesn't seem fair, me not reciprocating."

"I wanted to do this for you." He pushes himself back up on his feet and gives me his smile, which is the most beautiful one in the world. Maybe I'm biased, but I'll fight anyone who says differently.

"What if I want to do it for you?"

"There are plenty of nights to give it a try. Tonight, I just want to sleep off this headache in your arms."

I can't argue with that.

CHAPTER 12

Lex

We dry off and are in the process of climbing into bed when there's the sound of a loud explosion. I think for a minute they're trying to disrupt our sleep, to get us used to how it might be in a hot zone. But then the building shakes and our door, the wall it's in, and half our floor crumbles and falls away.

A crack runs along our ceiling, and Mike pulls me under my desk. I throw up a shield around it and us as the ceiling caves in and our upstairs neighbors come crashing down, screaming as the building just falls away and them with it. I can't help but watch the floor warily in case we're next. I shift the shield to be under us, as well as over. If we fall, we'll have a chance of survival, at least.

The dust in the air is choking and the roar of the building deafening, but I can still hear the screams below us that all die off abruptly. Our bed is under a pile of debris from above. A few more minutes and we'd have been sleeping and then dead. We barely made it under the desk as it was.

From a sound sleep, neither of us could have processed the danger in time to shield ourselves.

Mike's arms are tight around me, his lips near my ear. "Are you okay?"

"Yeah. I got the shield up in time, I think," I tell him. "You?"

"Not a scratch on me."

I breathe a sigh of relief, but there's no time to relax or drop our guards. The rumbling finally stops, but where our door was is a sheer drop off, the same as the window and wall that used to be parallel to the door. I can feel the cool fall air, the wind blowing through the debris and carnage of our barracks. We're trapped here for now, until rescue comes, because there's no way down except jumping, and my shields aren't strong enough to save us from falling into a pile of concrete, broken furniture and rebar. The wind is blowing some of the dust away, but also reminding me I'm still naked.

"Think you can generate a heating spell?" I ask Mike. "I'll keep the shield up."

"Yeah, I think so."

I feel as he taps into my magic and the space within the shield instantly warms. At least we won't freeze while we wait. Sirens are wailing and getting closer, so help is on the way.

"This would be the time when having a flying broomstick would be helpful," I say. "I mean, of all the stereotypes, couldn't that one be true?"

"You just want to play actual quidditch."

"Right now, I just want to find pants and firm ground."

It takes a few hours, but I finally hear the beeping of something just before a platform attached to a jib boom appears where our window used to be.

"Anyone here?" The voice calling out sounds dispirited and like he doesn't really expect an answer.

"Yes. We're here." Mike's voice is a little choked, probably on the dust.

"Okay. I need you to make your way over here, carefully. We think the floor is mostly stable now but stay along the inner wall as long as you can."

I draw on my inner reserves and strengthen our shield as we carefully crawl out from under the desk. We do as the fireman says, moving carefully, testing each step. It's agonizing how slowly we have to move, but we eventually make it to where our rescuer waits. He helps us onto the platform, and the boom lowers us down to the ground. I see other trucks lining the building, all equipped to rescue any survivors, but I don't see many safely on the ground. I can't process that, yet. Reaction is starting to set in, leaving me shaky and clinging to Mike.

When we're down, another fireman is waiting with blankets we wrap around ourselves before he leads us to paramedics to be checked out. I still haven't dropped my shield around us, and I only soften it enough for the paramedics to work, snapping it fully back in place when they're done, and they direct us over to where a small group is gathered—mostly our instructors and a few senior recruits who live in other housing.

Major Greeley greets us, but says they're still investigating, and don't know what happened, yet. Right now, the priority is rescuing survivors. My heart lifts a little when I hear a familiar voice calling our names. When I look, Isaac and Ronan come running and I hug both of them tightly, noticing they're also just wearing blankets and that the dust on them looks like it's hardened back into cement after getting wet. Isaac's curly hair is caked in it, sticking up at odd angles, but still wet.

"How...?" Mike asks.

"We were in the shower," Ronan explains. "The bathrooms on our side of the building all stayed standing, even when the hall wall fell away."

I look back at the building and realize he's right. "It gave us time to get our shields up, and then we just waited," Isaac adds. "What did you two do?"

"We hadn't gone to bed, yet, and were close enough to get under my desk and get shields up."

"Earthquake preparedness for the win," Mike quips. Why he'd prepared for earthquakes in Virginia is questionable, but his dad is big on all things survivor-related, so he'd regularly put Brandon, Mike, and their mom through all kinds of drills.

"Is that what it was? An earthquake?" Ronan asks.

"No," Isaac says with assurance. "Earthquakes don't feel like that." Being from California, he would know, though Ronan should, too. Maybe he's just rattled. "It was an explosion of some kind."

"Spell gone wrong?" I ask.

"Maybe. Or a gas leak."

"Gas leak should've taken down the whole building," Mike says.

"The building was magically protected from problems with the gas," Major Greely interjects. "That's what kept it from bringing the whole building down, I suspect. This...this was something we didn't ward against."

"Like what?" I ask.

"I don't know for sure, but I saw the initial explosion from my quarters, and it looked more like an IED than anything else."

"Someone rigged the building? On purpose?" I can't wrap my head around that kind of violence here at home. Yes, bombers have targeted federal buildings with catastrophic results, but no one even knows what these buildings are. We don't advertise where we train.

"I don't know, yet, but we'll figure it out." Major Greeley moves to go check on a few other survivors who are huddled together. Vera is one of them, and she's sobbing hysterically. Scanning the group and then the area, I don't see her brother or her soulmate. Fuck. Most people are huddled in pairs, holding on to one another, but here and there lone survivors stand or sit on the ground, looking shell shocked or crying like Vera is.

Someone finally brings us clothes, and eventually, we're shuffled off to local hotels to sleep. Mike and I curl up together for the rest of the night, but neither of us sleeps.

I never drop my shield from around us.

Mike

The next day we're transported back to our classroom building and all gathered in the auditorium for a briefing. I notice a lot of missing faces, and my heart sinks. All told, it looks like only about half of our company is here. Lex is pale and starting to look peaked. I know shock is probably part of it, but he's also risking depleting his core by holding these permanent shields he seems to have put up around us. He'll have to recharge soon, and I'll have to make sure he does, or he'll run himself all the way down trying to protect us.

Major Greeley and Captain Parsons step to the lectern at the front of the room and command our attention. The room goes silent, immediately.

"We're glad to see all of you here," Parsons starts. "And want to update you on what we do know about the events of last night. I apologize that it's still not much."

Major Greeley takes the microphone, breaking in. "The search for survivors continues. We've gotten everyone from the upper levels who managed to find a place of safety—that's most of you—and are beginning to search the debris below. We're using every available resource from technological to magical and to include specially trained dogs and some shifters who've volunteered. We've found a few people injured, but still alive, who are being taken care of in Medical. Their partners have been notified, and, for those of you missing someone, we will let you know whenever we have news. We apologize in advance that it won't all be good, I'm afraid."

I take that to mean they've found bodies in their search.

"We do know now what happened. Apparently, last night, across the country, there were coordinated attacks against supernatural families and communities. We were hit as part of that. An IED was wedged at the weakest part of the building, with a second in another weak spot that luckily didn't go off. We got it safely defused and removed and are studying it now for clues about the perpetrators."

Low murmurs start in the room, rapidly rising as the information and ramifications sink in.

"We know this is concerning for those of you with families who might be targeted, so we're releasing your cell phones back to you so everyone can check on their communities and warn them. We have no idea if this is all they had planned or if it is an opening salvo, but we have increased our warding on all MagCorps properties. We don't have the manpower to send help to every community, with so many of our troops deployed overseas, but, with early warnings, hopefully most communities can protect themselves."

"Except most don't know how to shield or do more than basic wards," Lex says to me in a low voice. I look at him and he's paler than before, tension tightening every muscle. I can't blame him; his family could be a target. I'm lucky in that way, I guess, except that I greatly prefer his family to my own, so now I'm concerned about them, too.

It takes about half an hour until the cell phones are all returned to us. Most of us haven't called home in the weeks we've been here, and we weren't scheduled to be able to do so for another two weeks. Lex gets his phone and hurries into the hallway where he can find a quiet spot. All around us, the others are doing the same.

I listen in on his conversation as much as I can, feeling a surge of relief when I hear Lex's mom's voice and see him relax when she tells him they're okay. He tenses back up after a moment and his mom's voice is lower, so I can't hear her. I can barely hear him.

"What? All of them?" He pauses, looking stricken, and I see tears gathering in his eyes. "But they were harmless." A beat and then he takes a deep breath, going into reassurance-mode. "Okay. Okay. Yeah, we're fine. Don't worry about us. They've got us locked up tight. I promise we're okay."

I can't help but think how close we were to not being okay.

Lex makes her promise to strengthen any wards around their house and make Lizzie practice using her shields. His dad was trained by MagCorps in a seminar they occasionally offer in defensive magic, so at least the Monroes aren't entirely helpless. He finally tells his mom goodbye, promising to be safe and then hangs up.

After hanging up, he sinks to the ground, pale and lets the tears in his eyes fall.

I squat down next to him. "What happened?"

"My folks and Lizzie are okay, but some guys in militia gear came by a lot of the community's homes last night, putting burning pentacles on their yards. They went to the Wilsons' house last. And they...they..."

"They what, Lex?" I put an arm around him, and he leans into me, his voice going softer like he can't bear to say it out loud and make it real.

"Somehow they forced them to shift, then they killed them and skinned them, taking their fur."

He barely chokes the words out, and I feel sick at the thought.

"The Wilsons?" I know the family through the Monroes, and from school, vaguely. "They have all those kids, right?"

"Six," he confirms.

"And the kids?"

"They killed them, too. The whole family."

He pulls away from me, and there's fury like I've never seen from him on his face. It eclipses what I saw the night we were attacked in New Orleans. "They were rabbits, Mike. Fucking rabbits. They couldn't hurt anyone. All they do when shifted is hop around and look cute. They weren't

a threat; they weren't even witches. They were just...just..."
He gets caught in the words in his own fury and makes a
break for the bathroom. I follow and find him getting sick.
He's not the only one from which I figure other people got
news just as disturbing. I go hit up the vending machine
outside the bathroom and get Lex a bottle of water for
when he's done. He's at the sink washing his tears away
when I get back and takes the water with a murmur of
thanks. The tears might have stopped, but fury is still riding
his face.

"Who would do something like this? Who?" his tone is
demanding, even though I'm just as baffled. "Us, maybe, I
get. If you're afraid of supernats, then hitting their military
makes sense and we're the most concentrated population
of MagCorps you can find. Most installations only have a
single platoon or even a squad until you get overseas."

"Yeah, but this place is supposed to be secret," I point
out. "How did they even find us?"

"How did they find the Wilsons? They were hardly out
and proud. No one dares to be in Staunton. But they
targeted multiple families in the community. Over half.
Someone knows and sold them out."

"But not your family," I remind him, hanging on to that
for something hopeful.

"Not yet. I tried to convince Mom to go to her sister's,
up in Maine, but she's worried they won't ever be able to
come back if they run. That it'll confirm for the bastards
that they're supernats. Plus, it might point to others they
don't know about, yet, but know my parents are close to."
He leans into me and rests his head on my shoulder, and I
can feel him trembling. "I just don't understand. How did
anyone know? How did they coordinate attacks in multiple

locations? Why do they hate us so much? We've never done anything to hurt them. What kind of psychopath kills baby bunny shifters?"

By the end, his tears are soaking my shirt, and I wish I had an answer for him.

"I don't know." Except I kind of do. I was raised by a man who wouldn't hesitate to kill a shifter, no matter the kind or age, if he thought he could get away with it. But he wouldn't know who they were, wouldn't know where this facility was, wouldn't have the influence to pull off this number of attacks at once. We're not looking for one man.

"It's someone with magic," Lex says after a moment. He's still sniffling with his tears, but that stony look is back that I don't like. If ever there were an occasion for rage, this is it, but I still don't like it on Lex.

"How do you figure?" I ask, puzzled.

"How else could they force an entire family of shifters to turn?"

"With threats?"

"But the biggest threat in that situation is confirming you are what they think you are. It'd be safer to swear you're human. How are they going to prove otherwise? But for the whole family, all eight of them to turn...something had to force the matter. There are spells that can do it."

"What?" I'm stunned, having never heard anything like this.

"Oh, no one uses them anymore, but, back when shifters weren't considered equals, when witches used them as laborers..."

"Slaves." I say the word he won't, part of the underbelly of the supernatural world.

"Yes, slaves. Back then, they developed this spell to force recalcitrant shifters to turn—either into animals or back into their human form."

"That's dark."

"It was a dark period in our history," Lex acknowledges. "But no one's used that spell in six hundred years or more. Like, not since before the Burning Times. It's forbidden to teach it or even write it down if you know it. Anyone found with a copy of it can be punished by the Queens. It's a capital crime to use it."

"For a single spell?"

"One that strips another person of their bodily autonomy, yeah. All those spells are forbidden, but this one has the highest penalty because of its history."

"But someone clearly knows it."

"Arcane knowledge rarely dies out completely. There's always some grimoire somewhere waiting to be discovered."

"So, you think this was a witch?" I ask, trying to incorporate this new knowledge into my paradigm of the world. "Maybe one that doesn't like shifters having equal rights?"

"The burning pentacles says not-a-witch to me," Lex says with a thoughtful frown.

"Unless they're trying to divert suspicion."

"Maybe, but that doesn't feel right."

"Who else, then?"

His words come out tentatively, like he doesn't want to say them. "A sufficiently powerful mage could probably pull it off."

"It wasn't me."

"Of course, it wasn't you. Obviously. But maybe someone like you. Someone powerful, with a grudge."

A throat clears above us, and we look up. Major Greeley is standing there.

"Everything all right at home, Monroe?"

Lex jumps to his feet, snapping to attention. "No, sir. My family is okay, but our community was targeted, sir."

The major nods. "I'm sorry to hear that, but it's starting to seem like almost every out community was."

"That's just it, sir. We aren't. Out, I mean," Lex explains rapidly. "The whole community gets by pretending to be mundane humans. But... someone knows the truth, or they wouldn't have been attacked."

It occurs to me, following Lex's logic about the spell, that a mage with magical sight like mine could also tell who was a supernat and who wasn't by their auras. Well, shit. Here I was, thinking I was the strongest mage out there, what with the ley line magic, but it turns out I might have deadly competition.

"You were saying you think a mage might be behind the attacks, Monroe?"

"Yes, sir. No witch I can think of would risk using the spell to force a shift. Not unless their life was threatened by a shifter who lost control in animal form. But the family attacked at home were rabbit shifters, sir. They couldn't have threatened anyone. They couldn't even fight back in their animal forms. A human can at least kick and throw a punch and put up a fight. Even kicking, small rabbits can't do real harm. So, if not a witch, then it has to be a mage. No one else could do the spell."

"You look like you've had a thought, Mathis."

"A mage might know what families to target, too, sir," I say, even though I'm reluctant to contribute to the theory. "He or she could see their auras."

"You can tell a supernatural on sight?" Greeley doesn't sound particularly surprised by that, suggesting he might know more about mages than Captain Parsons.

"Yes, sir. And even if a mage didn't have Sight, they'd have other ways of telling. It's how you ever find any of us, isn't it? Something about us signals our awareness of and ability to use magic."

"Hmmm." He studies us for a moment, like he's going to say something, then turns away, gesturing for us to follow. "Come with me." We do as we're told, following him to his office where Captain Parsons waits. "Close the door and sit down." Once we're sitting, he does, too, leaning forward with his elbows on his desk. "I wanted to talk in here because I don't want the idea that a mage or mages could be behind this circulating. We're going to have enough trouble without risking putting targets on the backs of a third of our fighting force."

Lex straightens abruptly. "Yes, sir, but it would have to be someone familiar with MagCorps, to know which barracks to target."

"Yes, but that's even worse for the mage recruits."

"Right, but, I mean, we don't know all the other mages, but I find it hard to believe any we've met would do this."

"No, I agree about our current recruits. Besides no one was AWOL to orchestrate or carry out these attacks. It's possible, though, that it could be a former recruit." Major Greely frowns, looking as troubled as he sounds.

"A current MagCorps member, sir?" Lex sounds like he can't fathom that.

"No. All current personnel are sworn to the Queen. But former members or those who washed out or were otherwise removed might be carrying a grudge."

"Do a lot of mages wash out?" Lex asks, while I just listen and observe. Greeley has an idea, I can tell, and the sick feeling of dread I had when Lex first mentioned mages is just growing.

"More than most, except pure shifters," the major confirms.

Lex looks like he wants to pursue that, but he keeps his mouth shut for now, only asking, "Why?"

"Lots of reasons, but the ones that concern us now would be the ones who couldn't cut it because they lacked the power or control. Or they refused a partner, refused to bond with their soulmates."

"But there are unbound mages in our recruit class, sir."

"For now, yes, but before they can be commissioned, they'll have to go through the binding. Most do without complaint. It gives them more access to power and raises their place in the social and magical hierarchy."

"Plus, they get to be bound to their soulmates," Lex says, looking at me and managing a smile.

"Yes, that, too, though usually those who want more power don't care as much about that."

"So, why refuse?"

"Some think they should be powerful enough on their own—they resent the implication that they are somehow subpar or lesser without a partner. Some don't want the permanent commitment, or to be in a binding where they are often, ultimately, subservient in their power to their partner. Some have shifters for soulmates and think they could do better with someone with a more powerful magical core."

"So, hubris?" I ask.

"Primarily."

"Does that happen a lot?"

"Not too often. Once every five or six recruit classes, if that."

"Still, given you go through that many classes a year, that's one possible suspect every year going back several decades," Lex concludes.

"Yes, but not all of them have the knowledge, power or wherewithal to carry out such a coordinated attack."

"What happens to them?"

"Most go back to their original branch of service and finish out their enlistment there."

"What about the shifters who wash out?" I ask.

"A regular shifter couldn't do the spell," Lex says.

"No, I know," I acknowledge. "But he or she might have information on the communities that were hit and have shared it with the mage or rogue witch."

"I'm with Monroe," the major says. "I don't see a witch doing something like this."

"What about a witch who's mentally ill or something? Can't witches be sociopaths, too?" It's a disturbing idea, given the kind of power magic can give someone.

"Well, sure, we have mental health challenges just like mundane humans, and it was a witch who first developed that spell," Captain Parsons acknowledges. "We can't rule it out. I'm less convinced by the shifter suspect angle, though. Most shifters who wash out of general MagCorps ranks aren't disgruntled about it."

"Why not? What do regular shifters even do?" Lex asks. "We've met a couple, but all the shifters in our company are also witches."

I remember Captain Parsons talking about regular shifters the first day, but now isn't the time to remind Lex.

"That's correct. The regular shifters are in their own unit, as the predators drill in animal form."

"What do the prey animals do?" Lex's voice is quiet, and I know he's thinking of the family of rabbit shifters again.

"They're trained in espionage and usually assigned to the CIA.'

"They're spies?" Now Lex looks delighted, if only briefly. The situation is too upsetting to sustain the delight, but I feel a flicker of hope when it breaks that dark look of rage on his face, even if it's just a momentary glimmer. He's going to want a spy kitten; I can already tell.

"No one pays any mind to a mouse in the wall or a house-cat sitting on a window ledge. They're often our primary source of information in hostile areas. Most of the intel the rest of MagCorps acts on comes from shifters. But every now and then one feels slighted because they aren't put on the front lines or like a second-class citizen because their partner can use their magic to be stronger."

"What if it's a mage and a shifter?" Captain Parsons asks.

"Now, that's a real possibility," Major Greeley replies, nodding a little.

"Anyone come to mind?" I ask.

"One pair, actually. Soulmates who never bonded: a mage who refused to vow fealty to the Queen and a squirrel shifter who was too impatient and scattered for espionage. The mage was insulted that his soulmate was not just a squirrel, but also male, and the shifter was insulted the mage was insulted. But they were united in being sure their lot in life was either our or the Queens' fault, and both made a stink when asked to leave."

"When was this?" Lex asks.

"About twenty-five years ago," Major Greeley says, watching me carefully. I meet that watchful, intent gaze. His too-green eyes reflect the light, I notice, and remind me of Andie's bodyguard—the panther who pounced on Lex. Huh. So, he's a shifter, too, though I can't tell what kind by looking. He's better at passing than any shifter I've ever met. There's been nothing in his movement to suggest shifter and, up until I catch that reflection of light, I would've sworn he was a witch like Captain Parsons. "Plenty of time to have built up a network of other aggrieved souls across the country and, with the Internet, coordination of the attacks wouldn't be that hard."

"Why are you staring at me?" I ask, feeling uncomfortable under Greeley's intent gaze.

"I find it curious you don't know this already."

"How would I?"

"The mage in question is your father," he says slowly, but clearly.

"No." It's not that I want to defend the man or say he's not capable of this much hatred, this much violence. I know him too well, especially his capability for hatred and violence. I feared for Lex enough to stop inviting him over a couple of years ago, because... Because I didn't like how Dad was looking at him. Like he knew something and hated it. I just figured it was Lex's bisexuality, but what if it was that plus his being a witch? But no. No, if my dad was a mage, I'd know. I think that again, like a lifeline, and this time, I say it aloud, insisting, "I would know. I'd be able to see or sense it."

"There are talismans a mage or a supernatural can use to hide the magic in their aura," Parsons tells me. "He could have been hiding from you."

"But why? He's never hidden his dislike for supernaturals, which I've always found funny since his best friend is a..." I break off because I realize the implications of what I was going to say.

"A shifter?" Major Greeley asks.

"Yeah. I just figured he didn't know. But Sam...Sam spews that same anti-supernatural, homophobic bullshit my dad does. I always thought that must be an epic level of self-loathing."

"It probably is."

Lex looks horrified at the possibility, reaching a hand out to me, then pulling it back. I'm not sure if it's because he can see I don't want to be touched, or if he can't stand to touch me. It hurts, either way.

The implications horrify me, too. If it's true, Dad knows what I am. He knows what Lex is. He knows about Lex's family. He knows we're soulmates. He knows I'm here. He...tried to kill me. If he was responsible for the bombs, knowing I would be in the barracks, my father tried to kill me. At the very least, he didn't care if I died, so long as I took Lex and all of our friends, our company, with me. I know my dad doesn't love me, but I never thought he hated me. Not really. Not when he didn't know about my feelings. But if he knew it all, then all those tirades about the evil of witches and magic and the sinfulness of the LGBT folks, all of those were meant to make me hate Lex and myself. To separate me from my soulmate. He wasn't just trying to get me to turn my back on my problematic best friend. He wanted me away from the other part of my soul, simply because he didn't have the power he craved. Power, I realize, I have now through Lex.

"My dad can't be a mage." I'm not really in denial, but I can't say my sickening realizations aloud. I can't bear to see Lex realize them, or for him to worry about his family.

"He is," Major Greeley says, not without pity. "We were recruits together. He was immensely talented. Could draw on the ley lines like you can. He's the reason for the theory that mages come from lost witch lines. We suspect your great-grandfather was the last Mathis witch. His mother and grandmother were both human, and then he married a human woman, as well. So did your grandfather. So, that was four generations of mundane human bloodlines intermingling with the magical Mathis blood."

"How do you know that?"

"Your father's second... no, third cousin, I think third," Major Greeley looks like he's tracing a genealogy chart in his head. "I always get cousins mixed up. Anyway, they share a great grandfather, your great-great grandfather. This cousin, Aaron, he's my soulmate and husband."

"So, what you're saying, Major, is we're in-laws?" I ask, unable to stop myself.

"Hardly the most important takeaway," he returns, dryly, "but yes."

"And cousin Aaron is also a mage?"

"He is."

"And my dad really is, too?" I still don't want to believe, even though part of me is already struggling to accept it.

"I'm sorry to say, but yes."

"And you think he did this, attacked here and all those families?"

"I don't know. It's just a theory I came up with while we were discussing possibilities. I know he hates us enough, mostly, I think, because he's bitter he wasn't born a witch, with power of his own."

"But with the ley lines, Mike's almost as powerful as a witch," Lex says, looking like he wants to defend my honor.

"You can't logic away resentment and hate, Lex," I say, reaching for his hand. Maybe I'm not really in the mood to be touched right now, but he needs it. Touch grounds him, helps him regulate his moods when he gets upset. His fingers latch on to mine, holding fast, though I notice they're trembling again.

"We're running some tests on the bombs. If we find anything conclusive, we'll let you know," Captain Parsons says. "But we won't mention this possibility to anyone outside this room and neither should you."

"No, sir. I mean, yes, sir," I say.

"Go get some rest and check in with your friends. Classes are cancelled for the rest of the day."

"Will you arrest him, sir, if you find out it was him?" I can't keep the note of hope out of my voice, and don't try.

"We'll turn the information over to the authorities," Major Greeley says. "But I don't know what they'll choose to pursue."

"Nothing back home; nothing for the Wilsons," Lex says. "The DA probably thinks they were just some animals. Maybe they get a slap on the wrist for hunting out of season, but doubtful."

Major Greeley and Captain Parsons look stricken, and it occurs to me that we didn't tell them about the Wilsons, so it must have happened to other shifters for them to seem to understand.

"Shouldn't it be a hate crime or something?" I ask.

"Morally, yes," Captain Parsons says.

"But, legally, being a shifter or a witch isn't a protected category for hate crime designations," Lex says, still sounding bitter. "Hell, we don't even have close to the same rights as mundane humans, if we're known to be supernaturals. It might not even be a homicide, let alone a hate crime. 'Witches and shifters are people, too' is just a slogan, not a fact under the law."

"But there are mages missing, presumed dead in the barracks, right?" I ask, holding Lex's hand tighter. I guess I knew that, technically, but it's never been a point of issue before.

"Yes," Captain Parsons says, looking sad.

"Well, then, they were human. Whoever set the bombs killed humans as well as supernaturals. And they were members of the U.S. military. That should count for something," I say, not ready to cede the point. "You can't just waltz in and kill human servicemembers on U.S. soil with impunity, surely? That's got to be domestic terrorism, at least."

"I would hope so," Major Greeley says. "But it will come down to politics and the pressure the queens can bring. I know the president has been pushing to provide supernaturals more rights, but next year is an election year, and he wants a second term."

"Right."

It's not their fault, but I can't help but think of all our missing company members. Some might still be found alive, but the likelihood of that drops with each hour. I stand since we've been dismissed and tug Lex out with me. He stops me in the hallway and wraps his arms around me, hugging me tight.

"We'll figure it out," he promises, even if I'm not sure how or what we're supposed to figure out. "He doesn't get to win."

"You need to call your folks back. Tell them their cover is already blown and to get out. I couldn't bear it if he hurt them."

He nods against my chest, and steps just a couple of steps away to make the call. He keeps his voice down so no one coming along will overhear. When he ends the call, he steps back into me. "They're taking Lizzie and going to Maine."

"Good."

I take his hand again and lead him back toward the main part of the building. Time to find out just how bad this is going to get.

CHAPTER 13

Lex

My head is swirling as I follow Mike back to where our classmates are gathered. I'm glad my parents and sister are safe for now, but heartsick at having to make that call. I'm in denial that Mike's dad could be part of this, though more for his sake than any real disbelief in the man's capacity for hatred and violence. I've seen the bruises Mike always tried to hide or brush off, and those were just from Mike being adjacent to queerness by standing by me and our friendship. I know his dad hates supernaturals even more than he does LGBT people, but this level of violence is not something you ever imagine coming from someone you know, someone whose roof you've slept under, someone who was a trusted adult through your childhood, even if maybe they shouldn't have been.

There's a hollow feeling in my stomach and a tickling at the back of my throat that's either tears or screams wanting to leak out. I can hear the sobs coming from other students before we even round the corner, and I know it's going to be bad. I can't believe our community has been attacked like this, that so much spilled blood stains the ground, that at least several dozen people hate us this much. I hold on tightly to Mike's hand, because I don't want him to think I'm pulling away or that I associate him with this horror as anything but another victim of it. If Major Greeley's suspicion is true, Mike's dad either just tried to kill him, or hated me and my people so much that his son's death was a price he was willing to pay to kill a bunch of teenagers who happened to be born different than him. I have fights with my parents sometimes—who doesn't?—but I can't even wrap my head around what Mike must be going through. I want to be supportive, but I don't know how, at least not until we can be alone, and he can talk freely. If he'll do so. He's not the best at using his words to sort out his feelings and problems.

We turn the corner, and my eyes are immediately drawn to Isaac and Ronan, sitting on a bench against the wall. They both look shell-shocked, pale and trembling, and I tug Mike toward our teammates and friends. Ronan looks up at us first; his eyes are red, like maybe he's been crying, but they're dry now.

"Is your family okay, Lex?" he asks.

I nod. "Yeah. At least my folks and my sister are. I don't know about the extended family. Mom hadn't gotten ahold of anyone but her sister, yet. There were attacks in our community, though, so they're going to go stay somewhere no one knows them for a while."

"Probably for the best," he says in a quiet voice.

"What about yours?" I ask because I do care even if I don't want more bad news.

"My immediate family's okay," Ronan says. "My folks, my siblings. But one of my uncles, the mage..." He pauses, voice catching, swallows and presses on. "Militia members caught him. Put iron handcuffs on him like he was a witch, then burned him at the stake." His voice drops to a whisper towards the end, like saying it aloud will evoke the collective memory of the horrors witches faced before they had lobbyists and PR firms on their side. But those memories are already evoked for all of us today.

"Jesus." I don't usually invoke the Son, for all I was raised a good Catholic boy, but the Goddess seems to be absent on this cold, horrible morning. "Isaac? Your family?"

He looks up at us, and the look in his eyes matches the hollow feeling in my stomach and the tickle in my throat. His voice holds almost no inflection as he answers me. "My aunt answered when I called. They're dead. My parents. My siblings. All but my big sister." Something flares in his gaze, and I recognize it as fury. "They were shifted, and the murderers took their pelts like...like some kind of sick trophy."

It's the same story my mom told about the Wilsons, but this guts me even farther, because this time I have a grief-stricken person I care about right in front of me. The fallout isn't theoretical; it's there in the tears that well up in Isaac's eyes and in the helpless look on Ronan's face, while he faces his own horror, and I feel myself flounder as Mike flinches. For a moment, I don't know who to reach out to, but before I can decide and move, I have a sobbing Isaac in my arms. I don't know why he chose me instead of Ronan. Maybe because I didn't lose anyone, and it doesn't feel like an imposition to ask for comfort, like it might from someone else also grieving. Mike lets go of my hand, so

I can wrap both arms around Isaac. Ronan looks stricken but mouths a thank you at me before sinking back on the bench.

Isaac's tears are a torrent, quickly soaking my borrowed sweatshirt. I'm no good at this sort of thing, don't know what to say. I want to make it better, but there isn't any making it better, so I'll settle for not making it worse. I don't try to shush him, just let him cry, holding onto him as tightly as he's holding me. I can't try to tell him it'll be okay. It's not okay, and it might never be okay again. Not for him. Maybe not for any of us.

I meet Mike's gaze over Isaac's head, and he looks as stricken as Ronan. He finally sinks down to sit next to the other mage, wrapping an arm around him as Ronan starts to cry silently. He's not sobbing, like Isaac, but his heartbreak is obvious, and his tears fall steadily.

The four of us stay like that for a long time, until Isaac cries himself out. More tears will come, inevitably, but for now, he sniffs and hiccups and eventually pulls back from me. I'm reluctant to let go until I see Ronan holding out his arms and Isaac crawls onto his soulmate's lap and lets himself be snuggled and petted. Someone comes and announces the bus being ready to take anyone back to the hotel who wants to go. Mike and I shuffle Ronan and Isaac down the hall and onto the bus, then off the bus and into the elevator. Mike takes Ronan's key and lets them silently into their room.

"We're right next door," I say, like that remotely matters right now.

Ronan nods and closes their door, and I almost collapse against ours. Mike gets us in, and then I can finally hug him tight. He grabs hold of me like he thought he'd never get to touch me again. It makes me feel guilty for just a moment, though I'm not sure for what. Then I realize it's not my guilt I'm feeling, it's his. More than that, I can feel more tears running down my neck and into my soaked sweatshirt. Maybe I didn't know what to say to Isaac, but I can start here.

"It's not your fault," I say softly, but as surely and firmly as I can.

"He's my father."

"We don't even know he's involved."

"Yes," he says around a sob. "We do."

"It could be a coincidence." I'm reaching, sure, but it's not like there isn't plenty of anti-supernatural sentiment out there.

"It's not. Major Greeley knows him. Knows he's a mage. He hid it from me. Had to be for a reason." The words come in short bursts, caught on sobs.

"Maybe rampant self-loathing, regret, or not wanting to admit to failure at something so tied to his image of fierce warrior hero?" I can't see Mike's dad being willing to admit he washed out of a military training program, after all, or having to defend why he'd left it.

"Somehow, I can't believe he thinks he failed," Mike argues. "That's not who he is, to admit that. More like his commanders and classmates were jealous or simply didn't understand his greatness."

That does sound more like the narcissistic asshole. "Doesn't mean he coordinated all of this, and even if he did..."

"He did. I just...feel it. I know it."

"You don't know it; you fear it and you're jumping to the worst conclusion," I argue, hoping to pull him back from the edge of despair I can feel him teetering on.

"What if it's the right conclusion?"

That's the question, isn't it? "Then we'll face that and deal with it. It's still not your fault. You didn't cause this, even if he's responsible."

"Will Isaac see it that way?" Mike asks, into my neck.

"He won't know. Major Greeley said they weren't going to tell anyone, and neither will we."

"I don't like lying to our friends."

"It's not lying. It's not protecting him," I insist. "It's protecting you from anyone who might want to tar you with the same brush, which is ridiculous, because you were attacked as much as the rest of us last night. You could have died like so many of our company have." The thought chills me and, while I've never liked Master Sergeant Mathis, I feel that dislike coiling into an ice cold, yet somehow still burning, hatred. Even if he didn't do this, he spent all of Mike's life trying to convince him he was wrong for being what he was, when, apparently, the Master Sergeant is the same thing. "Our—our—community is under attack, and we won't prevail against it by turning on each other."

"I feel even less like it's my community now."

"Well, you need to get over that. Make a choice to embrace us. Make us your own."

"Pick a side?" he asks, pulling back a little.

I meet his gaze. "I didn't say that. You already did that when you made your vow to the Queen and to me. That's why it's our community. I thought you just needed time to settle into that."

"So did I."

"Then what's...?"

"I'm human, ultimately, and everyone will always see that first, just like everyone sees people's supernatural identities first once they know them."

"Is that what you see first about me? That I'm a witch?"

"Of course not."

"Well, then. For most of these folks, the mages here are the first they've met. They're still getting to know you guys, to see you as part of us. But if you see yourself as separate, that's going to communicate itself to others, and they'll believe you. If you see yourself as one of us, they'll believe that, too."

"You really believe that?" I can't tell if he's hopeful, but I think that's the emotion I feel from him.

"Yes. Absolutely. You're mine and I'm yours, so. It's like what Ruth says to Naomi, you know? About your people will be my people..."

Mike doesn't know his Bible stories like I do, but he nods. "I don't think you want my people to be your people..."

"I love your mom and Brandon," I say, because it's true. "Let's be honest, your dad is hardly 'your' people, either."

"And I love your family," he says, finally seeming to agree with me, which I take as progress. "And our friends here."

"Who are kind of like family. Brothers, at least." I don't have any brothers, and it's what I hoped for in the military.

"Sure. At least potential brothers."

He's not signing on to my point as enthusiastically as I hoped. "So, I mean, Ruth's whole thing is kinda like our vows." It's one of the few bits of the Bible I bothered to memorize, because it was how I felt about Mike. Except for claiming his dad. "'Where you go, I will go, and where you stay, I will stay. Your people will be my people and your

God my God. Where you die, I will die, and there I will be buried. May the Lord deal with me, be it ever so severely, if even death separates you and me.'"

He finally smiles a little. "I like that part, the idea of not being separated in death... So much better than 'til death us do part.'"

I let myself relax a little. "I mean, it's kinda the whole soulmate principle, right? And that's a supernatural thing. So, being a soulmate, having this cord between us, that makes you one of us. You are my people. More than anyone else..."

"Except Andie."

"Except Andie," I say, allowing that, even if she still doesn't feel totally real to me. "But then her people will be our people, too, eventually, which means the shifters. So, see, you're tied to the whole community by sharing your actual, literal soul with a witch and a shifter."

I get a real smile, albeit a sheepish one, at that. "I guess I am. So, our community. And if someone threatens that, no matter who they are, we'll deal with them."

"Amen." I lift my head enough to seal it with a kiss. Like with our formal vows, I feel a piece of magic snap into place—one more vow, tying us to one another and a common purpose.

Mike

I can't say that my chat with Lex fully washes away my guilt and loathing, but it helps me separate myself from my father and his hate some more; whether or not he did this, that feels like a good step. I do realize that I've been holding myself a little apart from our new band of brothers and resolve to do better. I don't ever want there to be a question of where I stand. Maybe I feel a little outside-looking-in in this world, but that's at least partly my own fault for holding back. Lex is right—I swore fealty to the Witch Queen, and I went through a magical bonding ritual with him that's as sacred, if not more sacred, than a wedding.

His people are my people, and it's time I let my mind accept what my heart already has. Maybe I need to reach out, get to know the other mages better. That's somewhere to start, at least. With the eradication of the vampires, we're basically the third species in the supernatural world, the ones who span both worlds not just by living in them, but by blood, by family, and by history. If anyone can help each group understand the other, maybe it's us.

Now, I don't know how to even start that, mind you. We're mostly a secret for one reason: to keep from fostering the resentment humans already often feel at knowing magic is real and not being able to do anything with or about it. If my dad, with all his power, is really this bitter about not having the power of a witch, how much more bitter is Joe Schmo going to be when he learns his human neighbor can light his fireplace without matches or a lighter?

I realize Lex is staring at me when I haven't returned his kiss, so I duck my head to rectify that. "Sorry, I was thinking about what you said."

"Come to any conclusions?"

"I should ask Vera to sit with us at lunch." If her brother and soulmate are both gone, admittedly, now might not be the best time, or it could be that she might really need a friend. But better to think positively about them being okay, just not rescued last night when we saw her.

"Huh. Okay." Lex looks a little skeptical.

"Okay, really what I thought was that I should get to know the other mages and she's the only one whose name I remember."

"Her brother is Daniel."

"You sure? I thought it was David."

"Nope. Daniel." Lex sounds positive about this.

"Huh." I probably should be sure to remember that when I ask about him.

"Not that I think this is a bad idea, but why?"

"Because you're right. We're part of this community, but we're also outside of it a little because we're mostly just human, and maybe if we all acknowledge that and get to know one another and our soulmates, we'll feel more like part of it."

"So, you want other mage-witch couple friends?"

"Yes. We can't just have Isaac and Ronan as our only friends in the whole Corps." Even though they're technically a mage-witch couple, too.

Lex looks uncertain about that assumption, and I remind myself that we're both used to being insular with just one another. Our having one other couple as friends is already double the number of real friends, not just friendly acquaintances and teammates, we've ever had.

"Okay. I'm game," he says after a thoughtful moment. "But we also need to be there for Isaac and Ronan. I don't want them to think we're drifting away because we don't want to deal with their tragedy and loss."

I shouldn't be surprised that occurred to him, but I am a little mad at myself for being so. It's not fair to him. He's always been there for me, no matter what. Of course, he'd do the same for our new friends. I'm just not used to seeing him thinking of anyone outside of us. Maybe because he's always kept his distance back home, either because of being teased or because he's been afraid he couldn't play human if he was observed too closely. It strikes me again how much freer he's been here, and how much I took for granted being able to be free all our lives.

"We'll make sure they know we're here, whatever they need."

He gives me a beautiful smile, dimples flashing, and then a kiss that feels like I'm being given a reward. I'm glad I said the right thing.

After a moment, he tugs me toward the bed and flops down onto it, reaching for the remote. "Want to watch something?"

"Just you."

The smile I get for that puts the last one to shame.

I settle on the bed and tug him back into my arms, snuggling down into the plush mattress and holding him close. After all the tragedy and the upsetting news about my dad, I just want to hold him, to try and offer some comfort and maybe receive some in turn. He shifts around a little bit, pulling away to tug off his sweatshirt and tossing it aside before settling back against me in his t-shirt. Setting the remote back on the nightstand, he snuggles back into me and rests his head on my shoulder.

"What are we going to do?"

I want to ask about what, because there are so many possibilities to that question, from right now to a cosmic, philosophical question to a very pragmatic one relating to my dad. The thing is, it doesn't matter what he's talking about, because my answer to them all is the same. I reach and flip the switch that turns off the lamps, then wrap my arms back around him.

"I don't know."

CHAPTER 14

Lex

The first thing we do the next day is take a field trip to Marine Corps Base Quantico to get supplies and uniforms to replace what we lost in the bombing. No one made it out with more than what they were wearing, and Mike, Ronan, Isaac and I aren't the only ones to not have been wearing anything. There's only so long we can all run around with one sweat suit each, especially when we have to get back to training. I'm grateful for what we've been given, but it feels good, too, to have things of my own again. It feels better than I would have expected to be back in uniform again, honestly, when we all gather in the auditorium the next day. I notice a few people look a little calmer than they had yesterday, including Vera, while a lot more people are missing than had been. Major Greeley's announcement that rescue operations have determined there's no one left alive to rescue answers questions about the various reactions around the room. Apparently, several people had been saved, able to protect themselves with magic, even as they were buried in the rubble. So, some people who had been bracing for the worst news were spared that. However, in the end, over half of our platoon had perished in the bombing—nearly 30 souls were lost. Apparently, some of our people are on a modified bereavement respite, if not full leave, while others are in medical, with soulmates and friends. They will be briefed later, so everyone's on the same page.

Unfortunately, the news so far is that no one is sure what, if anything, is going to be done to find and punish the perpetrators, given they are most likely human and possibly even full citizens. To keep us from going on our own vengeance quests, our training pace is going to pick up with the likely goal of shipping us out sooner. Apparently, we should take our ire and aim it at Al-Qaeda. Or the Taliban, depending on where we're shipped. Even though neither had anything to do with our personal losses. Those who have lost family in the nationwide attacks are to get bereavement leave but will be expected to report back to base after the funerals and relative travel time. One assumes so they won't go off on a vigilante quest for justice.

Isaac's all but grinding his teeth as he sits next to me, and I can't blame him. It's not nearly enough, not even for the attack on us, let alone the lost families. I reach over and lay my hand over his, unsure how else to show support in this situation. I'm a little surprised when he turns his and grips mine tight, but I let him hold it as long as he needs to.

Some of our sped-up training means that some classroom work is getting reduced, primarily courses like Major Greeley's history class. We still have Captain Parson's magical theory class because that's considered essential knowledge, but we'll have to complete history by correspondence, on our own time. Mike is unimpressed by that, thinking they should just ditch the requirement if they're not letting us take it how it was designed, but I'm glad to still get to learn the information. We still have to write the papers. If he weren't so well-trained in respecting authority, I think Mike might walk out at that announcement, but he and Ronan just exchange a disgruntled look, while Isaac obviously doesn't care, leaving me alone with my delight. I'd already come up with my topic and started my research on the first paper, and I'm glad that work isn't for nothing.

"I worry about you," Mike murmurs as we file out of the auditorium on our way to magical theory.

"I almost have the outline done," I tell him, trying to tamp down my glee.

"How are we even friends? It's like AP US History all over again."

"You didn't have to take that, you know. You could've taken regular history class."

"But you wouldn't have been in there."

Sometimes, for someone who's really bad at using his words, he really does know just what to say.

"This is what being soulmates means," I say with a sigh.

"That I love you despite your freakish hard-on for history?"

"Yes." His words sink in. "Wait, what? You what?" He did not just drop the "l" word on me in that way, did he?

"I love you despite your freakish hard-on for history." He enunciates each word slowly even though I don't even really hear anything past the first three.

"You love me?"

Mike rolls his eyes. "Obviously."

"You can't just say that like it's not a big deal."

"Jesus Christ, Lex. You know I love you. I've loved you since we were five."

"You never said so before now."

"I thought my actions said it for me."

Well, huh, okay. That is a good point, I guess.

"I mean, we're soulmates. Of course, I love you. I bound my whole life to yours, swore fealty to a Queen I'd just met, agreed to join MagCorps, even though I had no idea what it entailed or might mean for my military career. Did you really think anyone would do all of that for anything less than love?"

"I-I guess not?" I hate that I sound unsure. "You've just never said so."

"Well, neither have you, but like I said, I thought it went without saying."

"It does." I don't want him to think I thought he didn't love me, after all. I just hadn't expected the words or the warm glow they brought. "I do, too. Love you, I mean." Because, I should totally say it back, to encourage these kinds of confessions.

"I know," he says, giving me a sweet smile, then a kiss.

"I'm not calling you 'Han Solo.'" Because I know that "I know" was a deliberate *Star Wars* reference, and he always had to be Han when we played *Star Wars* pretend as kids.

"Even in bed?"

"I told you, we're not ready for role play, yet."

He laughs against my lips, then pulls back and takes my hand. "You let me know when we are."

I can't help but grin, flashing back. "Yes, sir."

Mike

In an apparent effort to get us more combat ready, Captain Parsons decides today is the day I should demonstrate how I draw on the ley lines. Without any real warning, he doesn't just want me to demonstrate—he wants me to try and teach the other mages how to do it. Because mages don't have magical cores, we're all theoretically capable of the same things; hereditary parallels with my father aside, any mage should be able to do what I can do with the right training and enough practice. It helps me to remember that, to distance myself from my father. I can't draw on ley lines because he can; I can because the Monroes chose to train me largely along with Lex, always pushing me to try to do more, and I'm just competitive enough to push myself to practice something until I achieve it.

I try to convey all of this to the class of expectant mages and skeptical witches watching me. I don't want to be special, especially not if it's something my dad sees himself as being. I just want to be strong enough to protect my soulmates and my friends.

Captain Parsons takes us all to the meditation garden, built to tap into the convergence of the two ley lines that run through D.C. He nods, gesturing for me to take over, and I really wish I'd had the ability to prepare for this a bit more. I do my best, launching into a clumsy explanation.

"So, tapping into the ley lines as a mage isn't really all that different to how a witch does it. I mean, Lex and I learned how to do it at the same time. It's basically the same as pulling power from a witch or shifter." There are a few scoffs at that, and Lex looks ready to fight someone. "No, really. It's all about just being able to see the magic there, then reach out for it and pull it into yourself to shape and use. We can't store it the way they can, any more than we can store up the power we siphon off them, but if you can find it, you can use it for immediate power expenditure."

"How do you find it?" The question comes from a mage whose name I don't know.

"The same way you find magic in a witch or shifter," I say with a small shrug. "You just look."

"You can see it?" Vera asks, coming closer with a banged-up looking Daniel beside her.

"Sure," I say, a little confused by the question. "Can't you?"

"No," Daniel says.

"Then how do you pull any magic?" I ask, confused.

"I feel it," Vera says.

"I can hear its frequencies," says the mage whose name I don't know.

"Okay, so, how our senses interpret magic around us must be individualized," I say. This is why there should be more formal training for mages before this point. "I saw it first, so I tend to go the visual route, but now I agree with Vera that I can feel it, and I guess it's kind of a humming feel, but I don't hear it."

I get a few nods.

"How did you go from siphoning magic from Lex to the ley lines?" Captain Parsons asks.

"Clumsily," I say, more serious than joking, although I get a few chuckles. "Why don't we sit down here, in the garden? Everyone should get a partner, too. Someone you know how to siphon magic from."

I'm aware that several people seem to be here solo, but there are enough shifters and witches here to fill in for the exercise. It's not like mages can only siphon from their soulmate. Anyone with a magical core will do in a pinch.

"Okay, so, I'm just going to walk you all through the way the Monroes taught me. I don't know the theory behind it, sorry."

"I think we might be discovering a new theory," the captain says before offering himself to an unpartnered mage.

We all sit down on the cool stone with our partners. Lex settles close to me, reaching out a hand to touch my leg in support.

"Okay, so, however you do it, find the magic in your partner and start pulling just enough to form a witchlight or mageglobe." Same thing, different names, and the first thing I learned to do as a mage at around five years old, so I assume everyone can do it. They've been having us play with shields and offensive spells, after all. Creating light is a far more basic way to shape magic than a shield or pseudo-projectile. Everyone should be able to do this.

I pull some magic from Lex and shape it into a ball of light between one breath and the next, then glance around the garden. Some balls of light are brighter, some are sputtering a little, indicating varying smoothness levels of magic drawing, but everyone's done it.

"Okay, good. Now, hold that, like we've been doing shields, but shift your active awareness away from it. However you find the magic in your partner, use that same technique and...search the area, for lack of a better way of describing it. The ley lines are under the Earth's surface, so it might help to focus downward. Try and see or feel or hear past the grass and stones, more toward the heartbeat of the Earth. I can't actually hear it, but that's how I experience it, at least. Lex's aura glows with this pulsing light, in time with his heart that is his magic, and, to my eyes, Earth does the same. Finding the ley line is the trickiest part for anyone, even witches and shifters," I tell them. "Once you do, then just...reach out for it the same way you do your partner's magic. However you experience or visualize that." When I look around again, several people are frowning, their lights fizzling out. Others, though, are nodding. "Then, once you have it, try to feed the magic into your light, releasing your pull on your partner's magic the same way we do in shield drills."

A few witchlights flare bright enough to be blinding from the influx of power, until the mages find a way to smooth out and temper their use of the magic. About half of the class have lost their lights completely, but a few pop back into existence, and I suppose that shifting between power sources might still be an advanced skill. After about five minutes of playing with it, all but about a quarter of the mages in attendance have managed to at least form a pale mageglobe from ley line magic.

Now that he knows how I do it and can see it's largely the same way he does, Captain Parsons starts moving through the students who are struggling, coaching them one-on-one. At his signal, I leave Lex to meditate and recharge his core and do the same.

It's a lot easier one-on-one, because I can find out about each mage's practice and how they access magic and alter my instructions to take advantage of that. After about a half an hour, everyone's at least managed a small light, and everyone's looking pleased with themselves.

"Now it's just a matter of practice," I say. "It took me months to be able to consistently tap the ley lines and regulate the amount of magic I drew, but now it's something that I use more than anything else. It keeps me from worrying about draining too much of Lex's reserves and lets me keep my magical flow more even."

"All of which makes this great for your battle applications," Captain Parsons adds. "Thank you, Private Mathis. I want everyone to keep working on this today and tonight. We'll revisit it tomorrow to practice doing more than light spells with it."

He assigns some reading on ley line magic usually reserved for witches then dismisses class, making his way back to me and Lex. "I mean it —thank you. I don't know why we haven't been teaching mages to do this all along."

I don't either, especially if my dad showed them it was possible over twenty years ago, but I don't say that. The less said about him the better.

"I didn't know it was something others weren't taught," I say, instead. "The Monroes were teaching Lex, and I just wanted to try. If it meant his magic not having to fuel both of us, all the better."

"It will help with that," the captain said with a nod. "Witches and mages will be able to work more seamlessly together, and we'll be better able to pair mages with shifters and one another to make for a more flexible fighting force."

He's got that geeky light in his eyes that Lex gets when he's talking about history, and I guess that seems right—you must love something to want to teach it, surely?

"Thank you for being willing to just step in and not just demonstrate but explain."

"Of course, sir."

"You have a knack for it. I might just enlist your aid in helping the other mages apply other elements of magical theory, if I may."

"I'm happy to help, sir." A little more warning might be nice, but I don't say that. I've never really had a yen to teach, but I feel good about the class and more a part of the school than I had before.

Captain Parsons dismisses us to go get lunch and we head to the mess hall. Lex reaches out and takes my hand, squeezing it.

"Okay. Maybe we're ready for a little role play."

"Oh?"

"It was hot, watching you teaching and helping everyone," he says with a smirk. "I might need you to teach me something later."

"Hmmm...but we're still at the point where I am but the student when it comes to things we do together."

"I think you're catching up to me."

"I'll see what lessons I can come up with, then."

"They do say teaching is one of the best ways to learn."

I laugh, and he flashes me a grin before pulling me to hurry to lunch before we have to head out for field exercises in an hour.

CHAPTER 15

Lex

We're both tired when we make it back to the hotel and dirty enough that I feel guilty for walking through the lobby. A cleaning spell would be too obvious, and I'm too drained, but I manage a small flare of magic to keep Mike and me from trailing dirt across their floor in our wake.

"I feel that. What are you doing?" he asks, giving me a suspicious look.

"Just keeping us from making a mess."

"You don't have enough power to be wasting it on frivolous things right now."

"I'll recharge once we're in the room." There's no ley line directly under us, like there is at the recruit depot, but we're close enough to still pull magic back in with a lot of concentration in meditation.

"Do you need a refresher in spinning spells directly from a ley line?" my handsome teacher's pet asks.

"No." I can't help the scowl I send him. "Not in general, but maybe when there's a dozen things going on at once, including people shooting at us. I managed for the first couple of hours, and then I was tired, and it was easier to just work from my core."

"Easier, but problematic, long-term."

"Oh my god. You give one lesson, and now you're the ley line guru." I'm mostly teasing because I know he's right. "I will practice. It's not like I want to collapse mid-battle, but it's like switching shielding while firing offensive spells off – it's a new muscle that needs working. I hit exhaustion with it today. My endurance will grow, and I'll commit to using the ley line before my core from now on until I can sustain it indefinitely." It's definitely useful, and I don't know why I haven't tried doing so before. Granted, it's commonly taught that we can't, so maybe that just got in my head. But it always seemed to me that if a mage could do it, there was no reason a witch couldn't.

How I feel right now, it seems unlikely that anyone could sustain it indefinitely—it takes more effort to pull magic from elsewhere and fire spells at the same time, which is probably why most witches only do it when necessary, even with amulets and other artifacts. Our cores are there for a reason. But collapsing from a depleted core is just as bad. It seems reasonable to assume that, like most things in war, people weren't made to do things this way. It's why mundane humans are always making more and more efficient weapons. Witches and shifters haven't tended to be as warlike, except in human wars, and we're already more effective than they are, so we hadn't had as much reason to push ourselves once we were fighting for them rather than hiding. Maybe that's changing now, because a lot of people are pushing themselves and are looking beat as they trickle in from the bus. Granted, if we're being attacked again, and hiding isn't the option it was two hundred years ago, maybe we are all going to have to push ourselves harder. Add in the sped-up training, and there's no maybe about it.

"Seriously, Lex, let the floor get muddy."

"They shouldn't have to clean up after us when they don't have to," I say, objecting, and I don't know why I care, but maybe I just don't want to make more work for some poor housekeeper who's already underpaid and overworked.

I can see Mike wants to argue, but the next thing I know, I feel a spell from him supplementing mine, like we do with the shields, so there's less drain on me.

"Thanks." I smile; he grunts, and we make our way to the elevator.

I'd kiss him once we're inside, but Isaac and Ronan are with us, and they both still look so shaken with grief that I don't want to seem unsympathetic and like I'm just basking in joy, even though being able to just kiss Mike still makes something in me leap with glee every time. I feel an answering pulse of happiness even without the kiss and give him a sideways glance. He smiles a little, and I realize we're getting better at this sensing each other thing. I wish it were telepathy, too, so I could tell him what I'd like to do to him in the shower. It involves an encore of our performance pre-bombing. That part of our relationship has sadly been on hold since, besides the occasional kiss and the flirting. The hotel walls are thin and, again, we have grieving friends. Plus, I think Mike is a little shy about things between us, still. Tonight, I'm ready to dive back in. Yes, a lot of people died, but we didn't, and I, for one, think we need to celebrate that. We can try to keep it quiet to not disturb our neighbors.

Mike flashes me a smirk, like he can read my mind. I know that's not possible, so I wonder just what I'm projecting. I study the floor because it's just terribly interesting, and even Isaac snorts, not buying it.

"I'd say 'get a room,' but you're on your way to it," Ronan says, and I look up.

"What?"

"You've been undressing Mathis with your eyes since we got on the elevator," Isaac says, and he's almost smiling. "Don't let us deter you. I could use a good show, to be honest."

"Well, you can put your water glass to the wall in about half an hour, then," Mike says. "Because I, for one, need a shower."

I glance at him, huffing out a laugh. "I wasn't going to say anything..."

But, really, so do I.

"Thankfully, we're not sharing a bathroom, so you guys won't have to wait for us to be done," I say to Ronan and Isaac. "We might be a while."

"No might about it."

Mike's whiskey-rough voice is a little huskier than usual and it goes straight to my dick. I'm forced to wonder just what he has in mind and how long he's been planning it.

We all fall silent the rest of the way to our adjoining rooms.

"Have fun," Isaac says, and even if he looks a little sad, he's at least trying to smile at us. I can't imagine what that costs and reach out to squeeze his shoulder gently. Ronan opens their door and Isaac moves to drag him inside, like I'm not the only one who's impatient for privacy.

We barely get the door shut before Mike's got me pinned against it, kissing me. The move is sudden and unexpected—he's enthusiastic, usually, but hasn't really been as sexually aggressive as I know he can be. Apparently, that might be changing.

"Clothes, off. I'll go get the shower turned on."

I nod, a little dazed as he lets go, and put down another spell to protect the floor as I start stripping off my muddy boots and clothes.

When I'm naked, though still muddy, I make my way to the bathroom, and, really, how did I get so filthy under my clothes? Mike's equally naked and just as muddy when he pulls back the curtain to usher me into the already steamy shower. I moan a little as the hot water hits my chilled skin.

"You are a god among men..." I say.

"I haven't even touched you, yet."

"For how fast you got this on and heated up."

"I might've cheated a little."

I gasp and tsk at him. "Shameless."

"Just trying to take good care of you." He slips in the shower beside me, reaching to run his hands down my neck to my shoulders, massaging gently. "You need to recharge."

"I can do that and this at the same time."

"You can?" His fingers slide down my back and to the curve of my ass as he steps in close enough that I can feel his dick bouncing against my stomach.

"Well, not now..." He chuckles and lets me go, moving back.

"Don't go..."

"Recharge. Then you can have whatever you want."

"That's a mighty big promise, mister."

"I mean it."

I open an eye and peek at him, and he does look very serious.

"What if I want a pony?"

"Then we'll go horse shopping."

"What if I want a Ferrari?"

"Then you might have to wait until I get some hazard pay, but I'll start saving."

"I love you."

"I love you, too." He leans in and brushes a kiss across my lips before reaching for my shampoo and starting to wash the mud out of my hair. I moan again, pressing into his hands as he works over my scalp with clever fingers. "But seriously, tonight is about you."

I don't know what to do with that. "What if I want to take care of you?"

"Nope. I'm taking care of you tonight."

"What if I can think of something that'll take care of both of us?" It's a step forward, but one I think he'll be comfortable with. It's nothing completely new for him, at least, and I'm getting more relaxed trusting him to know his limits.

"What are you thinking?" he asks, tilting my head back to rinse out the shampoo.

"I want you to fuck me." I want to peek to see his reaction, but there are suds flowing over my face. His fingers still, so I imagine I've surprised him.

"You want me to fuck you." It's not a question, and he sounds pleased by my words.

"Sure. That seems like it's a logical progression, and you won't let me just take care of you again."

"But I wanted to take care of you."

Feeling the water be suds free, I chance a peek at him. He's looking a little bemused. "This will do that."

"It will?"

"I see I'm going to have to introduce you to a little thing called a prostate," I say before laughing.

"Right, no. I know that. Theoretically." I didn't mean to fluster him, but he's blushing. "It's just hard to fathom."

"Yeah, it is, until you feel it." I remember being sure there was no way bottoming could feel good until I tried it with someone who knew what they were doing.

"You really like it?"

"More than topping," I assure him.

"Okay. Well, I'm game if you are."

I laugh again at that, and he works the conditioner through my hair before switching places with me to start getting the mud out of his. I take the switch to lather up the washcloth and work on cleaning up the rest of me.

Once we're clean and dry and back in the bedroom, he starts looking nervous.

"It's okay," I say, sitting next to him on the bed. "You did this with Hannah. It's not exactly the same, but basically. If anything, it'll probably feel better to me than her."

I've read up on it and know about the G-spot stimulation it can provide for women, but still can't believe it can feel as good for a girl without the prostate stimulation.

"I just don't want to hurt you accidentally."

"I'll let you know if I need you to change anything." I give him a smile and fish the lube and a condom out of the nightstand drawer. "Here, we don't have to rush into it, and I can take care of most of it when we get there."

I shift and straddle his lap, pushing him back on the bed. Following him down, I kiss him, setting an elbow on either side of his head, framing his face. I can tell he's nervous in the hesitation in his kiss, but after I tangle our tongues and rock my hips against him, he relaxes. His arms encircle me, fingers caressing my spine, then gripping my ass and I hum my approval against his lips, nibbling a bit to encourage the kisses and touches. Just thinking about what's to come takes me from the half-hard the shower had me to full mast in no time, and I can tell his body's on board beneath me. To keep him from getting nervous again, I break the kiss and slide down his body, nibbling as I go until I'm kneeling between his legs and can run my tongue up his length.

"Lex... I thought this was going to be about you..."

"Oh, this is very much for me," I say against his skin. "I've been aching to get my mouth on you again since before the bomb went off."

"You'd just had..." He gasps as I swirl my tongue around the underside of his head.

"Yeah, and I immediately wanted to do it again." Well, once my jaw relaxed again, at least. But that's too many words from both of us, so I set to work to make him forget talking by making sure I'm not capable of it. I take him deep and swallow around him, adding in every trick I know until he's a moaning puddle with a leaking dick in my mouth. I slick up my fingers with lube, and set to work prepping myself for him, working myself open until I feel ready.

Only then do I ease my mouth off him. I manage to tear the condom wrapper open and slide it down on him before he can get nervous again. Then I slide back up the length of his body and kiss him, nipping at his lower lip as I straddle him again. "Since you're worried about hurting me, how about I just ride you this time?"

He blinks at me like he's searching for words and finally just nods. "Yeah. Okay…"

I give him a smile and reach behind me, positioning myself over his dick. As well as I prepped myself, there's still a bit of a sting as I sink down, letting him stretch me. It's not too much, but I make note for future reference—he's bigger than I ever quite think, as my aching jaw can attest. Still, he feels better than I hoped as I take him in inch-by-inch until I'm fully seated on him.

He's watching me with pupils blown wide, words forming on his tongue and dying on his lips before they make it to the air. I lean a little forward to rest my hand on his chest for balance and then I start to move, sliding up and down on him slowly, while his hands search for something to hold onto and eventually settle, as they should, on my hips. He's not really guiding me, more holding on to steady himself, but it steadies me, too. He lets me set the pace, but eventually, his hips roll up to meet me as I sink down. Our rhythm is a bit disjointed, at first, but it ultimately becomes perfect. I'm able to control the angle, which means he rubs over my prostate with each movement, leaving my dick red and weeping.

He keeps watching it, like he's going to stop me at the first sign I'm not enjoying myself, but that sign is not going to be forthcoming anytime soon.

I've always been told that sex with your soulmate is the best sex you'll ever have, but I wasn't sure I believed it. It seemed so woo-woo (says the witch) and out there, like some hippy-dippy flower child shit or maybe something parents make up to keep kids from having sex until they find their soulmate. Well, I owe all those people I scoffed at an apology. Because I've had what I thought of as great sex before, but I didn't know sex could be this good. Everything with Mike has been a revelation, and this is no different. I'm making sounds of pleasure I've never even heard in porn, and so is he, and I keep expecting someone to bang on the wall and tell us to shut up, but I'm not sure I'd hear them if they did over the pounding of my own heart and the roar of the ocean or something in my ears.

Mike finally wraps his hand around my dick and starts stroking in time with our still-kinda disjointed movements. That's enough to kick us into perfect sync, at last, and I'm fucking back onto his dick and forward into his hand and it's so perfect I want to cry. I don't want it to end, but that tingle starts at my back and my balls tighten and then I'm coming, spurting over his chest, startling us both, but it must be what he was waiting for, because the next thing I feel is him jerking inside of me, and we are going to have to get rid of the condom as soon as possible, because it's a sin that I can't feel him filling me as he comes.

I'm boneless in the wake of my own orgasm and his and collapse forward onto his chest, wincing a little at how slick it is with sweat and cum. I'm dripping with sweat, myself, as his arms wrap around me, and it seems like a trip back to the shower might be warranted. In a minute. When we're both not still gasping for air and trying to remember how lungs work and that hearts should stay inside of chests. Maybe in a few minutes, then.

Mike

We eventually separate and go get cleaned up again, but that inevitably leads to round two and shower three, and through it all the cord between us has done what Lex once surmised it might and lit up the room around us, at least to magical sight. We can't even watch television when we're snuggled back up together, clean and ready to bask in the afterglow, because the actual glow of magic in the room is too much.

"Guess that answers that question," Lex says, smirking a touch as he flips off the TV and tries to snuggle impossibly closer into my side. The only way he could be closer was if he were inside of me, and where that idea might have freaked me out earlier today, seeing how much he enjoyed himself tonight has made me more curious than not. I've enjoyed some ass play during blow jobs—I'm aware of the source of pleasure the prostate can be. I just wasn't aware it could be quite that much pleasure, but Lex is wrung out from it, and I think maybe, one day, I might ask if he'd be willing to switch. Not any time soon, probably. I need to manage to return the oral favor first, which I'd intended to try my hand at tonight until he'd upped the game.

Not that I'm complaining. I've never felt this close to anyone in my life, and I wouldn't change tonight for anything. But I would like my chance at making things all about his pleasure for once. I know that he might just be this generous of a lover, but I don't want him feeling like he has to only cater to my needs to keep me engaged. I'm in this.

Maybe I need to make that clearer?

"You're thinking too loud," he says, lips moving against my chest before he yawns and snuggles in again.

"Sorry..."

"Go to sleep." It's more suggestion than order, and I drop a kiss on his forehead.

"You first."

"Gimme five minutes and I'll be gone..."

"I love you." I've never found saying the words to anyone as easy as they come with him, maybe because, with anyone else, there's still always been him. He's been it for me our whole lives. I just didn't realize it until I got over my own preconceptions about myself.

"Love you, too." Another kiss to my chest, and I drop another on top of his head, and then, within two minutes, I can tell he's gone.

We're running a little behind in the morning, making it downstairs just in time for PT. We've been doing it outside the hotel, since our showers are here, but it makes for an odd morning, what with all the civilian traffic on the roads.

This morning is odder, since, as we jog outside, barely on time, and before we can fall into formation, everyone starts clapping. There are some catcalls, even, and when I look at Lex in confusion, he's started blushing, looking around for Isaac and Ronan.

"Were we that...?"

"Loud?" Isaac asks. "Yes. You also lit up our entire floor, so. Well done, you two."

Lex's face turns bright red.

"I mean, when we said get a room, we didn't quite expect that," Ronan says. "But honestly, I felt a little inadequate."

"We'll all feel inadequate for a while, I think," Daniel says, punching me lightly on the shoulder. "First time I ever wondered what it was like being gay."

"Oh, well, neither of us is actually..." Lex starts to say.

"Thank you," I say, instead, cutting him off. I'm a little embarrassed by all the hooting and hollering, especially as Major Greeley and Captain Parsons walk up, looking somewhere between amused at everyone's antics and annoyed we're off schedule before we've even started.

"At least they're laughing, son," Major Greeley says. "That's an improvement, and it sounds as if you had a good night."

I can't believe he's joining in on the teasing, even though I know his soulmate, too, is another man.

"Yes, sir."

"Excellent. Now fall in. You can use some of that energy you apparently have to lead this morning's run."

The run is the same no matter who leads, distance-wise. So, there's no downside here, but it does let me give the order to fall in, which feels good. I wasn't sure about the commissions that come at the end of MagCorps training for the top-performing recruits, but maybe it's something to work for. I know Lex is aspiring to hit some of those top spots, the better to show his parents that he didn't make a mistake going to the military rather than to college, so maybe I should work harder for them, as well, even if one part of it is the academics. I guess I can strive to do more than pass the papers. Not that leading men in battle is anything like leading them in PT, but I enjoyed teaching the mages more than I expected, too.

It's something else to think about as we run, at least, rather than just Lex's ass. It helps that he's running beside me, not in front, so I can't see it. I anticipate this new appreciation for his assets might become something of a problem. It's already a distraction.

CHAPTER 16

January 2011

Lex

MagCorps training is supposed to be for nine months. We were only one month in when the attacks happened. Nevertheless, with our accelerated training, we're deploying to Afghanistan three months later. They do let us go home for two weeks between graduation and deployment, which coincides with the holidays. Further investigation confirms with near certainty that Mike's father was involved in the attacks, so we go to Maine to see my family instead of going back to Staunton. Hannah had broken up with us both shortly after the attacks, though presumably in an unrelated move. She didn't really offer much of an explanation, so we figure she either met someone at college or her rooting for us to be together didn't hold up to the reality when we told her things had changed between us. Given our own near bliss with one another, and Andie on the horizon, we both decide it's probably for the best, no matter the reason, and hope that it won't be awkward when we eventually see her again. I like to think she's happy for us, not the opposite, but by the time we deploy, she's barely answering emails except to tell us to be very careful overseas.

My parents and sister are near distraught at the idea of us heading into a warzone and, once again, try to convince me—both of us, in fact—to get out. Even after I explain we can't even consider that for another two years without facing prosecution for going absent without leave, they are still trying to figure a way out for us. In their minds, the attacks on our community should give every supernatural service member a free out, especially since the government ultimately chooses not to do anything to pursue finding, let alone prosecuting, the perpetrators.

There's a lot of bitterness about that from people who lost loved ones, including Ronan and Isaac, but no one's talking about leaving MagCorps over it. By the end of our abbreviated training, we've been honed into a tight knit group. None of us might be thrilled about fighting for a country that seems unwilling to fight for us, but we will fight for each other. If some of us are going over there, then all of us are going. In a move that shows those making these decisions have some sense, we deploy as a company, together, to include Major Greeley and Captain Parsons, which surprises most of us who assumed they were permanent MagCorps instructors who'd be staying on to train the next class of recruits.

Then it turns out there isn't going to be another class of recruits for several months because a lot of the recruitment well dried up with the governmental inaction in the wake of the violence against our community. No real surprise, there, though I did sort of assume the Queens would try to keep some hold in the U.S. military. I guess those of us trained are considered enough of a hold for now. The rest is politics and that isn't my strong suit. Andie tries to explain the reasoning on one late night Internet chat, but it mostly sounds like excuses to me, when I think about the Wilsons and Isaac's family in particular. Andie swears her mother is furious at the lost shifter lives but can't act for retribution without inviting retaliation from the U.S. government that causes more harm to shifter lives. Andie's not as keyed into the Witch Queen's decisions, her relationship with Nick aside, but she assumes Esther's reasoning is the same. She joins my family and Hannah in fretting for us, angry that we're deploying so soon, and worried that we've missed something important in our training. I try to reassure her that we've just missed out on some academics, but that our theoretical and practical training, along with our instruction in strategy and tactics, was fully completed. I'm not sure that reassures her much, but she pretends that it does, at least.

By mid-January, we're in Afghanistan. We're stationed with a Marine Expeditionary Unit at Camp Dwyer in the Gamir district of the Helmand River Valley, technically assigned as support for the MEU, but everyone knows we'll be running our own missions in addition to providing them extra support and security. That's what MagCorps does. It's odd, being with the Fleet after so many months in our own pocket of the world, training in ways our compatriots can only imagine.

Ronan, Isaac, Mike and I are all commissioned as Second Lieutenants, while Major Greeley receives a long overdue promotion to Lieutenant Colonel. Captain Parsons is still a captain, but I have a feeling all it will take is a successful deployment and he, too, will be moving up the ranks. He tells us one night over a game of poker that it's his first deployment, too. I knew he wasn't much older than us, but it turns out that most of that age gap comes from him having gone to college and doing ROTC rather than enlisting straight out of high school.

Our first couple of weeks in country are uneventful, for the most part, at least for us. We've been warned not to go walking outside the camp or risk being shot or stepping on an IED. We follow that advice and stick to the patrol base. The most hostility Mike, Ronan, Isaac, and I see comes from a Private Mace who was in mine and Mike's Marine recruit company.

"Don't Ask; Don't Tell" might not apply to MagCorps, but we still tend to keep our same-sex relationships quieter around the Fleet—no need to antagonize anyone any further than our very existence sometimes seems to do. Mace, at least, seems to not appreciate that we exist, as he demonstrates when we run into him outside the small store for sundries that some enterprising local has been allowed to set up within our perimeter.

Mace recognizes us before I even notice him, and before I have a chance to react, he's in my face, shoving me then tapping on my MagCorps patch.

I freeze and can't help but flash back to the last days of basic training when we faced passing the Crucible. Despite part of the grueling test requiring teamwork to pass, Mace and a couple of his buddies almost caused our whole company to fail because they wouldn't work with me and Mike for fear, apparently, of catching our gayness. Luckily, the rest of the company wanted to graduate, so their bigoted rebellion was swiftly put down. I'd faced Mace the next day in the hand-to-hand combat segment and quite happily kicked his ass, a fact he seems to have conveniently forgotten as he gets into my face.

"So. Not just a fag, but a supernat? That fucking figures. Only reason they didn't kick your ass out for conduct unbecoming."

It takes me a minute to react, but that's a minute too long for Mike, who's hauling Mace away from me the same way he did Allan Thomas in tenth grade.

"I think you need an attitude check, Private Mace. Or a vision one. Because I know that you did not disrespect a superior officer. If you didn't notice Lieutenant Monroe's rank, allow me to point it out to you, so you can beg him not to report you to your sergeant for an Article 89 offense. That's a bad conduct discharge and up to a year's confinement, if I'm not mistaken."

I try not to gape at this defense, because it never would have occurred to me, and I'm not even sure if the elements of Article 89 apply in this kind of a situation. I suspect they don't toss someone out for calling a random officer a slur.

Apparently, Mace doesn't know, either, as he goes very pale, his gaze cutting to first my rank insignia and then Mike's, then on around to Ronan and Isaac's. Still, he gets points for bravado, though he loses more for his stupidity in not reading the room.

"No way they made the two of you cocksuckers officers for anything other than giving amazing head or taking it without complaint. Everyone knows you supernats are all just animals. You aren't even human."

Now that? That is a stupid thing to say, when you're outnumbered four-to-one, and the four are creatures you believe are not even human and thus in possession of powers you aren't aware of or prepared to defend against. It's not like he could've known that sort of ignorance would rub us even more the wrong way after the attacks we'd suffered. Isaac, in particular, is still very raw and starts to lunge toward the unfortunate Mace. Ronan anticipates this and holds him back, knowing we will be the ones in trouble if we start a physical altercation, especially if we use our powers against a mundane human subordinate.

Mike sighs, then tsks, grabbing Mace by the collar and marching him outside. "Take us to your squad leader. He can deal with this."

Ronan, Isaac, and I follow along; I'm more curious than anything. It's not that the slur doesn't bother me, but we're in a place where more people than ever want to kill us and where our training isn't going to be...training anymore. The next time I fire my weapon or throw an offensive spell, it will be at a living being, with the intent to kill and that's been weighing on me a bit in ways I haven't discussed with anyone. Nor do I intend to. We've been being trained to kill for almost a year now. Little late to get precious about it with the enemy not far from the literal gates.

Mace is reluctant to take us to his sergeant, but a few inquiries to onlookers soon sets us on our way. Unlike Mace, the sergeant does take note of our ranks and snaps to attention, saluting. We return the salute, then Mike explains the situation. The sergeant promises to deal with it appropriately. The look he gives Mace almost makes me pity the guy.

Almost. I'm not a saint. Assholes like Mace made basic training hell for me after one of my night terrors jerked me awake. Mike had tried to comfort me, as he has since we were kids, but when someone flipped the lights on in the squad bay and the company saw us snuggled together, they'd made the same assumption everyone always made about us. They couldn't discipline us, since hugging wasn't against regulations. It had made things rough the rest of the time, though. Even worse when I'd slipped and used magic carelessly, running late one morning and trying to streamline shaving and taming my hair, something that hadn't spread as far and wide, given Mace, Vera and Daniel all hadn't heard about it.

We head back to our section of the camp only to come to an abrupt stop not fifteen feet away at the sound of three loud explosions from outside the gates. Along with a dozen other Marines, we run toward the sound, pausing inside the gates and looking out. Three fires burn, one demolished car smokes, and three bodies lie in the street, two of them in uniform and one a woman in a burqa.

"IEDs," one of the gate guards says with a shake of his head. "Wasn't a thing to suggest anything was there. Then just one after another."

Medics come running and then move out cautiously, following the footprints from the gate to where the fallen Marines and the woman lay. They retrace their steps as they bring the stretchers back in and move quickly toward the Combat Support Hospital we're lucky enough to have in camp. There's too much blood on all of them to be able to assess their chances at a glance, but looking toward our area of camp, I see healers hurrying to meet the medics. Modern medicine can do wonders these days. Magic can do more. It's times like these when people wind up being glad we're here.

The next day, a new rule is instituted. No patrols go out without a witch or a mage. We've all been trained in sending out pulses of magic that detonate IEDs at a distance; the best of us can clear up to twelve yards in every direction. Shields help with insurgents firing at patrols, too, and casualties take a sharp drop. Several people might have shared Mace's sentiment when we first arrived, but, by the end of our third week in country, we've saved enough lives that no one's still complaining we're here or acting like we aren't valuable team members to have.

The end of the third week is when our squad gets its first mission, too. I don't know how the others feel, but they look as nervous as I feel once we've been briefed. There's a system of caves in the hills above the camp and intel says the insurgents who have been harrying us are coming from there. They want to send a strike team in to clear them out, and we draw the metaphorical short straws. They're pairing us and another MagCorps squad with a Marine rifle team, though the mission chain of command is a little unclear. I think we have point, but we've drilled with this team, and they aren't going to cede any control. That's fine, I think; we'll shield them and then move around them to clear the board like we do going out on patrols. The insurgents are dug in, apparently, but we've got shields and magic and highly trained Marines. I'm nervous, but I feel confident, overall. Not overly confident—it might be my first engagement, but I know getting cocky gets you dead—but I'm not freaking out and questioning my life choices, either.

That changes before we reach the caves the next day. As expected, the rifle team wants to make the approach, with us providing cover from behind and guarding the rear. We're content to let them, since we can shield effectively no matter where we are in the formation, and we've practiced shielding other teams both in training and out on patrols.

We lock the shields in, the four of us working as a well-oiled machine that fits in well with the rest of the MagCorps squad. The Marines are grateful, especially when the bullets start flying. The shields are holding like they should, and we have power evenly distributed through the squad, so no one's taking the brunt of the attack or responsible for any particular portion of the shield. Just when we make it over a ridge, though, I feel something puncture part of the shield. Before I can process that, the head of the Marine in front of me is sporting a hole, and I'm reeling back from the spray of blood and brains and a burning, searing pain in my shoulder where a bullet hasn't just hit but lodged.

I hear Mike shout my name, and the others yelling about them puncturing the shield. Adrenaline and training kick in, and the pain dulls as I slam power into the shield, trying to reinforce it. Isaac gives an order to fall back, and we retreat behind a rock outcropping.

"What the hell?" one of the Marines is cradling his fallen buddy, glaring at us. "I thought you witches had our backs."

"We do," Isaac says. "The shield should've held."

"It did," I say, leaning on Mike for support who is pulling my uniform away to check my wound which still feels on fire.

"No exit wound," he reports, "And look at this."

Ronan, Isaac, and another witch come over to stare at my shoulder as I start to get queasy. The pain and the nausea together trigger an unpleasant memory.

"He'll be fine," one of the Marines says. "Unlike David-son."

"Maybe, maybe not," Ronan replies. "Shit."

The dismay on my squad mates' faces mixes with the memory and I have the answer. "Iron. Their bullets are iron. That's why they could puncture the shield." And why I feel ready to hurl; I'm being poisoned by the piece of metal lodged in my shoulder.

"How would they know to use iron?" Isaac asks.

"Might not be on purpose," Mike says. "Could be what they have. Steel is an iron alloy, after all, made of some-thing like 97% iron."

"But we've deflected steel bullets before with shields," Ronan points out. "And it shouldn't poison Lex like it is."

"I don't know, then," Mike says. "But I don't think they're going to sit down and chat with us about it."

"Can you protect the rest of us or not?" one of the Marines asks.

"Not if they're going to use the same bullets that killed your friend and is poisoning ours," Isaac tells them.

"You were deflecting all of the other shots on the way up here."

"Sure, and who's going to take the chance on being the next one to go down because one guy's got iron pellets or iron tipped bullets or whatever he's got?"

"We go on the offense."

"They have the high ground and consistently defensive positions. We've got some rocks and vegetation that is likely infested with carpet vipers."

I reach up to fist my hand in Mike's uniform. "I did not come halfway around the world to get killed by a fucking snake."

"We can shield against the snakes," he reminds me.

"You can. I can't conjure sparks, let alone a shield, until you get this iron out of me."

A regular bullet, one of them could pull out with magic, but iron's immune, so no nifty tricks are getting rid of it.

"I can help alleviate the pain, at least," Isaac says, taking my hand. "And we'll shield you. If we're going, we're not leaving you down here alone."

"Maybe they have the tactical advantage, but we have magic," the Marine arguing for going on the offense says. "Can't you all just find a way to hurl fire at them or something so they can't shoot the fucking iron bullets? If not, what the fuck good are you all?"

"We're not dragons..." Isaac starts, but the Marine's question might as well have been fighting words. I even want to make him eat them, and I'm mostly hoping I didn't get Davidson's brains in my eyes and trying not to think about how someone I had a drink with last night is now never having a drink again.

"We're in just as much danger going back down again, unless we at least debilitate them," Ronan says, voice quiet. "They'll still have the cover, the high ground and the fucking iron bullets."

"So, we might as well get the job done," the Marine says with a nod, even though that isn't exactly what Ronan said.

That seems to decide it, though, and I feel useless for the next interminable period of time, unable to shield for defense, unable to throw any offense, barely able to support my weight with my injured shoulder to crawl each infinitesimal inch we gain. Bullets do keep raining down on us, though the new shields hold. I can hear explosions and screams above us where spells hit our opponents. The rocks are sharp under us, the bushes adding their own scraping when we scoot around them carefully. I can feel my blood soaking my uniform, can see a trail of it when I look back, and hear Mike cursing fluently and repeatedly. He has an extra shield around me, which is good when I scoot around a bush and do, in fact, come face-to-face with some kind of goddamned viper. If I wasn't about to piss myself, it'd be almost funny watching it try to strike repeatedly and bounce off the shield. Thankfully, before I can do something embarrassing, Isaac kills it with his wolf reflexes and a hand shifted into a paw with wicked claws.

"I bet you're so floofy," I say, to deflect from my whimpers.

"Bite me," he replies, with grand, original wit.

Eventually, magic prevails, and somehow, we make it to the cave without anyone else getting shot. A few bodies litter the ground outside, some shot, some burned.

I make it to my feet as we enter, trying to stay upright under my own power. It's easier than on the ground since I can't feel my arm anymore. Isaac's pain spell helped, but the numbness, I think, is the poisoning. We clear the caves slowly and are entering what appears to be the last chamber—no tunnels exit off the cavern and sleeping bags line the walls—when the guy with the iron bullets fires another one. This time it takes out Leroy Jenkins, a lion shifter in our squad. Everyone ducks for cover, including me, and, yet, somehow, I find myself facing the guy with the gun. He's young; maybe my age, probably not quite, yet. His tunic might once have been white, but it's stained with dirt and blood, now. His pants are ripped.

"Balaa," he says before spitting at me. His saliva hits the shield, but like with the snake, I still flinch back.

I don't know much Pashto, but they at least taught us the word for "witch." I freeze, staring at that gun and his disgusted look, lips curled and scowl sharp, pulling at his heavy brows; even as I stare, that look turns to one of a smug kind of glee, scowl lifting and lips curving in a smirk. He knows what I am, and he knows he can kill me with what's in that gun. I don't know how he knows, but he knows.

I still can't do any magic, but my luck comes roaring back when he pulls the trigger, and the gun seems to jam. Nothing comes firing out of it, at least. He curses and tries again, but the momentary reprieve unfreezes me and I remember my hand-to-hand training. I also have my Ka-Bar knife. I can feel my squad mates behind me, trying to help—the shield thickens around me which won't help if he gets the gun working, but the gun wrenches away from him and into the air, where it stays, floating out of anyone's reach, and that's one of Ronan's specialty spells, so I'll take it. The kid knows what he's doing in a fight, too, and maybe I should drop back, let someone not wounded take over, but I don't.

He hits my wounded shoulder, and I yell. The punch leaves his guard down for a second, though; not long, but long enough for me to get in under it and drive my knife into his gut and up to his heart. I feel the heat of his blood on my hand and see the shock on his face; I watch the life drain out of his eyes and let him drop, starting to shiver. With the magic-killing gun out of the way, the others can shield the Marines who take care of the few insurgents left alive in the camp.

Mission complete.

Mike

My heart doesn't feel like it's started beating back right, yet, as we make our way back down the mountain, shields in place in case of any rear attack. Isaac helps me support Lex as his legs don't seem to be working right after the fight in the cave. I'm worried he's going into shock. Two of our other squad mates carry Jenkins, and two of the Marines carry Davidson. It could have been more of us. We thought it was just luck, them having those bullets, but what if it's more?

After the attacks back home, and knowing mages were involved—mages who know the witches' weaknesses, I'm suspicious of anyone wielding iron in a non-standard way. Iron bullets just aren't practical—they'd ruin the rifling on a gun, aren't quite dense enough to make a good projectile, and iron is too brittle. The only thing iron bullets are good for is killing witches or getting past magic-fueled shields. And, yet this kid in a cave had at least two of them.

Lex is shaking a little against me, so I keep a tight hold and a steady stream of nonsense about home, anything to keep him moving and with me. Shock can kill as sure as the bullet poisoning him from his shoulder. We need to get him medical attention now. Thankfully, our Humvees are waiting at the bottom of the mountain, and we pile in and head for camp. Ronan and Isaac keep a steady flow of magic up to clear the road of any IEDs. The Marines follow behind us, which at least lets me hold Lex without dealing with any comments from the peanut gallery. His skin is pale and clammy, his breathing fast, and he keeps murmuring that he's gonna hurl, although he hasn't, yet. Definitely shock. I loosen his uniform and elevate his feet, trying to remember what they taught us in first aid. There's a blanket in the back with us, so I cover him and just hold on tight to try to keep from jarring his shoulder. I've got the blood slowed, at least, and don't want to restart it. I recall there are a couple of arteries there, after all.

Lex is covered in blood, and most of it isn't his, thank God, but I'm sure that's contributing to the shock. Even with the attacks in August, we didn't watch anyone die like Leroy and Davidson, and we've certainly never killed anyone before today. I'm still not sure if I have—I was throwing spells mostly blindly on the way up the hill and focused on Lex in the cave.

We make it back to camp, and LTC Greeley comes to meet us with medics from the Combat Support Hospital at the ready since Isaac had radioed in the situation. They take Lex away to the CSH, and I want to go after him, but know I should report first. Greeley takes pity on me, tells me the rest of the squad can report, and sends me after Lex.

They try to block me at the hospital, because it's a CSH, not a large metropolitan hospital with multiple waiting rooms, but all I have to do is point to my MagCorps patch and say he's my soulmate, and they let me through. I can't go into the operating room, of course, but they take me to the EMT's tent first, insisting on checking me out, too, probably since I'm covered in blood. Once I'm deemed healthy enough, they clean me up, then take me to one of the regular ward tents to wait there, and they give me regular updates. Apparently, he's doing well in surgery and the bullet didn't hit the subclavian artery. They're mostly worried about the poisoning and the shock, but that's all treatable once they get the source of the poison out.

After a period I can't gauge, Isaac and Ronan come to join me. I don't know how they got past the dragon-like nurse at the front of the tents, but Isaac could talk an angel into falling, so I don't bother asking. I'm just grateful they're there. Ronan is the calm and steady one. Isaac paces the length of the ward, past ten hospital beds before turning around and coming back. Then he does it again. It's what I want to do but decided against for fear of looking like a crazy person. Watching Isaac pace, I'm glad I decided not to.

"When are they going to be done?" Isaac asks, turning to walk past me again and toward the door that leads into the canvas tunnel connecting us to the next ward, before coming back to stand, shifting his weight back and forth in front of me.

"I don't know, man, but they've been keeping me updated."

"How is he?"

"As well as he can be from what they've said. Bullet missed the artery. I don't know about nerve damage, yet. They're just removing the bullet and then will start treating him for the poisoning."

"And the shock?"

"They're doing what they can while they get the bullet out, but they need to stop the bleeding before they can do much else, at least from my understanding."

To be fair, I understood about half of what the nurse told me they were doing.

"He's going to be okay," Ronan says, voice soothing, though whether that's aimed at me or Isaac, I don't know.

"Of course, he is," Isaac returns, like the alternative is unthinkable.

The alternative is unthinkable.

It's another half hour before the nurse comes to update me again. Once I give him permission to share the update with Ronan and Isaac in the room, he lets us know that Lex is out of surgery. They've got him on fluids and vasopressors for the shock, and he's responding well. The healers—the witches with healing magic who are part of MagCorps are going to take over to help with the iron poisoning. I'm not sure what that entails, and it looks like neither does he, so we just nod at each other. Another few minutes and Lex will be brought into the ICU ward to recover, he says. It's a sterile room, so anyone going in must change into scrubs and a gown and mask. I'm the only one given that option, though, which I can see Isaac almost object to until Ronan puts a hand on his arm and pulls him back down to sit on one of the hard plastic chairs next to the bed I've been sitting on.

It's closer to a half an hour rather than a few minutes before the nurse is back to escort them out and me to get decontaminated. When I finally get to the ICU ward, Lex is the only patient there. The rest of the severely wounded were flown out this morning to a fixed hospital. Lex is hooked up to too many machines, in my opinion, but I know they've all got a function in keeping him with me. It's just upsetting seeing him so pale. He looks small in the bed, hooked up to so many wires and tubes. His shoulder is bandaged, and he's got IV fluids flowing. Already, his color is better, though those angry red and black lines of his veins still radiate out from under the bandage. Healers come in to stand on either side of the bed, their hands over him. I can sort of see the magic they're working, can watch its golden tones sliding into him, pushing back the blackness of the poison that's darkened his aura.

One of them calls me over, telling me to take his hand, talk to him, let him know that I'm there. Soulmate magic is some of the strongest magic there is, she tells me, and she's seen people rally from things they shouldn't have, just drawing on their soulmate's strength.

I feel the connection between us thrum the second I wrap my hand around Lex's, careful not to disturb the IV there. It's not so much that he's pulling anything from me, but I can feel him unconsciously reaching for me, and I reach back, tightening my fingers on his hand as I let his magic drift over me through our bond. I'm not sure what to do, but the healer guides me. It's almost like meditation, and I find myself unconsciously reaching for the nearest ley line and funneling that magic back to Lex. It's not something I usually do—more often, I'm pulling magic from him, but we've practiced this in training for helping to restore our partners if they deplete their core.

Lex's core isn't depleted, but it is darkened, like his aura, like the poison is magical as much as physical. I say as much to the healer coaching me, and she nods.

"It's not so much that it is magical as it is the absence of magic. It's corrupting and depleting his, so until the doctors can come up with a physical antidote, we need to bolster his ability to fight it by cleaning and abetting his core."

I don't know how to clean the magic, but I know how to add to it, to replenish him, so I focus on that while they pull the sickly, black strands out. It takes a while before

I can see a noticeable difference, but, eventually, Lex's aura takes on his normal rainbow hues. They're still darker than usual, but not dull and dim, and the black threads are almost gone.

"Can you keep feeding his core?" the healer asks. "Your link to him allows you to do it more efficiently than we can, but I don't want to exhaust you, too."

"Replenishing him doesn't tire me out," I say, smiling a little. "If anything, pulling from the ley line gives me an energy buzz."

She smiles a gentle smile back. "Well, sit, at least. You're nearly as pale as he is. You should let the nurses examine you while you're here."

"They already did, thanks, and I'm fine. Just watching him get shot was upsetting, to say the least."

She nods. "I can imagine, especially when you were supposedly safe behind shields."

That takes me back to wondering about the iron bullets, over how they knew, when the doctor comes in a while later with something in a syringe.

"We don't see many cases of iron or silver poisoning here, so we don't have the usual antidote on hand you have access to back home, but I think this should do the trick."

I'm not impressed by her lack of certainty, but I appreciate them working to find a solution when the easy one isn't on hand. Like anti-venom, iron and silver antidotes are highly specific to the poison, made by healers with a knack for potions. I don't know the ingredients, but I guess they don't have access to them here. They're accessible, but hardly kept on hand in many places back home---poisonings, where the iron or silver gets into the body are rare and have to be deliberate, after all. She injects the serum into Lex's IV, then checks him over.

"He's looking better. If the antidote works, I see no reason he won't make a full recovery. He's young and healthy, and that's sometimes the most important thing for positive outcomes. His brachial plexus took some damage, so he might have to have another surgery or two to repair the blood vessels and help with pain. He'll definitely need physical therapy if he's going to go back to pitching no-hit-ters."

"How'd you know he was a pitcher?" I ask. I don't want to think about follow up surgeries or rehab—CSHs have limited beds and specialists, and they don't usually keep folks more than 72 hours, so both of those sound like a medevac to a larger, more permanent facility. They cater to soulmates a lot in MagCorps, but not so much that they'll ship me back out with him.

"Because of the poisoning, we used conscious sedation while we operated. He told us all about it when we asked him what he likes to do." The woman smiles at me, her cheeks flushing a little.

"And he said baseball?"

"Eventually." With a cryptic smile, the doctor pats my shoulder. "He should be waking up anytime now. He'll be glad you're here."

I nod, refocusing on Lex and run my hand through his curls which are damp with sweat. After a couple of min-utes, he turns his head into my hand, a smile curving his lips.

"Mike?"

"I'm right here."

"I know. I heard you fretting with the healers."

"I was not fretting," I tell him.

"You were fretting. It was sweet. Made me feel warm and fuzzy." Now, how can I argue with that? "I don't feel so good."

"Well, you were shot and poisoned, and a carpet viper tried to bite you, so I would suspect you don't." Just listing it out has me feeling not-so-well again, but I focus on him.

"You just had to bring up the snake," he complains. "I'm gonna have nightmares about that snake."

"We'll just have to comfort each other when we wake up with the shakes," I tell him. Because I'm going to have nightmares about this whole day. Probably for years.

"Did they get the blood off of me?" His voice sounds incredibly concerned about that detail.

I'm a little surprised he remembers the blood, drugged as he is. "Yeah, babe. You're all cleaned up."

"Wish it was that easy to wash it off the inside. I kinda get Lady Macbeth, now."

"Hmmm...?"

"Always washing her hands to get the blood off of them."

Oh. I don't know what to say to that, but it's about what I feared.

"Your hands are clean, physically and metaphorically, Lex. You didn't do anything wrong. You fought to survive, just like we're trained. You saved two lives."

"Two?"

"Well, yeah. Because I don't come back from losing you. I might've made it off the mountain, if Isaac and Ronan dragged me, but I doubt I'd have made it to this point in the day if you hadn't."

"Don't say that." He's frowning and trying to open his eyes at the same time, and I feel bad I've upset him.

"I'm sorry. You're right. I shouldn't say things like that."

"If something happens to me, you have to go on. Promise me." He's insistent, and finally manages to get his eyes open. They're serious as his gaze finds mine, intense and oh-so-blue, the way they get when he's doing magic, even though he's not calling on any power right now, except love.

"Lex..."

"Promise. I can't bear the thought of any of it otherwise. You have to take care of Andie..."

"We barely know her, Lex. I think she'll be fine without me."

"No. We're two thirds of her soul, Mike. She needs us, even if none of us knows what that looks like, yet. Promise me you'll take care of her. She's gonna be all swept up in the politics of royalty and forced into marriage and motherhood. Someone's gotta stand up for her right to control her life beyond that."

"And that's my job?"

"If I'm not here, yes." He gives me a solemn nod.

"So, otherwise, it's your job?"

"I'm appointing myself to that role." Another nod.

"Oh. Okay. Have you consulted her on that?"

"I might've mentioned it in my last email. She said I was sweet." He looks pleased by that to a ridiculous degree.

"You are sweet, but let's stop talking about what happens if you're not here, because the snake might be your nightmare, but you not being here is mine, and I was really scared today."

His gaze softens, and he turns his hand to hold mine more firmly. "So was I. I still am, honestly."

"Doc says you're gonna be fine. Arm will need some rehab, but you're expected to make a full recovery."

"That's hard to believe right now, with how I feel."

"Well, the antidote's still kicking in."

"Iron bullets don't make sense," he says with a frown.

"No, they don't," I say, the fact of this starting to bother me all over again.

"They'd mess up the guns, wouldn't they?"

"Pretty sure that saved your life." I'd had the same thought—the iron would screw up the rifling of the gun. Plus, iron's so brittle, the bullets would be nearly useless. That's probably why it shattered into Lex's bloodstream so easily. Then again, maybe that's the point. Easier to poison someone this way.

"Yeah. But someone should've thought of that before they made them."

"Unless..." I don't want to put my suspicions into words.

"Unless they were made specifically for us." Guess he's been suspicious, too.

"We think they were." LTC Greeley's voice comes from behind me, and I jump a little, hopping to my feet to come to attention.

"As you were, Lieutenant." I sink back down to my chair as Lex reaches for my hand again.

"What do you mean, sir?" he asks LTC Greeley.

"The medical staff turned over the bullet that was in your shoulder. We're still going to have to run tests, but from the way it burned my hand, it's not just iron. It's got silver in it, too."

"Iron and silver?" I ask, sure I've heard wrong. "How would you even forge them together to make a workable projectile?"

"The silver's easier to work with than the iron," Greeley says thoughtfully. "Hunters have been using it in bullets and arrowheads for centuries, after all. And there's no real reason you couldn't make an iron and silver alloy. That might even be how they can make the iron functional in a bullet. But they might still have to use magic to make the iron feasible as a bullet."

"Does that magic even exist?"

"Maybe. There's some indication that pure ley line magic, unfiltered through a witch's core, could stand up to iron."

"You mean like ley line magic a mage uses," I say, wondering if I sound as grim as I feel.

"Yes."

"Fuck." I have a few choice epithets I'd like to use to call my father, but not in front of my commanding officer.

"We found a site online offering 'witch and shifter killing bullets' for sale. It's on the dark web and some of the ads are in Arabic and Pashto, like the sellers are deliberately targeting insurgents and other terrorists who might be fighting coalition forces."

"Isn't that treason?" Lex asks. "Whatever else we are, MagCorps personnel are US servicemen and women. Helping our enemies must violate some law against treason."

"Technically, yes, but we've got to find the people responsible first," LTC Greeley says, voice gentler than I've heard from him before.

"You know who's responsible," I bite out.

"We suspect," LTC Greeley corrects me. "We don't have the kind of proof that will convict anyone of treason."

That's not good enough for me, but I don't know how to fix it. If my dad is responsible, he is showing himself to be perfectly content to sacrifice me, so I doubt he'd turn around and confess if I asked him. At this point, he might just shoot me himself. Christ knows I'm tempted to solve the issue that way.

LTC Greeley takes his leave shortly thereafter. They bring Lex some food, and I barely stop short of playing airplane with it to get him to eat. He finally eats most of it, though he says he's still queasy. He does ask for more Jell-O, which I take as a win. It's at least some calories, which he needs to have the energy to fight, even if they aren't the most nutrient dense calories.

Lex nods off shortly after dinner, and one of the nurses pulls one of the empty beds close enough to Lex's that I can still hold his hand while on it. The healers apparently did me a solid, telling the nursing staff that my being close by is key to Lex's wellbeing. I do leave before I fall asleep, letting a gowned and masked Isaac come back to sit with him. It gives me the time to run back to our tent and get Lex some warm clothes, something his own, so he's not stuck in that hospital gown tomorrow when he'll hopefully be able to move around some.

Isaac is sitting on the bed I vacated when I get back and re-decontaminated, holding Lex's hand and talking to him in low tones. Lex sees me standing in the doorway, though, and lights up. It might be my imagination, but Isaac seems reluctant to leave. He does yield the seat back to me, but he leaves only after promising Lex he'll be back to visit tomorrow.

"What's that about?" I ask, retaking Lex's hand.

"What?"

"Isaac seems suddenly more attached to you than he has been." I hope I don't sound jealous, but I am a little bit, so I can't argue the feeling out of my voice.

"I think he just got freaked out by people dying so abruptly, and my getting hurt," Lex says with a shrug of his uninjured shoulder. "He's still grieving his family, and we're kind of like brothers, so. I think it just triggered some of that unresolved panic and grief."

"That makes sense." And makes me feel like an ass for being jealous. "Was he close to Leroy?"

Lex shrugs. "I don't think so, but he was still one of us, and another shifter."

"So, close enough to be triggering."

"Yeah."

We settle in our respective beds for the night, and I hate the bedrail on his bed between us. It makes holding Lex's hand awkward, but I still find a way to manage it. I listen to the sound of his breathing and the soft beep of the machine measuring out his heartbeat, steady, sure, still going. You'd think that would be enough, but it's still a long time before I fall asleep.

CHAPTER 17

Lex

The 115th CSH keeps me for 48 hours before declaring I need more care than they can give. I'm doing well, but severe shock, a gunshot wound, and iron poisoning aren't things you just bounce back from, even as a healthy 19-year-old. Plus, they say I need another surgery, with a specialist. They try to reassure me that I will probably just need a few weeks to recover after that and then can return, but I have a sinking feeling that's not the case. I can barely close and open my left hand with the nerve damage, and even though it's my non-dominant hand, the US Marine Corps and MagCorps both prefer you have two working hands to serve at the front. Doc says I'll probably need at least six weeks of rehab.

I don't want to lose function in my hand permanently, so I don't kick up a fuss, but it's also not as necessary, given my use of magic. Either way, they're shipping me to Landstuhl Regional Medical Center in Germany, rather than back to the States. There's several of us being shipped back out, and I feel like a fraud for being the least severely wounded. Several are amputees—even with us out on patrol with them, scouring for IEDs, two caravans coming into camp got hit in the last week, and another two teams got hit with the shield-piercing iron bullets, with five casualties and four wounded the day after we were hit.

I pour out my angst about the move to Andie via email, once the doctors give me the news. I don't want to worry her, but I am trying hard not to hit Mike with any more than he's already dealing with. He held me while I almost died, after all. Andie only heard about it after we knew I'd be fine. Or that's how I justify my bitching to a fifteen-year-old girl to myself.

"I don't want to go," I tell Mike, who's brought my packed duffel to me in the CSH a day later. "Who's gonna have your back with me gone?"

"Our whole squad," he starts.

Before Mike can say more, Isaac, who's hovering by the door, aka, "visiting", interjects. "We've got him, Lex, promise."

"Yes, we promise," Ronan adds from beside him.

"As I said," Mike says with a smile at the shifter and mage.

"You guys are great." I don't want to seem ungrateful, but they aren't me. Maybe I have some trouble with delegating such an important duty. "But I joined up solely to take care of him."

"And look where you've ended up," Mike says, now frowning.

"Yeah, but you're fine." I shouldn't have to point this out.

The argument ends in a draw, but I do feel better that we have such good friends, who I know will do their best. I'm just now very motivated to ace therapy and get back here and on the duty roster as quickly as possible. Funny how I couldn't even have imagined that feeling a year ago.

The next morning, they wheel me out to the chopper that's going to take us to Kabul. It takes a bit to get everyone loaded and situated. Right as I'm about to be strapped in, the sound of heavy trucks and another chopper coming in drowns out the orderly's instructions. We're all straining to see the other bird when the radio crackles, ordering us to cut our engines and stay put. The pilot does as he's told, and everyone strains harder to see what's happening.

It's another ten minutes before we know anything—the chopper lands and several people spill out, dressed in battle uniforms lacking any rank or unit insignia. The trucks I can see from where I'm sitting are loaded down with what look like collapsed tents.

The curiosity sparks up higher around me. I frown because I can tell the newcomers are all witches, but they aren't wearing MagCorps patches. I watch as LTC Greeley comes jogging up and leans in to talk to them. I see a couple of glances at us, and I catch a glimpse of Mike on the other side of the chopper, frowning in concern. Another few minutes, and one of my doctors comes over. He shouts something to the orderly, who climbs back in and starts unbuckling me and helping me back out.

"What's going on?"

The orderly shrugs, lowering me back into the wheelchair. Mike tries to make his way over, but LTC Greeley holds him back. The newly arrived witches all fall in behind my wheelchair as we move back into the CSH, where I ask my question again.

My doctor steps forward. "Looks like you're staying here, Lieutenant. These folks are specialized healers, able to do what we can't, what we were sending you to Landstuhl for. They'll take over your recovery and rehabilitation, get you on your feet quicker and keep you here."

I don't have words for a moment and have to content myself with gaping at him. "I'm staying?"

"Yes."

"Why?"

The doctor shrugs and gestures to one of the witches, who comes around and hands me a folded piece of paper. I struggle to unfold it with one hand, and he does it for me after a moment. My bemusement grows as I read the hand-scrawled note from Andie.

Apparently venting to a fifteen-year-old girl has consequences when said girl is the Crown Princess of one of the two royal courts. She wanted to come, too, but her mother, thankfully, wouldn't hear of it, but Eleanor did persuade Esther to pull some strings. The witches are, as my doctor said, all healers who specialize in my type of injury. Esther sent out a call for any specialists who could be spared; she wouldn't call specialists away from other soldiers' care, apparently. Andie sounds a bit put out about that fact, but I'm grateful. But these four—a surgeon, physical therapist, occupational therapist, and skilled nurse—volunteered to take time away from their private practices to answer their Queen's call, and here they are.

To say I'm stunned is an understatement. The shifter guards with them fall to unloading the collapsed tents and then set to erecting an add-on ward to the CSH, so I'm not taking up a needed bed. Another truck rumbles in, and they unload beds and supplies for the new ward. It's nothing fancy, but it's set up like another ICU ward, kept sterile by what amounts to forcefield spells. There are ten beds in total, so my special treatment at least means the CSH can help more people if we have a mass casualty event. The orderly helps me back into bed, and each of the healers introduces themselves to me. The nurse unpacks my duffle into a canvas closet set next to my bed while the orderly re-hooks me up to all the monitors.

They get me out of the hospital gown and into sweatpants and a hoodie from my duffle. For the first time since I got back to camp after being wounded, my ass is fully covered and not in danger of hanging out of a gown that ties in the back. The whole process from waking this morning until now has worn me out, and the healers seem to realize this—it's apparently a common complicating factor of hypovolemic shock. My shoulder is killing me, but they give me a pain-killing potion that's better than the morphine the docs had me on. They promise Mike can visit for supper if I'll sleep for now and follow their instructions. I'm certainly not going to complain at that news, or my reprieve from being shipped out, so I make sure to be good as gold the rest of the day. Given the sedative in the potion they gave me knocks me out fast, I'm a model patient all day.

Mike

After they take Lex back into the CSH, I hurry to the communications tent and pull rank on the private manning the equipment so I can commandeer one of the laptops here for our use, even though I'm not signed up for a slot until tomorrow. I need to thank someone, and I have a good idea who. Apologizing to the private, I launch the chat program and ping Andie. She must have been expecting it because she answers right away.

M. Mathis: I could kiss you.

A. Lafayette: Promises, promises.

M. Mathis: Seriously—how did you convince Esther to do what was needed to keep him here?

A. Lafayette: A lady never reveals her secrets. But let's just say she has a vested interest in keeping me happy if she wants me to stick around and marry Nick, not head to Maine to find Lex's family when I turn 16.

M. Mathis: I thought you were okay marrying Nick?

A. Lafayette: Things change.

M. Mathis: What changed?

A. Lafayette: He's an objectively terrible kisser, and I have significant concerns about my ability to enjoy my wedding night if that is any indication.

M. Mathis: I think all teenage boys start off objectively terrible kissers, sweetheart.

A. Lafayette: Yes, well, he thinks he's great at it, courtesy of his vapid little soulmate who has him convinced he's great at sex, too. Let's just say, I have doubts about her judgment. How is Lex doing, really? Your last email was vague, and his was just bitching about going to Germany.

M. Mathis: The docs say he's doing as well as can be expected given everything he's been through. They let me in to have dinner with him and spend about an hour, then run me out again. I hate to go, but, honestly, he's still just really exhausted. Last night, he almost fell asleep in his food and was totally out when they made me leave.

A. Lafayette: Is he supposed to be that fatigued?

M. Mathis: Yeah, they told me it's normal and will probably go on for a while, yet. Physical therapy will supposedly help build up his energy and endurance again. Get this, though, when I got there last night, he was chatting with the chaplain.

A. Lafayette: I've heard the chaplains are good about ministering to everyone equally, so what's so strange about that? Not the statistically-probably-Christian part, right? Lex is a practicing Catholic, isn't he?

M. Mathis: Technically, yes. In practice, though, Lex is whatever church has the best youth group this year.

A. Lafayette: So, a non-denominational chaplain might be exactly what the doctor ordered.

M. Mathis: For what?

A. Lafayette: Counseling. What he went through was traumatic, and I've heard the mundane human shrinks don't know what to do with supernats sometimes, because our brains/thoughts don't fit into their boxes and diagnoses. They don't know what a baseline for a witch is, let alone a shifter.

M. Mathis: Yeah. School counselors and a couple of shrinks back home never could figure out what to do with Lex. Was he hyperactive? Bipolar? Something else? He did good at school stuff, though, so, eventually they stopped trying to fix what they figured wasn't broken. His folks weren't ever concerned enough to take him somewhere with therapists for supernats.

A. Lafayette: My mom and Esther have been recruiting supernat shrinks for MagCorps, so our troops have psych services abroad and at home. It's slow going, though, and I've heard that a lot of times the chaplains will step in to provide at least emergency counseling.

M. Mathis: Lex is fine. Just tired and still jumpy about the snake.

A. Lafayette: What snake?

M. Mathis: The viper that tried to bite him while he was down on the ground after getting shot. We had the shield back up by then, so he wasn't in danger, but he still saw it lunge at him, and Lex has a thing about snakes.

A. Lafayette: Ick. So do I, and I have claws, enhanced healing abilities, and can often strike fast enough to decapitate them before they bite. I can't imagine being injured on the ground, behind a shield that already failed once, and seeing one strike with no way to fight back.

M. Mathis: Isaac killed it with his wolfy claws. Now Lex wants to keep him as a fluffy puppy.

A. Lafayette: ...

M. Mathis: No offense?

A. Lafayette: Oh, I'm not offended. I'm laughing so hard I can't see the screen. Only Lex would take one of the most vicious predators since the vampires died out and want to make him a pet.

M. Mathis: I'm not even sure if Isaac would object all that much.

A. Lafayette: Oh?

M. Mathis: Just a sense I have.

A. Lafayette: Doesn't he have his own soulmate?

M. Mathis: Yes, he does, and they're very much in love, but love is complicated. Lex was in love with me for years, I know now, but I also know that he fell in love with other people at least a couple of times during that time. Maybe not soulmate-level love, but it was real.

A. Lafayette: You mean Hannah.

M. Mathis: For one, yes.

A. Lafayette: Have you talked to her recently?

M. Mathis: Not really, not since she started dating a guy at UVA. I wrote to tell her about Lex, because I thought she'd want to know, but she hasn't responded, yet.

A. Lafayette: Huh. Weird. Maybe she's got finals or something...in February. Midterms? I don't know. Elias had a bunch of tests last week at Tulane. Even Kelly didn't see him for days, and they *live* together.

M. Mathis: Maybe. I tried to tell her she was right about us while we were still stateside, and she responded to that, but just to say she was happy for us. And to threaten me if I ever hurt Lex.

A. Lafayette: Oh, she won't get a chance at you if you ever hurt him. I won't leave enough for her to bother.

M. Mathis: Why is everyone assuming I'm the one who'd do the hurting?!?

A. Lafayette: Because Lex couldn't hurt you if he tried. He'd die first. And you were oblivious to his feelings for a minimum of six years, after all. You're the wild card in this.

M. Mathis: I would die before I hurt him. I couldn't hurt him without destroying myself.

A. Lafayette: Good. Keep it that way. I gotta go—we're doing the fealty ceremonies in smaller groups since the Massacre, and we've got one tonight. Mom wants me there, so they can see me as their future Queen or something. I have to wear the Crown Princess crown instead of my circlet. I hate that crown. It's got sharp pieces that dig into my head.

M. Mathis: Go be a princess. Tell your mom and Esther that Lex and I are deeply grateful. I couldn't stand the thought of him half a world away, even if he'd be safer.

A. Lafayette: On their behalf, you're welcome. I didn't want him to be alone in a strange country, separated from his family and both of us, either. Give him my love when you see him next?

M. Mathis: You got it, sweetheart. Good night.

A. Lafayette: Night! XOXO <3 ;-)

Smiling more than I realize until I see my reflection in a monitor's glass, I return the laptop to the waiting private and head out to my assigned duties for the day.

CHAPTER 18

Lex

They do my second surgery the day after the healers arrive and let me just rest and recover from that for a few days. With healing magic, they're able to put me on the road to recovery faster than a mundane human would be. By two weeks after the healers arrived, everything has settled into a routine. I get up, go talk to the chaplain over breakfast, then go to physical therapy for an hour. That's usually exhausting, so I get to go back to bed until lunch. After lunch, I have occupational therapy. Then, I have "free" time until dinner. I usually spend some of it napping again, but along with the healers came a dedicated, approved laptop just for me, along with a satellite modem, that I can use without draining the camp's resources. Video games, even on a laptop, are deemed good for my fine motor skills, so no one minds that I play. Mike comes to join me when he gets off duty, and we have dinner and hang out until bedtime. They've made up the bed next to mine for him, if he wants to stay, but the nurses coming in to check on me all night keep him awake. He doesn't complain, but after I notice the dark circles under his eyes, I start sending him back to our tent to sleep.

I'm wearing my own clothes, which is great, although I'm still not supposed to get out of bed without calling for a nurse. Something about fall risks. I tried pointing out that my arm was injured, not my leg, but apparently it has more to do with the shock recovery and lingering fatigue and weakness from that. Part of my rehab will be building back up my endurance. They got treatment before my organs were damaged, but my body still went through so much that I apparently can't push myself too hard.

I've been in the newly designated rehab wing for two weeks and am finally allowed to move from the bed to a wheelchair on my own, courtesy of my physical therapist downgrading my risk level. I am finishing up lunch when I hear a familiar voice outside the door, in the hall.

"It'll be fine, promise. He probably doesn't know what to do with a ward all to himself anyway."

I smile to myself, swinging out of the bed and to the stupid wheelchair—how am I supposed to build up endurance if I barely get to walk around a gym for thirty minutes a day? I'm intending to roll out into the hall, caught between delight and worry, when a bed is wheeled into my up-until-now private ward and there lies Isaac, who I haven't seen in a week.

As my soulmate, Mike's allowed to visit daily, but the rest of my friends only get a half hour a week. They're still on the duty roster, after all, and LTC Greeley is already confused by the special treatment I've been given. Isaac's pale, with his face is bruised up and head bandaged.

"Looks like you're getting a roommate, Lieutenant Monroe," the orderly says just a touch too cheerfully, like I might take it out on him if I object. The special treatment confusing LTC Greeley has given rise to animosity in others, especially those already not fans of MagCorps. "He says you're friends...?"

"We are," I confirm, backing the chair out of the way so they can roll Isaac to the other side of my bed and get him settled.

There's a bit of fuss and bother before the orderly leaves and then the nurses are in the ward, introducing themselves and checking his vitals, and all I want to do is ask what happened and if Mike's okay. I saw him yesterday, but who knows what's happened since then?

Finally, after what seems like forever, we're alone.

"Not that I'm not thrilled to see you, but what the hell happened?"

"Iron shielded IED," he says, making a disgruntled face. "Or, if not shielded, enough iron in it to absorb the magic we sent out to disable them..."

"So, not disabled, then, when..."

"Not disabled when our caravan ran over it," he confirms, making a face.

"Mike...?"

"Mike's fine. He was here with Parsons when we went out and never in harm's way."

"Ronan?" That matters, too, even if it's not my primary worry, but Isaac's cheerful enough that I figure his soulmate's okay, a fact which he confirms quickly.

"Ronan got a bit banged up, but we were in the second vehicle, back from the blast. I'd be fine, too, but I hit my head on the side wall when we flipped. Even with my helmet on, I rang myself up a pretty severe concussion. They had to do surgery to relieve the pressure, and they're worried about neurological damage, so they wanted to keep me for observation for a while. Normally, they'd have medevacked me out, but the guys here for you were willing to work with me, too. So, I get to stay."

"So, Mike and Ronan can commiserate now? Or rejoice at having double the room in our tent?"

"Yep. As can we." I get a grin from the wolf shifter, before he yawns and stretches. "So, how did you score all this prime treatment, anyway? Mike seems to know, but he's not saying, and LTC Greeley's downright cranky at not knowing why you rate so highly with Queen Esther."

I shrug because we don't generally talk about Andie and who she is to us. I feel we could trust Isaac with it, but still can't bring myself to explain. I'm a little embarrassed, truth be told, like I asked for special treatment, or think I deserve it or something. "I dunno. Someone liked my smile, I guess."

"Right." Isaac looks skeptical and a little hurt I won't say more. "I promise not to snore," Isaac says, crossing his heart like a dork.

"That's the only reason I let you in here," I say, like I had a chance of stopping them bringing him in from my wheelchair. No one has taught me how to do anything cooler than back up in it. "If it had been Ronan..."

Isaac laughs, because Ronan's snoring is legendary. "I don't know how I'll sleep in the silence."

"Nothing is ever silent here," I say. "There's always beeping, even at 3AM, and bells calling the nurses to patients' bedsides in the other wards. But it's not snoring."

Isaac smiles a little sadly, then gives me a curious look. "What's with the wheelchair? It was your arm that was hurt..."

"Apparently having gone into fairly severe hypervolemic shock, I was still considered a fall risk until I proved to my therapist's satisfaction that I could be trusted to transfer from my bed to the chair without falling and without trying to take off walking unsupported or unsupervised. My first few days here, an alarm went off if I tried to get out of bed. But now I've got this baby." I hold up my wrist, showing off my orange wristband, in contrast to the red one on Isaac's wrist. "Another week and I might get downgraded to yellow, which'll let me take the chair down the hall to the bathroom alone and then, maybe, just maybe, I might make it to green and be allowed to go take a piss completely alone and on my own two feet."

"Wow, seriously?"

"That's the dream, man. That's the dream."

In truth, I'm grateful for the good care they're taking of me, but it's a little degrading to have to call a nurse every time nature calls. Sure, I can transfer to my chair and get out of bed alone now, but I'm still not supposed to go anywhere unsupervised, including the bathroom.

"I'm guessing the red band means...?"

"Getting out of bed alone will make you feel like you're trying for a prison break," I assure him. "You won't like the results, my friend. Nurse Jennifer is pretty and sweet, but she doesn't mess around. If you behave, though, she'll sometimes sneak you extra pudding."

"For real, though, how are you doing? Mike's been pretty quiet and uninformative, and you were so sleepy last week, we barely talked when I visited."

"Okay," I say with a shrug. "They've got me doing like three hours of therapy a day. Other than that, I've been catching up on my reading, listening to war stories from the Master Sergeant in the main ward, who comes in to visit with me, and Skyping with people back home." That part's sweet, but I don't say that because his family is gone, so I don't know who Isaac has to call.

He smiles again, though, and nods. "I'm glad you're recovering. You gave us all a real scare."

"I won't lie—I was pretty scared, too." It's a quiet confession, but I make myself say it, because the chaplain says you have to talk about this shit, to get it out before it can develop into PTSD. Sometimes it still does, anyway, but counseling is supposed to help forestall that or catch it early, at least.

"Yeah, I was, too, when I saw you guys go down, and then we walked into that cave..." He shudders. "I was terrified when the IED went off."

I scoot to the edge of my bed and reach across the space between us for his hand. "We survived, though."

"But now the men we love more than anything are still out there, just without us."

"Yeah, that's been the hardest part of being confined in here," I say. "But it's also the thing that makes me push harder in therapy every day. The faster I get better, the sooner I can get back out there and be there for Mike."

"Heh. I almost wish Ronan had been hurt just a little worse. Not badly, of course, but enough they'd have sent him in here, too, y'know?"

I nod. I do know. I don't want Mike to be hurt, not for anything, but I'd also give anything to have him safer here with me. We're still in an active combat zone, after all, nowhere is fully safe, but we're not out there, out in the open.

"War was always this thing we trained for, but somehow it never felt real until that bullet pierced our shield," I say. I start to pull my hand back worried I'm overstepping, but Isaac holds on tight. So, I let him. "Even after..."

"Even after the bombing and the massacres," Isaac finishes for me.

"Yeah."

"That was the work of party or parties unknown, but the enemy in Afghanistan is one we have to look in the eyes. It's different," Isaac says, voice quiet. "Although if I'm never in another bombing again, it'll be too soon."

It's not funny, but we both laugh anyway. He finally lets go of my hand. I settle back on my bed, reaching for a tin on the table beside it, then turn back to him.

"It's not much, but my mom sent peanut butter cookies."

"My favorite." Far from looking crushed at the mention of mothers, Isaac looks delighted and steals two cookies. "They didn't let me have solid food for twelve hours after surgery for fear my ability to swallow would suddenly disappear."

"But you're cleared now?" I look over my shoulder, half afraid the nurses will come storming in and confiscate the cookies.

"Yep, I got three squares of solid food yesterday, though they'll probably want to watch me eat again, or so I was told before breakfast this morning. I think it's like your fall risk thing—always standard operating procedure."

I pull the cookie tin back. "Well, then, after you're officially cleared, you can have more."

Mike

I haven't been sleeping well in the weeks since Lex was shot. I was never one to be bothered by nightmares before, but now they wake me every night. The empty space in the cot connected to mine doesn't help. Neither do Ronan's snores, a less-than-charming quirk I've been able to ignore since we got here by assiduous use of ear plugs and focusing on the rise and fall of Lex's chest as he breathes. Now there's just emptiness and silence broken by snores that are more like a freight train than anything else. I hoped he'd stay with Isaac at the hospital, but the nurses send him away after we all finish dinner. Apparently, his snoring disturbs the patients in other wards.

The iron shielded IEDs have everyone shaken, like everything we can do to protect ourselves is just being stripped away, piece by piece. Ronan's distraught over Isaac's injury, something I understand all too well. We don't talk about it, or not much, but we do spend a lot of time we're off duty talking around it.

Tonight, we're playing some card game I've already forgotten the name of.

"Lex still feeling tired all the time?" Ronan asks, discarding a card carelessly.

"He says most days are better, but some days he still just wants to sleep." I don't know nearly enough about recovering from shock, and my limited computer privileges here don't give me enough time to research much. I tried to get Lex to let me use his shiny new computer to look things up, but he just cradled it to his chest like it was his precious. Granted, most people use their computer time to Skype with family, and since I have no desire to talk to mine, I get some time to learn things. And try and write the damn paper for LTC Greeley that Lex and Isaac were so excited about and now have indefinite extensions for.

My lack of an extension is just another reason to wish I'd been the one hurt. The main one, of course, being that I still have nightmares about watching Lex fall and about that hellish ride back to camp when I was sure he was going to stop breathing at any moment.

"Isaac doesn't say much about how he's feeling or how his recovery is going," Ronan says after a lengthy silence. "Surely if it were going well, he'd say?"

"Maybe he's not sure. Or they don't want to give him bad news, so they just don't tell them much of anything? Lex doesn't talk about his overall progress, either just little things about his day in general." And when he talks to Andie, which seems often. I get four or five emails from her a week but haven't asked about video calling her. I'm not sure if her mother would okay that, but apparently Lex gets to, so maybe I'll ask. It'd be nice to have something more to tell him about my day than 'Another caravan got hit today' since the insurgents seem to be taking this iron thing and running with it. Of course, any time we get hit, the wounded are rushed to the CSH. He knows, even if we don't talk about it.

"Do you and Isaac talk about the continued iron laced IEDs and bullets?"

"Fuck, no. He knows they're happening, obviously, but talking about it makes him damn near go out of his skin with worry, and I need him to focus on getting better. So, I just don't tell him when I'm scheduled to go out. You talking to Lex about it?"

"No. Same reason. He's already a nervous wreck since Isaac told him about y'all getting hit. And the attacks since then haven't helped. Almost every day he asks if I'm going out. I tell him no."

"So, you're actively lying?" Ronan looks a little shocked.

"So are you." I'm not defensive.

"I'm omitting, there's a difference."

"Not if he's asking."

"He's not."

"What would you say if he were?"

Ronan sighs and sinks down in the chair next to mine at the desk. "The same thing you're saying."

"Hmmm."

"Okay, fine. I'm also lying."

And I feel vindicated. Ronan seems to realize this, but he hands me a beer anyway.

"Where'd this come from?"

"I don't ask questions, man, I just deliver."

So, we're both underage and in a country that doesn't sell beer, on a base of an American military that actively bans alcohol here, but those are just details we're not going to discuss. Kind of like we aren't discussing how much we miss our soulmates, even if they are just across camp. Or the lies we're telling them, ostensibly for their own good, when we know it's really for ours. The lies let us pretend we have some illusion of control in the long nights when we've each been stripped of the one person who gives our lives meaning. What are we even fighting for, if not them? Surely not a country that hates us—both countries, our own and the one we're serving in, now? Beer might be sinful, but we're anathema, and we know it.

I've never felt more like a member of the supernat community than I do right now.

CHAPTER 19

Lex

Another month of rehab goes by. It's nerve-wracking as fuck, sitting here in a heavily shielded hospital, hearing it every time there are explosions out there. Sound carries a long way in the desert. Even more unnerving is when the engines of vehicles gun coming in, and we hear the shouts as the EMTs go running out to get the wounded and the sounds of the OR being prepped. The wounded scream sometimes, and I hate that more than even the memory of the damn snake. It's raw and immediate and it brings back the scent of blood and smoke and the screams of the men up the hill from us.

Still, none of that is what I'm dreaming of the night the real nightmare comes back—the one that's always been there. I've woken up shaking, thinking Mike's been hurt, or woken myself up with a yell as a dozen snakes strike at me, but tonight, tonight there's no jerking awake, no yelling I hear.

It's so stupid, I've never told anyone about the details, not even Mike. He's woken me up from the dream several times in our lives, and I always tell him I can't remember the dream. He thinks I'm just nightmare prone, not that I have the same nightmare. But even if I tried to explain it, it would sound so dumb. My parents tried to get me to talk about it for a while, but I refused. I wouldn't say a word to the human shrinks.

See, nothing happens in the dream. There are no macabre or terrifying visions that haunt me, no villains, no guns, no snakes. I don't see horrible things happen to people I love. Nothing horrible even happens to me. No one dies.

I don't know when I first had the dream. Can it even be called a dream if nothing happens in it? It's this thing that's always been there. All I do remember is the darkness. It's absolute, like in a sealed, lightless room, though I'm usually outside, I think. It's nighttime, but in a city. I don't know what city, just that it's a city. Everything will be okay, except this sense of foreboding, and then the lights go out, like a city-wide blackout, only they go out slowly, in a wave. From there, all other light sources go out—the moon, the stars—darkness rolls across the sky, extinguishing them, and then it's just me, there in the darkness. Maybe it's like the inside of a sensory deprivation tank with the absolute dark? Not perfectly, though. It's silent, too, sure, but I can feel the wind on my skin, and then I know. I know there's something there in the dark. I can't hear it breathing, I can't feel it move, and I can't smell it or anything. I just know it's there. I don't know what it wants, but I know it's nothing good. It doesn't ever do anything, but I know it wants to destroy me and everything I love. I start to run but I don't know which way to go, and it doesn't matter. This isn't something you can outrun. I can't get away from it, can't make it stop, not even by waking up sometimes, which generally involves a lot of screaming and thrashing about that's mortifying once I'm myself again. I used to refuse to go to sleepovers for fear of it happening.

The worst thing is that even after I wake up, the dream doesn't really end. The terror follows me. The darkness stays wrapped around me. I used to beg my mom to leave the light on when I went to sleep, and she did, but when I'd wake up sweating and shaking, it was like I couldn't see the light on my nightstand, like the darkness had followed me. My parents would hold me, my mom singing hymns as she rocked me, and sometimes, I just kept screaming. Night terrors, one doctor told them, and we tried all he said should prevent it, but nothing ever worked forever. The darkness always comes back for me. Mike's the only one who's ever been able to really help. When he's holding me, the darkness can't get to me—the light between us is too bright. He can drive it back, calm me down like nothing else ever has.

It's a shame he's already gone back to our tent the night it finds me in the CSH.

I'm vaguely aware of myself screaming. Arms are tight around me with a voice telling me it's going to be okay. Not Mike, but the voice is a soft murmur, and it pulls me to it with some magic. Fingers brush through my hair in a soothing pattern, and when I open my eyes, I can see the light on in the ward illuminating the nurses' worried faces.

"It's okay," Isaac murmurs from behind me, and I realize he's the one holding me. Some of the tension eases. "I've got him. He'll be okay now."

He's reassuring the nurses, I realize, even as I feel his magic wash over me again. It's lulling, whatever he's doing, pulling me back under, toward sleep, even though I try to fight it. It's useless, and I feel myself slip away. This time, though, there isn't anything dark waiting for me.

Mike

I wake up abruptly, panic tight in my throat. I'm breathing hard, and I'm confused by the silence. When I look around, I see Ronan, holding a book on his bed, staring at me.

"Something wrong?"

"I need to get to Lex..." I recognize the feeling, now. It's not my panic; it's his. I've always felt at least an echo of it, but since our binding ceremony, his strongest emotions echo through me almost like my own. The flavor of this panic is familiar at least. He's had one of his nightmares. The ones so bad he won't talk about them.

I pull on my boots and head out of the tent, Ronan on my heels.

"What's going on?"

"Lex needs me." Too much to try to explain.

"How do you know?" Ronan could be irritated, but he's not, sounding genuinely concerned.

"I just do."

The nurse at the front of the hospital waves us through, though she frowns. We're halfway to the private ward when I see one of Lex's nurses hurrying toward me.

"He's okay, Lieutenant. Everything's fine..." She seems to know why I'm here, even though it's confusing her. Then again, mundane humans don't really understand soulmates and there are a lot of misconceptions out there—like that we feel everything the other feels or can communicate telepathically. Sure, there are spells for that, but it's nothing inherent.

"I need to see him."

She nods but moves along beside us. "I promise he's okay. Lieutenant McCall was able to calm him down. We would have sent for you if anything were wrong."

I want to dispute her assessment. Lex can't be okay. Isaac couldn't calm him down. Only I can do that.

But when we burst into their ward, sure enough—Lex is sound asleep, curled up in Isaac's arms. Magic I don't recognize glows faintly around them. Isaac's awake, but barely and blinks up at me and Ronan.

"Sup, guys?"

Ronan is just staring. I try to find words.

"Wh-what happened? I felt his terror…"

"Yeah." Isaac's fingers run through Lex's hair gently. "Night terrors or something. I'd barely fallen asleep, and he just woke up screaming. Almost threw himself off the bed. I got him calmed down. I-I was just about to try to go back to my bed."

He looks a little abashed now, as if just realizing what this could look like.

"How?" I demand. "How did you calm him down?"

He shrugs, trying to untangle himself from Lex, who murmurs a sleepy protest. "It's a spell my mom taught me, that my dad's mom taught her. My dad and grandfather got night terrors, too. It's something my grandmother worked up herself. A family remedy if you will. I didn't know if it would work without a blood or binding connection, but I had to try." He finally can ease away from Lex, and Nurse

Jennifer helps him back over to his bed. The magic stays wrapped around Lex.

"Oh... thank you." I can't really say anything else, can I?

"I can teach it to you," Isaac offers, as Ronan comes around to perch on his bed.

"Yeah. Thanks. That'd be good..."

I decide to stay the night, squeezing into Lex's bed, over Nurse Jennifer's objections. It's a tight fit, but once I've got Lex wrapped in my arms, where he belongs, it's almost comfortable.

Ronan and Isaac talk for a little while before Ronan heads back out, and I finally fall asleep, listening to Lex breathe.

CHAPTER 20

Lex

When I wake up the morning after my night terror, no one is holding me, but my pillow smells like Mike's aftershave. Isaac is looking a little sheepish, and I remember my fear the night before.

"I'm sorry if I woke you last night." My skin feels hot with embarrassment, and I hope he doesn't ask questions I don't want to answer.

"No worries," he assures me. "I was used to it growing up. My dad had night terrors, too."

"What did you do? You were with me when I woke up, yeah? You calmed me down?"

"Just a spell my mom taught me," he says quickly. "Mike showed up a little later. Guess he felt your panic. They let him stay the night with you."

"Why'd he leave?" I look around, like maybe he's just in the corner of the corner-less ward or something.

"He's leading PT this morning, apparently."

It's such a mundane thing, a thing I hated before but find myself missing now. I want that slice of normalcy again. I clearly was not meant to be an invalid.

My healers must agree with me—or I disturbed everyone too much with my screaming—because within the week, they're clearing Isaac and me both for release. We're not cleared for a full return to duty, and the healers are staying with their equipment, but we can be downgraded to "outpatient" physical therapy now. They tell us after our occupational therapy sessions, and we're able to tell Mike and Ronan the good news at dinner that night.

Strangely, they don't seem as excited as we are.

Mike

One night with Lex in my arms, and the next night is hell without him, so, you'd think I'd be thrilled to find out he's getting out of the hospital. I'm not thrilled. Out of the hospital is, eventually, back in the field. Back in the field is back in danger. I don't want him here for that. I want him with his family, safe on an island off the coast of Maine. Or I want him in New Orleans, with Andie, playing bodyguard to one of Queen Esther's kids, like a supernatural Secret Service agent. That's not too far off—they do use MagCorps for those roles, especially after the Massacre.

Still, I find myself smiling at the sight of him coming out the door of the CSH, duffel bag slung over his right shoulder. He grins at me, knocking into Isaac to point out me and Ronan waiting for them, and then they're racing to see who can get to us fastest. Isaac wins the race, but I still barely have time to brace for impact before my arms are full of a warm and solid Lex who wastes no time in kissing me enthusiastically. The President repealed "Don't Ask, Don't Tell" a few weeks ago, and it never really applied to MagCorps, anyway, but we did try for some discretion, usually. Apparently, we're saying "fuck discretion" today, and I can't even complain. I do glance sideways to see Ronan and Isaac having an equally enthusiastic, if slightly more discreet, reunion.

Yeah, okay, maybe we've seen them every day, but there's a big difference between an hour or two for a meal and spending most of your days together. I know I've missed Lex like he really is my other half. I've missed holding him, missed kissing him, missed...other things.

Ronan and Isaac break first and tell us they're going for a walk and the tent is ours for the day—they'll see us for dinner. I have no idea where they're going to go, but I'm not asking questions as I start to tug Lex toward the tent, anxious to thoroughly reconnect with him in multiple ways.

LTC Greeley passes us and starts to say something, but just grins and waves us on. Lex laughs and races me for the tent, where he crashes our mouths back together even more hungrily than before.

We still haven't mastered getting undressed smoothly together, and I'm blaming all the buttons, but we are getting faster about it. I haven't hit complete impatience, at least, before we're both in our boxer briefs and tumbling onto one of the narrow cots we have as beds. I try to take the brunt of our tumble, cautious about his shoulder, then roll him to his back, hovering over him.

"This thing is going to collapse under us," Lex predicts, and I can't argue with him.

"As long as the tent doesn't go with it, I don't care." I slide a hand down to grip his ass and pull him more firmly against me. "I can fuck you just as well on the floor as the cot."

Lex blinks, stares at me for a long moment and then bursts out laughing. "Is that what you're planning to do, then?"

"Uh...after this long in separate beds, I thought that was obvious. Unless you don't want to." This thing between us isn't brand new anymore, but it's still new enough for me to be learning to read him in new ways.

"Oh, I want to," he says, tilting his head up to kiss me again. "You've just never been that direct about it before. It took me by surprise."

"I can go back to fumbling around for the words to say I want to kiss you if you'd like?"

"No. Christ, no. We wasted years like that, and I missed being with you too much to wait for you to find the words. The ones you said will do just fine." He hooks a leg around my hips, bringing us into closer contact.

"I should get the lube..."

"That would be appreciated, yes." He doesn't help by not unwrapping from around me, causing me to awkwardly squirm with him down to the footlocker at the end of our cot.

"I need you to let go to be able to get it, though. You can finish getting naked while I do that." It's half suggestion, half appeasement to stop his pouting before it can form.

He sighs, but acquiesces, and, by the time I've fished the lube out, he's out of his boxer briefs and lounging naked on the bed. If you'd told me six months ago that such a sight would leave my mouth dry and my hands a little shaky, I might have believed you because I'd been sneaking peeks at Lex for years, but I could never have imagined the effect of all that golden skin laid out just for me to touch and savor. My chest tightens because he's just so damn beautiful, and my cock starts to harden in anticipation just from the view. It brings me back to something I've thought about a lot while he's been sleeping across the camp, and that I think I finally have the nerve to try. When I stretch back out on the bed, I settle myself between his legs, hands on his hips, at right about eye level with his dick.

"Wh-whatcha doing?" When I glance up, his eyes are wide, pupils blown, and he looks a little nervous—excited, but nervous.

"I thought about it a lot while you were gone, and I want to try this."

"You don't have to." His words are almost so fast as to trip him up.

"I know I don't have to. I want to. You do it for me all the time. I should return the favor." At least once.

"And if you hate it?"

"Then I have ten fingers very willing to be put at your disposal."

He chuckles, then suppresses the smile. "Seriously, Mike..."

"Seriously, Lex...the bigger deal you make of it, the more nervous I get. I mean, I was nervous going down on a girl the first time, too. At least I know what feels good on the receiving end, with this."

That must be a convincing enough argument, because he lays back against the pillows and brushes his fingers through my hair. Now, I'm just faced with his dick in a close-up view I haven't really had before. Hell, I've never had this close of a look at my own dick, and I find myself compelled to touch more than anything else. I run one finger up his length, tracing the vein on the underside and watch, delighted, as it twitches under my touch. Lex is holding very still—almost too still, and I don't want him to be afraid to move, so I move my hand to his hip to massage there in hopes of getting him to relax. When he does, at least a little, I take a deep breath to steady my nerves and lean in to lick a wet stripe up him from root to tip. There's a bead of pre-come at his slit. That's what I'm most nervous about, afraid I'll gag at the taste of him, so I test that out first, lapping it up. It's not really what I expect, this mix of salt, musk, and a touch of sweetness. Hardly the disgusting concoction my fear made it out to be.

More confident, I call on the memory of every blow job I've ever received and slide my mouth over him. I'm not expecting the immediate stretch for some reason, and the tension that wrapping around him puts on my mouth. I don't know why it surprises me. Exhaling, I slowly sink my mouth down on him, feeling him get tense again under me. I steady his dick with my hand wrapped around his base and decide I can take him in until my mouth reaches my hand. His dick hits the back of my throat, just as I reach my fingers, and I gag a little, pulling back up until it's comfortable.

"Don't try to take too much," he murmurs, like he's going to walk me through this, which will be kind of awkward. "It feels good, even if you keep it shallower."

I know this from being on the receiving end, but I think it's a point of pride to be able to take all of him. Maybe, however, it's something to work up to. I slide down again to the point right before he's at the back of my mouth and that's more comfortable. Eventually, I remember to use my tongue, as well, as I suck back to his tip and then sink back down. It takes a few more slow explorations before I feel ready to set a rhythm, bobbing down and up his length, taking him deeper for a stroke or two, then slipping back to something more comfortable.

I'm surprised to find that the overall taste of him isn't unpleasant—it's less of an adjustment than the first time I did this for a girl, actually. What I'm not expecting is how soon and how much my jaw starts to ache. Lex wriggles a time or two, but mostly stays still, any roll of his hips aborted, and I realize he's trying to not make me gag by thrusting too deeply. While I appreciate the gesture, I don't want both of us overthinking this, so I tug on his hip a little to encourage him to move.

Eventually, he thrusts up into my mouth, just a bit, and, as he probably worried, I do gag the first time. He murmurs another instruction, encouraging me to relax my throat. I don't really know what that means, but I try to implement the instruction, willing my tongue and throat to just relax, and the next time he thrusts up, I'm able to take him deeper. Not all the way, but I feel surer that I'll be able to work up to that. I test out different things that I like having done—different amounts of suction, different moves with my tongue—gauging by his moans to learn what he likes best. He's as responsive as ever, encouraging my efforts, and I find a rhythm of suction on his length and tonguing around his head that seems to suit us both.

I reach for his hand to grab the lube and slick up my fingers. I was serious about wanting to fuck him—I need to be inside him, to feel that connection—and now seems like as good a time as any to make sure he's ready for me.

This is something that I've learned to do since our first time but coordinating my mouth and my fingers makes me feel like I'm trying to pat my head and rub my stomach at the same time. I have to pause my suction to just hold his dick halfway in my mouth until I'm able to press a finger into him. Once I'm in and have found his prostate, I start moving my mouth again until I'm able to match the rhythm of mouth and finger, pressing in as I take him in.

My jaw is seriously starting to ache, but the sounds he's making encourage me to keep going, because I can't imagine stopping at this point. He's leaking pre-come into my mouth, and it's still a weird taste and texture, but I'm getting used to it. My own dick is aching in response to what I'm doing, and I figure that's a good thing. I don't have a hand free to do anything about it, but I roll my hips into the cot below me for some friction. It at least takes my mind off the ache in my jaw. The pace of his hips changes as he fucks himself back on my fingers and into my mouth. They stutter and he murmurs a warning that he's close. Unsure about taking his whole load in my mouth, I pull off and take over with my hand. It lets me lift my head for a better view of him as he starts to come undone. His moans get sharper, escaping on panting breaths until he tenses and starts to spurt, covering my hand and his stomach. I keep stroking him through it, taking the opportunity of his relaxation to stretch him just a bit more until I'm sure he's ready to take me.

Wiping my hand off on the blanket, I wriggle up to stretch out against his side. I clean him up with his discarded shirt, then wrap an arm around him, content to hold him until he's ready for more.

He pries his eyes open and gives me a dopey smile. "Not bad for your first time. Not bad at all."

I'm probably inordinately proud of myself for that and smile back at him. "It wasn't really anything like I imagined."

"Your jaw aches way more than expected, huh?"

"Yeah. Any way to lessen that?"

He huffs out a laugh. "I'm sure there is, but I haven't found it, yet. If you figure it out, let me know. A lot of the time, I just get so into it, I forget about it, I guess, until it's done."

His eyes drift closed again, and I will my dick to have patience. Even if he falls asleep, he rarely stays that way for long before he wakes up, ready to go again. That's true this time, too, as maybe ten minutes later his fingers start sliding up and down my side. He rolls to his side, facing me, and slides his fingers around my hip to stroke up my aching dick.

"I should probably do something about this, hmm?" he asks, giving me a teasing smile.

"You could just roll on up to your hands and knees." I hold up the lube and wiggle it a little.

"Sounds like a plan." He leans in to kiss me, then does as I've suggested. He winces, though, and eases back down to his elbows. "Not sure I can support my weight on an extended arm, yet. This do?"

"This'll do," I assure him. I push up onto my knees, too, to slide around behind him. Like all the other views of him, this one is spectacular, especially when he glances over his shoulder to give me another smile. We've tried a number of different positions, all with their charms. This isn't actually my favorite, because I like being able to watch him and see his reactions, but it is where I feel like I have the most control. After how out of control I've felt since we started up that mountain, a little control here won't go amiss. Impatient to be connected to him again, I slick myself quickly, line up with his hole and slowly push inside, moaning at how hot and tight he is around me. Maybe too tight.

"You okay?" I ask, pausing my forward motion.

"Fuck. Yes. Don't stop." As if to assure me he's all on board, Lex pushes back onto me, taking me deeper.

I've been proud of my restraint and self-control for what feels like hours now, but as I am fully sheathed in him, my body remembers how scared I was that I'd finally found him only to lose him, and my ability to hold still flies out the window. I'm still careful in the force behind the pace I set, but I do set a pace that's not going to let me last that long. I angle my hips downward the way I've learned will let me thrust against his prostate, and it's only a short time before his moans are echoing my grunts and there aren't really any more coherent words as we let our bodies take over until I feel my orgasm rush through and out of me. I spill deep inside him, and just manage to catch myself before I collapse against his back. He might have been released from physical therapy, but he shows his shoulder is still healing when his bent and braced arm still gives out a bit beneath him and he sinks back down to the mattress, trembling. Only when I pull out and settle on the bed again to pull him into my arms do I realize that he's come again and is already drifting toward a far deeper sleep. I get us both cleaned up as best I can, then pull the blanket over us before I follow him into the best sleep I've had in weeks.

CHAPTER 21

September 2012

Lex

They keep us in Afghanistan for a little over a full year. We get a few days of leave here and there, but not enough to go home. Instead, we travel around Asia with Ronan and Isaac, visiting places I never really expected to see, like Tokyo and Hong Kong. When our deployment to Afghanistan is done, our human counterparts are sent home for at least a few months before they can redeploy again. Not so much for MagCorps. There haven't been any further attacks back home, at least not on a large scale, but the attacks in Afghanistan continue steadily and our tour holds the record for the most losses of MagCorps personnel in history. Even that doesn't win us any reprieve, and it's never been more obvious that we aren't seen as people, but commodities to be used but not protected.

Instead of sending us home, they send us to Iraq. At least the active fighting has largely died down here—we're mostly here to provide backup for Iraqi forces and keep the ever-precious oil fields of the Middle East secured. It's menial, mind-numbing work and not the best use for our skills, but I suppose it keeps us out of trouble. We still do find ourselves in firefights on occasion. Once, even, we find ourselves facing magical attacks, which should be a game changer. Only us and our Western allies have had anything like MagCorps. That the insurgents are using magic users comes as a shock and costs us a couple of people. We aren't trained to fight our own, but we learn on the fly, and the attacks slow down and then stop.

We've been in country almost a year, are finally preparing to ship back out home when things go sideways again. It's movie night, and we're set up in the tent we've set aside for recreation. The projector is aimed at the big screen up front, and the smell of popcorn fills the air in the tent. Spirits are high, everyone looking forward to being back stateside, as the movie starts. Mike and I are sharing a bag of popcorn, lounging on a ratty blow-up sofa with Isaac and Ronan on the ground in front of us. The movie is some cheesy action flick, utterly forgettable in how it blurs into every other action flick, but it keeps us entertained until we're headed into the final big showdown. Just as the scene starts, when we're all leaning forward, eyes fixed on the screen, there's a swell of magic that flares up from the ley lines. I've never felt anything like it, even when using ley line magic and pulling it into myself, but for a second, it almost pulls me back under with it as it ebbs. I hear Mike calling my name and shake my head to clear it. I look around to see if anyone else was affected, but it's utterly dark in the tent. Anything giving off any light is out, including the movie. There's a rise and fall of shocked voices around me and then several witchlights pop into existence. I call up my own and see my friends blinking in its glow. Everyone looks stunned.

"What was that?" Isaac asks, even as voices behind us demand the movie be turned back on.

"Power's out," the sergeant running the video equipment says with an apologetic shrug.

Voices are yelling outside, though I can't make out what they're saying. My mind goes to what seems the most obvious.

"They found a way to use the ley lines against us," I theorize, "And it sounds like we're under attack."

I get up and move to the tent door, ducking out into the camp only to find it nearly pitch dark in the desolation of the desert. A few witchlights glow here and there, but not many and not enough to let me see well. The stars are still visible, and I can feel Mike's hand on my arm, which keeps me from utterly panicking at thinking my nightmare has come true. I don't hear any shots being fired, at least; everyone just seems thrown into confusion as they scurry around trying to restore power—the majority of the witchlights are shining near our generators, and I make my way over there, the other three trailing behind me.

Lieutenant Colonel Greeley is overseeing a squad at the generators.

"What happened?" Mike asks.

"Hell if I know," the colonel responds. "Some kind of magical power surge and the generators all died."

"Yeah, we felt the surge, too," I volunteer, glancing at Ronan and Isaac, who are nodding. "Should we station extra security, sir?" It still seems most likely to be a new attack tactic, like a magical EMP. Confuse and disorient us, then come in and pick us off.

"Already done," Greeley says, giving me a nod. "Stay alert tonight. I want the four of you on second watch, east side of camp."

The east side is opposite the generators and faces the mountains.

"Yes, sir," we all say before heading for our tent. Second watch will come quickly and take up most of the rest of the night. We've learned to sleep when we can these past two years.

After we're all settled in our racks, none of us find sleep.

"I've never felt anything like that," Isaac says into the pitch dark.

"Me, neither." We all agree.

"I never would have thought to use the ley lines themselves as any kind of targeted conveyance," Mike adds.

"I don't know how it's even theoretically possible," Isaac says. I can hear the frown in his voice.

"Based on the theory we've studied, it isn't," I say. "But maybe Captain Parsons will be able to explain. Maybe it's just theory we haven't learned, yet."

"Maybe we should," Ronan says. "As far as battlefield applications go, it's powerful."

We discuss it a while longer, though we reach no conclusions as one by one the others drift off. I can hear Mike breathing slowly and deeply next to me and roll over and into him, snuggling close. His arm automatically wraps around me and that helps as I try not to panic at this development. Something's really wrong, but we're not going to figure it out tonight. I just know, somehow, this won't have an easy solution.

Mike

Second watch is uneventful except for the impenetrable darkness. For security, we're all allowed to use only the bare minimum of witchlight to do what we need to do—no need to make ourselves a target in the dark. Our senior officers have warded the camp as best they can, and it's part of our job to keep the wards charged and shields up. But for all our precautions, no attack comes before the sky starts to lighten and the sun peeks over the mountains to illuminate a camp still on the edges of chaos. Everyone emerges from their tents, expecting for shit to be fixed. When it isn't, they all start milling around, asking questions no one has answers to. No one falls into formation for PT, and no reprimands come for that failure. The further disruption of routine just makes the volume of the voices grow.

We head to the mess tent after our watch ends to discover breakfast is cold cereal—there's no power to cook anything and we need to drink the milk before it goes bad. We've all had worse breakfasts in the field, so no one complains about their Cheerios.

After breakfast, we stay where we are for a briefing. The news isn't good. All our physical communication equipment is useless—nothing worked to get the generators working. What's more, there's nothing wrong with the generators that the mechanics can find. They've just stopped working. Everything has, even things with fully charged batteries. Luckily, supernaturals have other ways of communicating, even long distance. Such magical communication has let us contact other camps in the area and even back home, and that's where the news gets worse.

It's not just us.

Everyone we've been able to contact is in the same boat—nothing that relies on electricity is working. The magical surge that hit us hit everywhere and, at least temporarily, has knocked working technology to what existed pre-Industrial Revolution. It's not just the United States, either. From what we've been able to determine, it's a worldwide phenomenon. The loss of life is already catastrophic and only predicted to grow—automobiles abruptly stopped working, but momentum didn't, leading to countless traffic accidents and fatalities. Planes fell from the sky, killing passengers and people on the ground. Life support technology and other medical equipment stopped, too. No one had any warning or time to prepare, so the outlook is dire the longer the power is out—water treatment plants aren't working, which will lead to a lot of disease. The looting has already started for food and bottled water. The only lucky thing is that it's spring—no one in the main temperate zone of the globe is going to freeze or die of heat exhaustion. Everyone hopes this is just a temporary situation, obviously, but the entire power grid of the world is down, and no one knows why or how to fix it because no one understands what caused it. "Magic" is all anyone has, and we all groan at that, practically able to hear the bigots blaming the supernatural community from here.

We exist in what feels like a state of suspended animation for the next two weeks, waiting for the power to come back. It doesn't. It's clear our superior officers are as stumped as we are—no one knows what to do, because there are no orders coming in. We've had some communication with HQ, but things are dire back home. The government is in chaos and unable to tell anyone what to do with those of us deployed. The Queens are less in chaos, but equally baffled. The general consensus seems to be to keep waiting, but, as the days tick by, that becomes less tenable. The hard fact is there's nothing else we can do. There are no planes or battleships coming to take us home. No one's coming to refill our supplies, either, and they're starting to run low. Luckily, we had the foresight to dig a well when we established the camp, so we have water. We also have the shifters, who are master hunters, though even they are taxed with trying to bring back enough game for everyone. At least where we are there are herds of fallow deer and wild boar, so the game is plentiful enough that we're unlikely to starve. Fig and apricot trees will help keep scurvy at bay.

Still, the longer we're waiting for orders, the more restless everyone gets. After three weeks, there are fewer people present each morning. Even LTC Greeley starts to look restless.

"I'm not sure how much longer we can stay here," he confides in us one night over a campfire meal of wild boar and figs.

"Where would we go?" Ronan asks.

"To the city, to see what evacuation we can coordinate," LTC Greely responds.

"With all due respect, sir," Lex says. "The Iraqis aren't likely to be considering evacuating. To where? They're home. And the cities are probably far deadlier than out here."

"I'm open to suggestions," LTC Greeley says with a sigh.

"We head west," Isaac says, sounding decisive. "To the Mediterranean Sea. Once we get to Syria or Israel, we find a boat."

"Why west?" I ask. "Why not head up to Turkey or through Iran to the Caspian Sea, or even south to the Persian Gulf?"

Isaac sighs. "Because the Caspian Sea and Persian Gulf will require a lot more navigation to get us to the Mediterranean than if we just head straight there. We're more likely to be able to find a suitable boat—something seaworthy—on the bigger body of water, too."

"You want to, what? Sail home in a fishing boat?" LTC Greeley scoffs a little.

"In a sailboat, yeah," Isaac returns. "I don't care if it was used for fishing or not, but. Yes, it's crazy, and it won't be easy, but it's been done. People sail across the Atlantic all the time to challenge themselves. And we'd have the advantage over most of them. All of us working together can at least partly control the weather to keep it in our favor, and we can purify and desalinate the water with magic."

"One major problem with that is that I don't know how to sail," LTC Greeley says, though he sounds more thoughtful than before.

"I do," Isaac replies. "I practically grew up on sailboats—it was my dad's great love, after my mom, and he made sure we all knew how to handle a boat with a skeleton crew. I can do most of what needs doing and show you all how to help me. We make it to Tel Aviv or Beirut, and we'll find a boat that can make the trip."

"What if everyone with a boat has taken it and fled?" Lex asks.

"As you said—to where?" Isaac leans in, clearly warming to his idea. "Most people aren't prepared to undertake a long journey without an engine, but engines are a fairly recent invention in the world of sailing. My dad never liked using one except in an emergency. We can carry MREs with us and fish along the way. It's about 500 miles to Beirut, so, we plan on 12 to 15 miles a day, for maybe 40 days on the road. Crossing should take us another 40 or 50 days to Charleston, depending on how good of wind we can get," he pauses, doing some calculations, if the way he counts on his fingers is any indication. "So, we're home in maybe three months. Four if we suck at weather control, even when using collective power."

Three to four months sounds like forever of a journey, but we've just been sitting here for almost one month already.

"Unless the power comes back, there's really no other way home," I say. "So, even if orders come through, they'll end up being something like this."

"And if power comes back while we're on the road, ex-cellent," Isaac says. "Someone can pick us up, pop us on a plane."

"We do this, and technically, we're going AWOL," Ronan interjects.

"I'd rather be court martialed for being proactive than sit around here waiting for orders that might never come," Lex says, looking over at me.

"Same," I tell him, before glancing at the others. Isaac and LTC Greeley are nodding, though Ronan seems unsure. "Do we tell anyone else? Take anyone else?"

"Boat the size we can man won't hold more than a couple more of us," Isaac offers. "Six at most."

"Then just the five of us," LTC Greeley says, sounding decided.

"Six." A familiar voice speaks from the darkness before Captain Parsons steps into the glow from our firelight. "I know a bit about sailing, so I can help teach the rest of you."

"Six," Isaac agrees.

Lex is still looking a little unsure, and I find myself reaching for his hand and squeezing, giving him an inquiring look.

"Maybe we can't take any more," he says, quietly, looking around. "But we also can't just abandon them without any explanation. We're the officers; they're looking to us, and they're our responsibility. Do we know what the Queens are doing? I know, theoretically, there could be a magical way home that none of us are powerful enough to do. Or... historical tall ships that could hold a lot, if not all, of us. Further, we're not the only camp, even. What about the others? What about those that don't have a MagCorps contingent? They might not even know what's going on."

He breaks off, looking a little surprised at his own out-pouring of words. I'm not, though. He might not be overly altruistic, but he's always cared about other people. Everyone else looks a little chagrined in the firelight, with Isaac frowning in thought.

"*We* don't know what's going on," Ronan says into the silence, which just deepens it in some ways, because what we do know isn't something we probably should share with mundane humans, for our own safety.

"Tall ships could work," Isaac says, finally. "I don't know of any on display in the Middle East, but there are several in the U.S. that are probably even still seaworthy or could be made so. Maine still has a ton of shipyards working with wood. Same for Europe. We'd need several to evacuate all American servicepeople here, and it would be a slow process, but it could be done."

"The logistics would be the hardest part," LTC Greeley muses. "Coordinating it without working communications equipment..."

"We could send witches as volunteer communications officers," Lex says. "Set them up with the spell work you have to talk to MagCorps HQ."

Captain Parsons finally takes a seat, nodding. "That could work."

"What about steam engines?" Lex asks, sitting up more, looking almost excited as he pulls out some U.S. Naval history. "The USS Kitty Hawk was just decommissioned a few years ago. She ran on steam, not electric generators."

"Steam's a possibility," LTC Greeley says with a nod. "We don't know if enough steam engines would still function after whatever this is, because there are so few left. I don't know of anyone who's checked, at least. We'd have to reengineer a lot to make them viable long-term."

"I'm not talking about long-term, yet, sir," Lex interjects. "I just mean to get folks home. And, surely, we can help things along with magic? MagCorps often did that in the old days, right?"

LTC Greely nods at him, an approving smile curving his lips, and I have to acknowledge that maybe all that history studying is paying off.

"That's all well and good for the future," Ronan says. "But what about now?"

"Now...for now, we tell people our plan," Lex says, tone more commanding than I've heard from him outside of talking strategy in the locker rooms before games in high school. I'm reminded of why he was inevitably the captain of most of the teams he was on. "We can't just disappear. There might be other sailors who can do what we're doing, and maybe we take more than one boat to go home and start working to get everyone else home. With the Queens' resources and the technical and magical archives in New Orleans, we can figure out a plan and then send word back." He looks at the Lieutenant Colonel. "Can you do what's needed to set up more of those who stay behind as communications officers?

LTC Greeley nods. "It's a simple spell, much like the interpersonal ones and squad ones we already have. It just needs a focus and anchor to work over long distances and across the ocean. The saltwater weakens it otherwise."

"We could tether it to the ley lines here, if we need to," I add, feeling like I need to contribute, too.

Captain Parsons takes my idea and runs with it, and by the time we turn in, we have something that looks like a workable plan in place. Lex even sketches out how to get word to camps without a MagCorps contingent. He declares we should try and get everyone in the Middle East to a central location, like Baghdad. Isaac collaborates with him and suggests sending shifter volunteers to the human camps and to Baghdad, to extend their food supplies and maybe generate a little goodwill, while we're at it. That way, they are not over-relying on the civilian population for resources. Lex even comes up with ideas about central locations for troops deployed or stationed in other areas of the world: Europe, Japan, Korea, even Hawaii. Isaac and Captain Parsons settle in with maps to chart our course to the sea. Ronan's the least enthusiastic about our endeavor, but he still accepts his assigned tasks willingly, helping LTC Greeley induct new communications techs, while I start getting Lex and myself packed.

CHAPTER 22

Lex

It takes us nearly a week to get everything finalized to leave. LTC Greeley gets the communication spell set up on about twenty volunteers—witches and mages who agree to stay behind and help the other camps. Several shifters stay behind, as well, to keep hunting for the camp. But three more groups of six choose to join us, with enough folks able to sail to make it possible. We're all able to carry our own gear, though we also acknowledge that finding some pack animal might be useful.

We've got at least one shifter in each group, though, which will make finding a pack animal able to stand traveling with us hard. Shifters make animals nervous. Granted, we have nothing to trade for it, and probably no one wants our currency in a world that can't really be tracking it that well anymore, so we resign ourselves to nearly 1000 kilometers with 40-pound packs. I'm glad none of the mundane humans around choose to join us—they might all be Marines, sure, but the distance on our feet is intimidating.

It's impossible to not draw comparisons to the Crucible. It seems laughable now that we felt like 40 miles was a lot to do in 56 hours, even with events interspersed between marches. Our packs are heavier this time—we need more than 2 MREs each and have to carry our ammunition with us, rather than having it waiting at each station. It helps that we can use magic to lighten the weight of our packs and expand our carry capabilities.

It helps, too, to have the shifters. Just like in camp, they hunt most days, so we can supplement our food rations. We witches can find water sources and purify what we find. They're not as regular as they would be out of the desert, but there's enough to keep us from getting severely dehydrated. At least the weather isn't as brutal this time of year—temperatures are usually in the upper 70s to low 80s Fahrenheit, while we're moving, which, after a summer of over 100 actually feels good, which helps with both distance and need for water. At least it's not humid. Some of the witches, including me, can manage to multiply the water supplies, as well. I'm left in awe, still, when I think of the desert nomadic tribes who have lived and traveled out here for thousands of years, without any supernatural abilities. When the temperatures drop at night, they don't go far below 65, plus we have fires and the ability to heat our tents with magic.

At first, it feels like an adventure, but after a week, we're all sick of it. However, we're also aware that compared to crossing the Atlantic Ocean in a small boat, in the winter, this is probably the easy part. After we find our rhythm, LTC Greeley estimates we're managing around 20km a day. We stay on the road for about ten hours a day, breaking early enough for a good dinner and to get some sleep.

We don't see anyone else as we walk. A few abandoned cars litter the road, and even the few villages we pass are abandoned, animals and people both gone. It's desolate, giving a feeling like we're the only ones left, and I get a chill when I wonder how many places are like this back home. Surely not many, right? We have so many more people that you'd have to run into someone, walking for days.

Mike and I share a tent at night, as do most of the other soulmate pairs in the groups, but even allowing for distance between tents and soundproofing spells, there isn't much privacy, and by the end of the second week, I'm missing it. We're generally too tired to do anything more than fall into our sleeping bags and sleep, anyway, but it's still difficult to feel like we're so close but still so far. There's still the intimacy of touch, sleeping close together once cleansing spells take the worst of the day's grime away. But the daily sameness leaves us with little to talk about, no moments that are just ours. As a group, we take to telling stories both as we walk and around the campfire at night, something we've come to excel at to amuse ourselves in the last two years. Turns out Captain Parsons is a fount of lore about the magic of the region with its roots running back to the dawn of human civilization. Isaac and I are fascinated. Mike and Ronan, not so much, but they seem to find it better than silence, coming up with questions to ask when Parsons falls quiet.

Isaac and Captain Parsons estimate it will take us between three and four weeks to make it to Jerusalem at our average pace. Our route takes up through Damascus, where we plan to pause to try and restock some supplies--it ultimately seemed safer to head for Israel than Lebanon. Syria's not precisely friendly territory since the

Syrian Civil War broke out, but apparently a lot can be forgiven when the world shuts down.

Even so, when we're just a mile or so outside Damascus, we pause and LTC Greeley tells us to take off our Mag-Corps patches.

"There's a strong local coven here that has garnered political protection, somehow," he tells us. "But witchcraft is still technically a capital offence. They made allowances for foreign troops before the war, but I don't think we want to test anything now."

The suburbs of the city aren't as empty as the villages we've come through, but people run inside as we approach, casting wary glances at our weapons. The abandoned cars just get thicker the closer we get to what should be civilization, until we're forced to walk on the side of the road rather than on the pavement. Instead of fear, we get some hostile looks as we near the city, but no one gives us any trouble. Occasional shouts—and even screams—in the distance tell me others aren't as lucky as those of us marching in an armed group of twenty-four.

The city is terrifying in its silence. No traffic, no radios, no TV sets. It's dark, as night falls, though someone has rigged up lanterns where the streetlights were, so we have more light than we did in the desert. Flickering lights—candlelight, I realize—illuminate occasional windows, but too many others sit dark and broken. Storefronts we pass gape open through shattered glass. Fires burn here and there, with no one to put them out. It feels like we're walking on the set of some postapocalyptic movie, but this is real life. LTC Greeley directs us through the streets until we reach one that's well-lit. It hits me after a moment that the lights are witchlight and seem to be spilling primarily from a very well-lit building ahead of us—a hospital, I realize. Rising out of the darkness, it almost looks normal.

"It's all magic," Mike murmurs, and LTC Greeley nods.

"My sources say it's how the coven is trying to keep safe—keeping medical services running as best they can by offering up their own healers. Magic can't get the generators to run any more than it could back at camp, but it can make the physical parts of things like ventilators move or replace their purpose."

"They're making themselves indispensable," I murmur to Ronan.

"Good for them," Isaac offers.

Across from the hospital is another well-lit building. It takes us a moment to recognize it, but the steam venting out finally clues us in that it's a hammam—a Turkish style bathhouse we're all thrilled to see is still functioning.

"The local coven has been running it for years," LTC Greeley tells us before suggesting our squad visit—a couple of others choose to push on and camp on the other side of the city, wary of coming in to a place known to be run by witches, which may be wise, but I think is foolish the second I get a look at the steam in the bathhouse. "They're able to keep the water running and hot, at least."

They're also, as it turns out, happy to help out fellow supernaturals in a part of the world where they're more persecuted than anything we've seen back home. That's not in evidence now, with the hammam doing a lot of business when we arrive.

It's heaven to sink into the hot water, but even better are the soaps and shampoos available. Cleansing spells might have made it bearable to be around each other, but we all spring for the scrub by a bathing attendant. Night has fallen by the time we're all clean, and we're further delighted to find that the coven members have even laundered our uniforms for us—no pulling back on grungy, salt and sand encrusted clothes over our freshly scrubbed bodies. The coven priestess comes to greet us herself and offers us lodging at a nearby inn owned by her family. LTC Greeley gives the group that pushed on our ETA for the morning.

"It may not be the luxury mattresses they have at the Hilton," I tell Mike, falling back onto the bed in our room—bonus of staying with supernaturals in a country where our relationship could get us up to three years in prison, if not worse. "But it's still the best thing I've ever felt."

I pat the bed, inviting him to feel, and he throws himself down next to me with a moan. "We could just move here. Join this coven..."

"Medical outreach notwithstanding, the authorities here make the militias back home seem like children playing at witch trials," I remind him. "But I think we should enjoy it to the fullest, while we're here, if only for tonight."

I pull out a little vial of oil the priestess gave me for any "rituals" I might want to perform and wiggle it at him with a smirk. "Who knows when we'll have a real bed in a room to ourselves again? Maybe Jerusalem, but maybe not until we're back home..."

I've barely finished speaking when he's already pulling off his boots, followed by his uniform.

Mike

I didn't think that I could be this sex-starved after just a few weeks, especially when I've gotten to hold Lex every night, unlike when he was in the hospital, but when he pulls out that oil, the only thing I can think about is being inside him again.

We've still got our pants on, barely, when a knock interrupts us, and a shy young witch enters with a tray of food. I think it can wait, but Lex lays the dishes out on the small table in our room and pulls me to it.

"We should make sure we keep our strength up," he tells me, almost demurely, the tease.

The food is fantastic, though, prepared rather than just spit-roasted over a fire or eaten out of a vacuum sealed package. But as soon as he's finished, I tug him back to the bed, and work on taking our pants off.

He pushes me back on the bed, stretching out between my legs before sliding his mouth over me. It might not be where I'd intended to go, but we'll get there, and I'm never going to complain about sliding into the wet heat of his mouth. After weeks, it's like heaven, like when he was finally healed enough to come back to our rack with me all over again. His tongue makes me forget the hardships of the road, and the wet suction sends me flying. The sound of him jerking himself off to the same rhythm he's set with his mouth is just as heady. Part of me wants to stop him before this is over too soon, but he feels too good and my orgasm hits hard and fast. A few moments later, he moans around his own orgasm. In a move I still can't quite believe comes from me, I tug him up to lie on top of me while I kiss him, shivering a little at the salty taste of myself on his lips.

"Missed this more than I thought," he murmurs against my lips. "After waiting years for it, I guess I hate feeling like we're forced back to where we were before you told me how you felt."

"We'll never go back to that," I promise rashly. "Even if we aren't able to get in quality naked time, we still can feel each other, are part of each other in ways I still don't fully understand."

It's the right thing to say if his smile is anything to go by. I hold him for a while, just running my hands over his skin until my cock remembers this might be its only chance for action for a while and takes a renewed interest in the naked Lex pressed against me.

With the urgency dampened, at least, we're better able to take it slow, the way we used to be able to before we deployed, were sharing a tent with Isaac and Ronan, and had to schedule private time in advance. Lex's skin is warm when he settles under me, smelling sweet and spicy from the soaps at the bathhouse. His body moves with mine when I press into him, and I wonder how I let so many years go by when I could have had him like this but was too scared to try. Never again, I vow, as his lips take mine in a hungry kiss, and his legs wrap around me, pulling me deeper into him. The languor eventually wears off, the urgency to climax taking over, and I grip his hips tightly as I thrust harder and faster into him, marveling at how he matches me. I don't want to hurt him, but he's urging me on with grunts and pleas. When we come, this time, it's just as intense—I feel him spending between our stomachs and the clench of his body sends me over the edge into my own climax.

As usual, he's the first to pull away, fetching a wet cloth to clean us both up, then curling up against my side again. Our legs tangle, and he keeps up lazy kisses and murmurs of love until we both fall asleep.

The same shy witch wakes us with breakfast and assures us the others are just getting up. We eat, then take advantage of the shower across the hall, not turning down a chance to be fully clean again. When we meet the other four in the inn's lobby, they look similarly refreshed, and Ronan's got a bruise on his neck that suggests Isaac let his wolf-side out just a bit last night. They both look very satisfied. LTC Greeley and Captain Parsons appear well-rested, at least. After effusive thanks to our hosts, we gear up and head out again to meet the other squads on the south side of the city, so we can continue to Jerusalem.

CHAPTER 23

Lex

"I wonder if this is the same road Paul was on," I ask, an hour or so after we've left Damascus behind.

"What?" Ronan asks, and I shrug a little.

"When he was on his way from Jerusalem to persecute the Christians in Damascus, but spoke to Jesus instead and converted," I explain.

Isaac and Ronan look like they don't care, but a panther shifter from the squad behind us double times it forward to fall in beside me.

"I was just wondering that, too," she tells me with a smile.

"You're a witch," Ronan says. "Why do you care? You don't actually believe he saw Jesus, do you? It's probably just a myth."

I don't really want to get into a theological debate. I know the fact that I was raised going to church until we left for New Orleans is rare among witches, but I don't think Christianity in its pure form automatically clashes with being a witch. The Goddess is real. Why not Jesus?

And their core message is largely the same. Maybe they're both part of the same true thing that none of us will ever know for sure until we die. Just...people suck and mess shit up a lot of the time.

"Maybe," I acknowledge, nodding at Ronan. "But I like a good redemption story, and Paul's conversion is a doozy. He, at least, existed. There's historical proof of that. And he did convert to Christianity after being one of their prime persecutors. Something happened on this road."

"That seems to be a logical conclusion," Captain Parsons interjects. "The historical record absolutely supports him being a real person, as well as people he met in his ministry."

"Jesus, as a person, was real, too," Mike says, which surprises me to hear him chime in. "Whether he was divine, I guess, is the matter of faith."

"Which leads back to the question of what happened on this road," the panther shifter says.

Ronan sighs, but doesn't push back, clearly not thinking it worth arguing, if no one's going to insist it was a divine visitation Paul experienced. I smile at the shifter and go back to trying to recall other stories that might be linked to this road. She falls back to her squad, and I can't think of anything specific to add.

"How long do you think it will take to find and supply the boats?" I ask Isaac.

"I'm estimating about a week, especially with needing four of them."

"And the port is how far outside the city?"

"About a two-day march."

"So, we won't actually be staying in Jerusalem for long?" I can't help the flicker of disappointment.

"Probably not. Why?" Isaac sends me a bemused look.

Mike answers for me, "He wants to play tourist in case we never make it back here."

He's not wrong. Isaac rolls his eyes at me.

"We should be able to do some of that on the way," Captain Parsons offers. "We'll be going right by the Sea of Galilee. Cutting through Nazareth would be easy. The River Jordan—we'll be along it for a while, too. Bethlehem is past Jerusalem, though, so that's out of our way."

"Nazareth would be cool," I say, sure Isaac is going to shut me down. I think he starts to, but a chorus of agreement rings out from the squads behind us.

Overruled before he can voice objections, Isaac nods. "It might add a couple of days to the trek, but it would also give us a chance to rest with easy access to water."

"Let's do it, then," LTC Greeley says, and it's a plan.

Mike

Lex has a renewed bounce in his step as soon as he's got Captain Parsons and LTC Greeley on his side. I wouldn't have made the suggestion for myself, but the history buff in Lex just can't resist, and I'm glad to walk a bit more if it makes him happy.

So, we play tourists for a while. When we get to the Sea of Galilee, we discover there's a Jesus trail for hiking that goes to Nazareth and passes through several areas of Biblical interest. Lex and Captain Parsons are delighted. Several of the rest of us just eye the beach wistfully, but it's too cold for water activities, and it's not like the jet skis or ski boats are running anyway. No music, no ice cream. We picnic on the Mount of Beatitudes, camping by the sea for the night, where Lex insists we eat fish and bread—a nice change bought with a gemstone the high priestess in Damascus gave us to better barter with on our journey. Lex's sheer fascination and delight turns even Isaac around, and the wolf starts playing tour guide, reading off the importance of each stop along the trail from the detailed map we pick up from an abandoned tourist hut in Capernaum.

There's a suggested four-to-five-day itinerary. Isaac might have come around, but he still gets us to do it in four. We spent a full day in Nazareth, finding the supernatural community there to be as welcoming as that in Damascus. The town itself is nearly as deserted, but somehow not as bleak—maybe because so much of it existed before the area had much access to electricity. They insist on sending word to the coven in Jerusalem, so they'll be prepared to welcome us.

And welcome us, they do. We're taken first to the al-Ayn hammam which is just as wonderful as the one in Damascus. The coven splits us up to let us stay in members' homes, and Lex and I end up in the home of a witch and shifter pair who treat us like family.

LTC Greeley must talk to Isaac about the need for keeping up morale or something, because those mainly responsible for sailing leave the rest of us in Jerusalem to keep playing tourists while they go on to Ashdod. We're meant to follow in a couple of days, but until then, Lex goes fully into tourist and historian mode. Ronan's gone with Isaac, but the panther shifter Lex has been talking to stays to sightsee, too, so she, Lex and Captain Parsons can talk about the Biblical sites that we have largely to ourselves without causing a debate. Ronan had been good about not saying anything on the Jesus Trail, but it was clear he was biting his tongue in Nazareth. Lex is almost reverent when we visit Golgotha, and I remember how he loved to talk about the stories he learned in Sunday school. Religion in my house is less wonder and love and more fire and brimstone, so I don't feel the same surge of emotion on my own. I can feel Lex's, though, and I find myself fighting back an echo of unexpected tears when we visit the Garden Tomb—the presumptive tomb where Jesus lay.

Israel isn't really thrilled about their supernatural community, either, but there's less of a sense of fear here than the undercurrent in Damascus. The city is just as freakishly quiet, and while we weren't in Damascus long enough to feel it, the eeriness has time to sink in here. Magic can make up for a lot—our hosts have light and hot water and even refrigeration but few of their neighbors do, and, despite the thousands of people still in the city, it feels deserted.

More than that, funeral pyres burn outside the city, put into service when the cemeteries couldn't bury people fast enough and the crematoriums no longer worked. When we ask about any of it, though, all we get are shrugs and eyes that look away. No one wants to talk about it, and the reality of what the world is facing is impossible to dismiss—not that we've been dismissing it, of course, but it suddenly feels crushingly real.

When our two days are up, we head back out on the road to the sea, getting into Ashdod two days later. The others haven't been slacking on their own, it soon becomes clear, as Isaac and the other sailors have procured us four ocean-worthy sailboats and have started gathering supplies. Better than that, they've used communications through the local coven to find out that the Queens have taken Lex's ideas about the tall ships to the European community, and they are going to do what they can to muster the ships and crews to help get any Americans stranded in Europe and the Middle East home. It's not perfect, and it will take a while to get all the pieces in place, but there's hope, and Lex and Isaac are both thrilled their ideas are proving workable.

CHAPTER 24

December 2012

Lex

The boats look very tiny to hold six people for almost two months, especially when the supplies are loaded—we stock up heavily on dried fruit, nuts, hardtack, something like jerky, and have tanks for water. There's no way to carry enough water for the trip on the boats, but, unlike the Ancient Mariner, we'll be able to access the water everywhere, desalinating it with magic and making it fit to drink. We also have fishing poles, and the cabin of our boat has a small gas stove in it.

Once the boats are loaded, the sailing lessons begin. Two people will always need to be on duty, which is fine since there's only room for four below. Isaac turns out to be a good teacher, deeming us ready to at least be able to venture out and learn more as we go.

We tether the boats with magic, so we'll always be in sight of each other and can help if anyone has trouble. Three days after our sightseeing contingent arrived, we head out.

As I imagined, the quarters are tight. If we thought we were close after two years in warzones, the trip across the ocean is either going to render us into nearly one organism, or we'll all kill each other. For the most part, we stay up top in the fresh air, except when we're sleeping, and, even that, we tend to do in shifts. Mike and I stretch out in our sleeping bags in the stern of the boat when it's not our turn in the cabin. We find an astronomy book tucked on a small shelf, so we make a good stab at learning more about the stars and constellations than we ever did on childhood camping trips. Mike splurged a couple of his gemstones on a used guitar in Jerusalem, which proves to have been a wise investment. Music joins storytelling in our nightly entertainment, and teaching Isaac to play gives me something to do while Mike and LTC Greeley challenge each other to chess game after chess game. Ronan, meanwhile, is determined to up my poker skills, insisting on what turns into a tournament playing for pistachios.

After a week, right before we leave the Mediterranean for the open Atlantic, we pull the boats in closer and do a bit of a rotation—two people from each boat migrating to another one, so we all have some fresh faces to stare at through the interminable days on the water. This works so well that we make it a weekly practice, and it's a month before Mike and I are back with our squad. I find I've missed them more than I realized, though Mike looks ready to haul me back to our last boat when Isaac stretches out with his head in my lap that night. Similarly, Ronan looks ready to toss me overboard, but when we bed down for the night, and Isaac and I happily part company back to our respective soulmates, they both calm back down. If Mike is a little more physically possessive for a few days, I'm not complaining. I'd never actively try to make him jealous, but I'm still not used to the idea of him being capable of it, at least over me.

Like on the march to Jerusalem, we fall into a routine on the boat, each with our own jobs. Captain Parsons does most of the navigating, while Isaac makes sure the boat goes in the direction Parsons tells him. Mike does the fishing; LTC Greeley does the cooking. I take care of desalinating and purifying the water, while helping Isaac and Captain Parsons with whatever other tasks sailing the boat requires. Somehow, Mike and I wind up on the third sailing shift, in the darkest and coldest part of the night, through sunrise, when Isaac and Ronan take over.

We're able to keep up a good wind, even before we hit the trade winds, keeping us moving at a quicker pace than we'd hoped, but the fact that none of us are particularly skilled in weather magic becomes apparent about halfway across the Atlantic, when a storm catches up to us. As is normal for this time of year, we've had fairly rough seas since entering the ocean proper, but we've been able to use magic to protect us from the worst of it, save for some seasickness. This storm is different. Rough seas aside, we haven't had the issues with extreme seas that can happen in the Northern Atlantic. The winds from this storm are high enough that we have to drop the sails and tie everyone into the lifelines. Then the waves get high enough to be terrifying to even look at, towering over us by more than a dozen feet, looking like they'll crash down and crush us at any moment. Prudently, we throw shields up around the boats to ride the waves out without capsizing, but it's still more frightening than I want to let on. The storm only lasts a few hours, but it's enough to leave all of us grateful to not be attempting this in hurricane season.

Mike

In the aftermath of the storm, we're all thoroughly drenched and chilled. We might be angling for Bermuda, but the middle of the Atlantic still has colder winds than we could wish for, especially at night. The witches bust out warming and drying spells, but we're all sneezing within a couple of days anyway. Isaac and LTC Greeley are the only two of our squad to not wind up with a cold. Shifters almost never get sick, with their enhanced healing. It's rare enough for witches, given the home remedies and magic they brew up at the first sign of a sniffle, but our magical supplies are geared more toward emergencies than congestion and witch physiology is ultimately more like mundane humans than not. It does occur to me, though, that in fifteen years, I've never actually seen Lex sick until now.

Honestly, I quickly realize that has been for the best. Turns out, he's an even more miserable patient when sick than he is when injured. LTC Greeley at least packed some lemon and ginger tea in the supplies, and one of the witches on another boat has more healing skill than the rest of us, so he cycles through the boats, offering advice for natural remedies we do have access to. Thankfully, salt water is one of those remedies, once we're able to rig some of it into a kind of nasal spray. The small stove proves helpful for steam, and the tea helps, too. Still, God save me from a boatload of miserable witches for the foreseeable future. I try to be sympathetic, snuggling Lex when he gets feverish and chills, making sure he and the others stay hydrated, but Isaac, LTC Greeley and I all are about out of patience by the time the other three start feeling better. My own cold lingers a few days longer, and Lex proves to be far better at coddling me than I am him, bringing me tea as soon as I even start thinking I might want some, keeping cool water on hand for when I'm thirsty, and pouring his own magic into my reserves in a slew of what healing spells he knows in his efforts to help.

By the time everyone's well again, the temperature is warming, and the water is taking on an aquamarine hue. A few days later, we spot land. Even Captain Parsons has gotten a little discombobulated in his navigation by then.

"It should be Bermuda, right?" Isaac asks. Lex, I see from the corner of my eye, perks up.

"Should be," Captain Parsons agrees after consulting his navigational map and instruments.

"Are we going to stop?" Ronan asks from his seat on the bench by the cabin.

"And, what? Ask for directions?" I can't help teasing, before he flips me off.

"And make sure we're on course."

"Unless we went too far south, it's got to be Bermuda," Lex chimes in. "Otherwise, we missed it, and that's got to be the first of the Bahamas."

Humming "Kokomo" kind of seems required at that point, which at least gets a few chuckles.

As we get closer, LTC Greeley pulls out his binoculars and peers at the island.

"It's Bermuda," he confirms. "I can see Fort Saint Catherine."

"I don't think we should stop," Isaac opines. "We're okay on supplies, and we don't know what conditions there might be like. Better to press onward. We could be in Charleston within the week."

Where to put in has been a point of contention and LTC Greeley, Captain Parsons and Lex are all quick to contradict him.

"We promised to come straight to New Orleans," Lex reminds him. "We need to talk to the Queens about bringing the rest of our people home."

"Charleston's got more ships we can use," Isaac says.

"But not the authority," LTC Greeley says with a sigh. "I know we're all anxious to be off this boat, but we're expected in New Orleans, where we also know we'll be welcomed. South Carolina—who knows what atmosphere we'll find there? Never mind having to restock supplies for another 850-mile march."

The reminder of the militias is probably enough to convince everyone to sail on, but the distance to walk clinches it. When we chart the course more certainly toward New Orleans, we do lose one boat that decides to head to Charleston, since its occupants are all from the Carolinas, but the other two venture on with us. We drop anchor just a mile or so off the island and get in some excellent fishing for dinner, though, spending the night in calm waters for a change.

"We're heading into the Bermuda Triangle, aren't we?" Lex asks as we head out the next morning.

"We are," Isaac tells him, "But we'll be fine. Cruise ships came through here all the time without incident."

Lex doesn't look reassured and pops up another shield around the boat, along with some wards. The others smile but indulge him, and, once we're as protected as we can be, he settles in close to me.

"At least if we disappear, we'll go together," he murmurs.

"Always," I murmur back, pressing a kiss to the top of his head.

We make it to the Bahamas without incident, sailing through tropical waters of a brilliant hue. We keep up the habit of dropping anchor closer to shore, near vibrant harbors. The islands, like Damascus and Jerusalem, are dark, but we occasionally catch faint music on the breeze that feels welcoming. There are other boats in the water, as well, and the people on board wave, though everyone looks a little shell-shocked, still—no party boats carrying snorkelers out to gaze at tropical fish among them.

The battleships still anchored in Guantanamo Bay are jarring. For all it's a US military base, LTC Greeley vetoes pulling in there. Anyone who's gotten stranded there can feasibly make it at least to Florida, and there's never been a MagCorps contingent there. No need to court trouble or risk sanctions for going AWOL, even though we technically have leave—we checked in with and got permission from both HQ and the Queens before we left Iraq. Still, no point in risking it, even if being wary of our own fellow servicemembers feels strange. A couple of more weeks, and we'll be in New Orleans. I don't want to think about what comes next. Lex wants to find his family, but even if they've gone back to Virginia, that's still 1000 miles. If they're still in Maine... maybe, we can take the boat? Even to Virginia—we can get to Richmond by boat, at least, and then it's less than 150 miles home. Spring is coming upon us, and I don't want to think about walking that far, not knowing what we'll find. But I will, for him. I push that off, for now, focusing as we finally make the Gulf of Mexico, with Florida off to our starboard side.

CHAPTER 25

February 2013

Lex

Sailing from Cuba to New Orleans, we see more signs of civilization than we have since we left Baghdad to trek to our camp when we first got to Iraq. Granted, most of it is silent and bleak—the oil rigs are all still, which is nice but eerie. We see a lot of dolphins, who love to play alongside the boat, and a few sharks, which keeps us out of the water, even now that it's warming up again. It takes us a little over a week, and, it turns out, there's very little question about when we're close. Unlike anything we've seen since everything went dark, New Orleans is lit up, the glow of her lights brightening the horizon even while we're still miles out to sea. Ronan and I call up a little extra wind, redirecting it to push us north, out of the Gulf. We let it up to slow us down as we need to navigate into the river and up to the port itself. Cargo ships still linger, along with a few silent and dark cruise ships, but the pier is lit up, and we can see a large group of people waiting on it.

"I guess my message got through that we'd be in today," LTC Greeley says with a chuckle.

It takes a few minutes to get situated and get the boats all tied up, but I notice both Queen Esther and Eleanor at the head of the crowd waiting for us, and can't help but feel a little frazzled, given the length of our journey. At least I started shaving again after we hit Bermuda, and we've had enough water to stay reasonably clean across the ocean.

Mike helps me onto the ladder, and I reach down to help him once I'm up on the pier. Once he's climbing steadily, I turn to face the crowd, only to almost fall back down into him below as I'm hit in the chest by someone flying into me. I put my arms up reflexively, only then realizing that I have a girl in them, practically wrapped around me.

"I didn't think I'd ever see you again!"

It's only when she speaks that I realize who she is. It's one thing to note that Andie has grown up through seeing her on video screens. Having my arms full of someone who's very clearly a woman, not a child, is disorienting.

"Andie...?" I hug her close, feeling her trembling. "Hey, it's okay. We're here now. We're—"

Before I can finish my reassurances, she shuts me up with a kiss, and I freeze, unsure what to do. It's an innocent kiss, at first, I realize after my momentary freeze, just a sweet press of lips to lips, though once I relax into that, I feel the tease of her tongue and let her deepen the kiss. Still, even the simple one rocks me to my core, and I'm still trying to catch my breath from the more sensual one when she pulls out of my arms and Mike gets basically the same greeting, kiss and all.

Ronan clears his throat, so he can get onto the pier, and Mike breaks the kiss with Andie, looking as sucker punched as I feel.

"Hey, kid," he manages, earning him a glare that's so familiar from all our Skype sessions that I have to laugh.

Isaac looks as stunned when he makes it to the pier, but hastily sketches an awkward bow.

"Your Highness."

Andie considers him a moment, then gives him a hug, too, though he clearly has no idea what to do with his arms, seemingly not willing to dare to hug her back.

"Thank you," she tells him. "Thank you for bringing them home."

"It... it was pretty much a joint effort," he tells her, but she just kisses his cheek.

"Come on. Mama wants to meet you."

With that, she drags him down the pier, leaving the rest of us to follow. Both queens are looking amused and indulgent and we're almost to them when I hear my name called in a far more familiar voice. I stop, straining to see past Queen Esther, who smiles and steps out of the way. Then I'm the one running, and my mom meets me halfway, pulling me into a hug that cuts off my breath.

I knew I missed her, but it still hits me harder than I would have expected, and I feel tears well up and start falling down my cheeks. It's been almost three years since we left for MagCorps. So much has happened that I can't seem to grasp that fact and just hold tight to her.

"Hi, Mom," the words are quiet, barely making it out around the tightness of my throat.

She kisses away my tears, hugs me again, and then turns me over to my father so she can hug Mike. My father's greeting is more restrained, but he's got tears in his eyes, too, and when my sister—who's grown up far too much—pushes her way between us to wrap her arms around me, she's openly sobbing already.

I can still see the Queens out of the peripheral of my right eye and pull back from my sobbing sister to greet them. Further to the side, LTC Greeley is enthusiastically kissing a man about his age with dark brown hair and a look of Mike about him.

"Cousin Aaron, I presume," Mike murmurs.

"It's so weird to see him kissing someone," I say, meaning LTC Greeley. It's kind of like...well, I don't even know, because my parents were always kissing when I was growing up.

"Like when Miss Burton got married to Coach after Junior year?" Mike suggests, naming our tenth-grade English teacher.

"Yeah," I agree, shaking my head before turning to greet Queen Esther.

"Welcome home, Lieutenants," she says as we step forward and bow. "Well done, all of you."

The witches from the other ships have joined us, with the shifters moving to greet Queen Eleanor.

The formality of the greetings breaks down again after that as others in the crowd behind them cry out, and more families come spilling forward to welcome their children home.

"How is everyone here?" I ask, not even sure who I'm asking.

"Once LTC Greeley let us know who all was coming with this first group, we tried to find their families and have them here," Queen Esther replies. "Not everyone's made it, yet, but everyone is on their way, at least. Travel, as you well know, is much slower now, and some had a continent to cross."

Mike

I shudder at the Witch Queen's words to Lex, having no desire to even think about the real-life game of Oregon Trail that's sprung up again. I'm not disappointed that my own family isn't here—Lex's parents, not to mention Andie, are welcome enough. I miss my mom and brother, but still can't think of my dad without fury I don't want to cloud others' reunions with. Isaac looks a little sad to have no one here, but Andie still has his hand and is looking at him like he's her personal hero, while Eleanor beams at him with a ton of pride. Lex's mom moves to meet him, as well, giving him a tight hug, even as Andie still refuses to let go.

Mrs. Monroe kisses Isaac's cheek, and Lizzie hugs him as enthusiastically as Andie had. She twirls one golden curl around a finger as she steps back, blushing, and that'll need to be cut off before she breaks her heart on his and Ronan's bond. If I can't believe how grown-up Andie's gotten, Lizzie is a wonder. Lex's little sister was barely twelve last time we saw her, and now, at fifteen, she's clearly a young woman, growing up way too fast. Andie finally lets Isaac go, turning him over to her mother. Lizzie and she join hands and move back to us, one snuggling up on either side of Lex, their linked hands pressing at his lower back to keep him close. Andie reaches out her free hand, pulling me in to join them. It's a little awkward, what with the queens watching and all, but I push that aside, meeting Lex's eyes and smiling over Andie's head.

After a while, the enthusiasm of the first greetings dies down, and Esther directs everyone back toward the street where honest-to-god carriages wait. Our boats have already been emptied of our personal possessions while we said our hellos and loaded onto a waiting wagon. Andie dodges her mother to climb into a carriage with me and Lex, settling herself on Lex's lap when he sits next to me. I'm still not sure what to make of her greeting, but she seems intent on marking us as hers. I remind myself she's still only seventeen, but that kiss was a little disorienting.

"Where are we going?" Lex asks her as he wraps his arms around her waist to stabilize her.

"All the families are being put up in hotels around the Quarter, and they all have extra adjoining rooms, so y'all can stay with your families," she informs him. "Isaac and Ronan are supposed to come back with me and Mama, since they don't have families here, and Mama wants to talk to Isaac about the tall ships and getting everyone else home."

"We heard Europe was going to help with that," I say.

"Oh, they are," she assures me. "But I think Mama and Esther want Isaac and Lex to help coordinate, since it was their idea. But I told them to let you and Lex have at least one night with the Monroes before they put you back to work. You deserve a break."

Lex is staring out at the streets as we drive, and I follow his gaze. Everything is well lit, with even some neon showing here and there.

"Witchlight?" he asks, pointing at one neon sign.

"Oh, yeah." Andie sits up a bit. "The human authorities basically ceded the city to Mama and Esther. We haven't been able to keep everything the same, obviously, but we've done what magic can, courtesy of the ley lines. The old water pump house was a museum, but we were able to get it working again. New Orleans has the oldest plumbing guild in the nation, and we had indoor plumbing in 1836. A lot had been modernized since then, of course, but with everyone pitching in, we basically..." she shrugs a little. "Switched it back? The covens have been working overtime to make sure everyone has working refrigeration for food, and a lot of things that electricity ran are working on spells now, ones that are set in place and synced up to triggers that humans can activate. We're working on mosquito suppression, now, so we don't wind up with another yellow fever epidemic." She gives us a smile, clearly proud of her city and her people.

"It helps that we have more witches per capita here than anywhere else in the country. Other cities, even those with active covens, aren't doing anywhere near as well. From what we've heard, Baton Rouge has had mass casualties—nearly half their human population already, even though the covens and packs there are doing their best. There just aren't enough witches, and we get a steady trickle of refugees each day. Eventually, we'll have to figure out what to do if we reach capacity, but, for now, we're doing okay."

I can see some of the tension easing out of Lex as he takes in the near normalcy around us, and I smile as I feel relief flicker through him.

Andie points out the innovations they've put in place as we ride through the streets, sounding more like a princess than I've ever heard from her. She clearly cares about her people, and she's grown up so much more than any of our calls have indicated. Lex asks astute questions about implementation, tying to the ley lines, and scale, and I can see the wheels turning in his head.

Andie sighs when we get to the hotel, getting out with us, but saying she has to go meet up with her mother. She gives us both another quick kiss, blushing as she says goodnight, before climbing back in the carriage. Our packs are waiting with the Monroes outside a hotel far nicer than we could afford last time we were here. It even still has working bellboys—humans who seem to be well-fed and content at the end of the world. Despite our protests, they carry our packs and my guitar up to our room. We don't have anything to tip them with, but they just tell us when the dining room closes and wish us a goodnight.

The Monroes give us time to grab a shower—oh, blessed hot, clean water again—and then take us downstairs for dinner. Apparently, the Queens are still figuring out what to do about currency, but Esther is taking care of any of our expenses while we're here.

Despite us swearing we never wanted seafood again, not two days ago, Lex talks me into crawfish bread as an appetizer and a low country boil for dinner. Everything is cooked to perfection—we even have drawn butter to dip our seafood in, and aside from the light all being from witchlight, it's even easier than it was in Damascus to pretend everything's okay, or normal, here. Still, that's not the case everywhere.

"The federal government has basically collapsed," Mr. Monroe tells us as we sip actual cocktails poured over actual ice. "Looting and illness have made any city without a strong supernatural community a death trap. Places with a strong coven, with healers, and shifters to help provide food are hanging on. However, from what we've heard, most cities are just places to die, and small towns aren't always better with a scourge of bandits and undisciplined militias roving. People are starving and more than happy to kill their neighbors for food, let alone strangers on the road."

"For Lizzie's sake, I think we're going to stay here," Mrs. Monroe says after we've all fallen silent. "We haven't been back to Staunton since the Massacre, anyway. Supernats are protected here, respected even, where in other places...we're being blamed."

"What?" Lex asks, even though reports from HQ suggested the same.

"The ley line surge before the power went," his father says. "They're saying magic caused this, that witches caused this."

"How would humans even know that?" Lex asks.

"I'm not sure," his mom admits. "Maybe they overheard witches talking, or..."

"Or mages felt it and are spreading it," I interject dully. It sounds like something my dad would do.

"Oh, Mike, I'm sure that's not it," Mrs. Monroe protests, reaching to hold my hand. But she doesn't know everything about my father, so I can't take any comfort in it.

We finish supper quietly before heading back upstairs. I let myself into our room while Lex says goodnight to his family. He's only a few minutes, but I'm already stripped down to my boxers, with the mini-fridge open and two cold beers out. I hand him one as he pulls off his boots.

"What do you want to do?" he asks me, watching me while he undresses and settles on the bed with his beer.

"We have to see what the Queens want before we do anything," I point out.

He nods. "First priority has to be getting our people home from overseas. Then...something. We can't just hide here. I mean, I'm glad my folks want to stay, but that's not what we trained for. They wouldn't let us do anything after the bombing and the attacks, but if there are supernaturals out there being blamed for this, being attacked--we have to do something."

I've never heard him quite so resolute before, and the seriousness of his gaze burns through me.

"We do," I agree. Especially if my dad is one of the ones persecuting people. I owe it to them to protect them from him.

Lex holds his hand out to me. I wind my fingers through his and let him tug me onto the bed, setting my beer aside as I reach for him.

"Tomorrow," he murmurs before kissing me, "We'll find out what the Queens want, and then, we'll plan. Together."

I kiss him back, pulling him close against me. He fumbles to set his beer aside, then wraps both arms around me. Our legs tangle, and he fits against me perfectly, our edges slotting together like two puzzle pieces.

"Together," I agree, and it feels like our vows all over again, or a new vow for a new world. Whatever it is, I feel that now-familiar surge along the silver cord between us. It pushes back the fear flickering at the edges of my mind. The fear I have been burying since the night darkness fell, the fear that I've fought since the night the bomb went off.

Alone, I can't imagine bearing the weight of it, but as long as Lex is by my side, I know I can face anything.

Lex nips at my lower lip, running a hand up my spine as he shifts to sprawl atop me. He soothes the sting with his tongue, then lifts his head. "Is it just me, or has Andie gotten super-hot?"

It's so incongruous with the solemnity of our discussion that I'm startled into a laugh. I shift him onto his back, following until I can hover over him and start getting rid of the last pieces of clothing between us.

"You're hot," I tell him as he wriggles into a place where he can rock against me and make us both moan. "Andie is still too young to be hot."

He wraps a leg around my hips, his own rolling so our dicks drag against one another in a slow slide. "Agree to disagree, but we can add it to the list of things to discuss tomorrow."

I can't deny him that any more than I can deny him anything else.

"Tomorrow," I agree, kissing him deeper. Tonight, I have other things to think about, like how bright I can make the cord between us glow. Surely, we can light up the room again. And I can't think of any better way to push back the darkness.

THANK YOUS

Thank you for reading *Darkness Falling*! I hope you enjoyed getting to know Lex and Mike and witnessing the start of their journey. Rest assured, they'll be back soon to continue on their way as they try to save what's left of the world—you can get a sneak peek at Andie's perspective starting out Book 2 at the end of this. If you enjoyed the boys and their world, please consider leaving a review to help other readers find them. You can find ways to connect with me at the end of the book. I look forward to hearing your thoughts and getting to know you.

There are so many people without whom this book wouldn't have been possible. First and foremost, I want to thank my mother for all her support while I was struggling to put this book together. You were unerringly on my side, even when I surprised you with requests and information you weren't expecting. Thank you for always being there and encouraging me when I get overwhelmed. Thank you for reading to me and always encouraging my bookworm habits. My love for reading led me to writing, and that came from you and Daddy.

Thank you to Michelle and Mary for letting me bounce ideas off of you and for asking all the right questions as I was working out the kinks of the story. Your response and interest kept me going.

Thank you to the wonderful team at All Write Well: Maria for your constant encouragement and belief in my story. Knowing you cared about Lex and Mike's journey got me over the hump of self-doubt and to the end of the book. You've been a wonderful mentor on this journey. LeAnn for your thoughtful and encouraging edits, helping me shore up the weak spots in the story and making sure it read coherently. And Carrie Anne for taking the final look at this, making sure none of my careless errors remained—for seeing the things I missed. I couldn't have done this without you.

Finally, thank you to Kimberley Killion at The Killion Group for your gorgeous cover design. You really helped capture my vision of Mike and Lex and their world.

About the Author

Bria was surrounded by story from the time she could understand language, nurtured by a family tradition of oral storytellers who made fantastic worlds come alive. She has been writing since the time she discovered that was the way her beloved books came into being. Her first book was a non-fiction story about her beloved cat, Boots, written in first grade for a county-wide contest. It won an honorable mention, and that set her on her path. She started writing down her imaginary adventures soon after and always turned in fiction when that was an option for an assignment.

She wrote her first paranormal story in college, turning it into a play she then produced with friends from the theater department. Seeds that story sowed will be sprouting in later books in the Darkness series.

When she's not writing, Bria teaches writing, science fiction, and literature at a university in Virginia, where she lives with her two cats, Holly and Lily, and explores the beautiful area she's made her home. She does her best story generation while swinging on the swing she hung under her deck, listening to playlists for the characters who've taken over her head.

COMING SOON

Pick up Lex and Mike's adventures in Book 2 of the Triune Souls trilogy, *Darkness Creeping*, which adds Andie's perspective into the mix as they and their friends try to navigate this new world and all the challenges of rebuilding civilization after the world falls apart.

Can their relationship withstand the trials and tribulations of leadership? And what was up with Marguerite's prophecy about the darkness and pain in Lex's destiny? Find out in Fall of 2023, but until then, here's a sneak peek of *Darkness Creeping*, which backtracks a little to give us Andie's perspective on things as the boys were trying to get back home, starting with how the power going out was experienced in New Orleans.

Darkness Creeping

Chapter 1
Andie
Six months ago/September 2012
The magical surge that floods the ley lines like an incoming high tide is the strongest magic I've ever felt and

almost knocks me off my feet. I hear Becky cry out over the pounding music of the club we're in, and Lizzie's hands fly to her head, like it hurts. Tia seems as unstable on her feet as I am, reaching out to steady herself and me, even though, as snow leopards, we both usually have perfect balance, even in human form. My stomach flips like I'm on a roller coaster, and sitting down, even on the wet and sticky dancefloor sounds like a good plan. Even though I've lost count of how many hurricanes I've had, I'm not drunk because it's nearly impossible for shifters to get drunk. Still, I imagine this is what it feels like. I see my bodyguards, Grégoire and Gervais, step closer, reaching for me just as Tia does, and between the three of them, I stay upright.

Then the music abruptly cuts off, leaving my ears ringing in the sudden silence. The lights pop and crackle, sending down a shower of sparks before they go dark. A few land on me, singing my little black dress and burning my arm. Where a second ago, we were encased in bodies sweating and moving to thumping beats, half-blinded by the flashing lights, suddenly the room is almost preternaturally quiet, and the only illumination comes from the glow sticks scattered through the cavernous room. It's been nearly three years, but as if to prove everyone is still on edge from the Massacre, it's only a couple of heartbeats before the pounding bass is replaced by scattered screams.

Two hard bodies crash into me— Grégoire and Gervais on either side, flanking me with their arms tight around me. They lost me a few years ago, and they are never doing it again. A few moments later, some witchlights pop into existence, lighting up the room, like the numerous young witches in the club finally remembered they have magic and can use it to see. I'm grateful because, even with my superior eyesight, I can't see in pitch darkness without any light source at all. I glance around me, registering that Becky, Tia and Lizzie are still right with me. Becky's bodyguards are pushing through the crowded chaos to get to us, fighting against the crowd of clubbers who are trying to flee outside. Only once they reach us and secure Becky do Grégoire and Gervais deign to move. The four bodyguards work seamlessly together and, through a judicious use of magic and brawn, cut through the crowd and reach a side exit in moments. They make us stay inside while they clear the alley, then escort us into the balmy night air redolent with the scents of alcohol, exhaust, and magnolia trees.

The situation isn't much better out here, though. Less crowded, at least, but just as chaotic. I can hear scattered screams up and down Bourbon Street, along with the thunderous sound of multiple car crashes. I watch as a town car careens by the mouth of the alley we're standing in before stopping courtesy of the corner of the building housing the club. The Quarter—usually brightly lit—is as dark as the club. Maybe for the first time ever, I can see the moon and stars in the sky from the heart of downtown. Another car crashes into the town car with a squeal of breaks—honestly, no one should've been driving that fast down here to begin with.

"Oh my God, that plane is going to crash!" some girl on the main street screams, and I look up reflexively. Sure enough, a plane—completely dark, visible only by moonlight, seems to have lost all lift and is gliding right toward one of the banking buildings on Canal Street. In a scene that's eerily reminiscent of the planes hitting the Twin Towers, the plane crashes into the building, sliding half into it. The building itself starts to crumble and collapse, and it's impossible to know how many people might be in there because, like everything else as far as my eyes can see, the windows of the building are completely dark.

"It's worse than Katrina," Tia murmurs, looking at me with wide eyes and horror on her face.

"Katrina didn't blackout the cars and planes," Grégoire says, apparently in agreement.

"Is it an attack?" Lizzie asks, reaching to wind her fingers through mine. "Terrorists or the start of another Massacre?"

"I don't know." I force the words past my lips as I squeeze her hand. Pulling out my phone, I look at it, only to see it's dead. "My battery was fully charged before I left home.

Everyone else pulls out their phones to the same result.

The bodyguards decide, whatever is going on, it isn't something four teenage girls should be out in and start hustling us in the direction of Lizzie's hotel, since it's closest. They don't have a way to check in with either Esther or Mama, so, after dropping Lizzie off with the Monroes, they make a command decision to hustle the other three of us to the Witch Queen's house. Tia's mom is probably with mine, but our Court is outside of the city, and we're now without transportation. Grégoire, Gervais, Tia and I can all shift and run home, but we need to make sure Becky's safe first.

So, we do. At her house, Esther doesn't know any more than we do. They've got communication spells going all over the first floor, checking in with the High Priestesses in charge of other areas. Grégoire and Gervais insist on getting me and Tia home before we learn anything, though. We leave our clothes with Becky, shift and the head back out in our feline forms—snow leopards for me and Tia, a panther for Gervais and a lion for Grégoire. Perhaps unavoidably, the sight on big cats on the streets causes more screaming from the tourists, and then bitching when they realize we're shifters, and probably royals, and their phones aren't working for them to get our pictures. Once we cross Canal St., we're able to move more swiftly, and it's less than an hour before we're back home—which is just as dark. Not silent, with all the people talking, but at least no one's screaming here. Yet.

CONNECT WITH ME

Facebook Reader Group: https://www.facebook.com/groups/briafergusonmusebox

Instagram: https://www.instagram.com/bria_ferguson_author/

TikTok: https://www.tiktok.com/@briafergusonauthor

Website: www.briaferguson.com

www.ingramcontent.com/pod-product-compliance
Lightning Source LLC
Chambersburg PA
CBHW030131310726
48970CB00005B/1394